MURDER IN COLD MUD

A Churchill & Pemberley Mystery Book 2

EMILY ORGAN

First published in 2019 by Emily Organ

emilyorgan.com

Edited by Joy Tibbs

Emily Organ has asserted her right under the Copyright, Designs and Patents Act 1988 to be identified as the author of this work.

ISBN 978-1-9993433-6-1

Chapter 1

"THAT'S ENOUGH SCRAPING for now, Pemberley. Come and have a jam tart."

"But I've just started on the 's', Mrs Churchill," replied her thin, bespectacled secretary with scruffy grey hair.

"Can't the *'s'* wait? It's been there so long that one more day is hardly going to bring about Armageddon."

Mrs Annabel Churchill was a large lady with silver hair so well lacquered that it didn't budge in even the briskest of breezes. Her crimson lipstick matched her twinset and she wore a string of pearls which she had proudly possessed for over fifty years.

"If I leave it, it will look wrong," said Pemberley, frowning at the office door. "It will say *'s Detective Agency'*. If I scrape off the 's' it will just say *'Detective Agency'* and that'll look far better."

"I see your point, my trusty assistant. And call me over-sensitive, if you wish, but after a while the relentless scrape of scissor blade against glass leaves one feeling as though someone is hammering rusty nails into one's head."

"Oh dear, you should get that seen to."

"It's not serious enough to be *seen to*, Pemberley, it's merely a common human reaction to an incessant and irritating noise."

"Well, I don't know how we're going to get the rest of the letters off then," said Pemberley, helping herself to a jam tart from the plate on Churchill's desk.

"Any idea what type of glue Atkins used when he stuck the letters onto his door?"

"He had a man come and do it."

"Perhaps we can ask the same man to put the name *Churchill* on the door."

"We could, but given that he has died he is unlikely to respond."

"Oh, that's a terrible shame. Perhaps he was poisoned following a career of overexposure to extra-strong letter adhesive."

"I think he was, in fact. Poison was definitely mentioned at the inquest."

"We'll have to find someone else then. In the meantime, Pembers, I'm rather concerned about our empty-looking incident board." Churchill pointed at the map on the wall hanging next to the portrait of King George V. "Only recently we had photographs and drawings and pins and lengths of string connecting everything up, and now it all looks rather bare."

"Probably because we're not working on any cases at the moment, Mrs Churchill."

"Well done, Pembers, that's exactly what it is. Not a single case. I don't like being caseless; it makes my thumbs twitchy."

"'You never know when the next case is going to come in.' That's what Atkins always used to say."

"Well, he wasn't wrong on that score."

"But then he did have an extensive client base, so he was never without a case for long."

"That's what we're missing, Pembers, an extensive client base. How does one acquire one of those?"

"Through years of hard work and reputation-building."

"I meant quickly, though. How does one acquire an extensive client base in a matter of, let's say, a week?"

"You could advertise."

"Oh no, I would never do that. Advertising has a cheapening effect on one's services, I find. I would prefer clients to find us through recommendation and word of mouth. I tell you what we could do with and that's an upper-class customer. Aristocratic, even, like my friend Lady Worthington in Richmond-upon-Thames. She once happened to mention, in passing, a favourite little haberdashery of hers just off Sloane Square, and you couldn't move in the place the following day! They sold out of every single button cover before lunchtime. *That's* the sort of recommendation we need. In fact, we should try to ensure that we're a little choosier in future. We should only service an upper-class clientele."

"How can we be choosy when we don't have any clientele at all?"

"It won't always be like this, Pembers. Not once recommendation and word of mouth have spread themselves around the village."

"Within a week?"

"I would certainly hope so."

"The upper classes are riddled with criminality, so hopefully we'll have no shortage of cases once word gets out. Those large inheritances, priceless heirlooms and secret passageways practically encourage intrigue and murder."

"They do indeed, Pembers. I pray that our next client is in possession of a generous fortune." She brushed the jam tart crumbs from her ample bosom.

"*S Detective Agency?*" called a coarse voice from beyond the door. "What's the 's' for?"

Into the office stumbled a wide-framed, heavily bearded man wearing a tweed cap.

"D'you mean *Sdetective?*" he asked.

"No, we do not," replied Churchill haughtily. "Are you lost?"

"Oh, I see what's 'appened," continued the man as he surveyed the door. "It used ter say *Atkins's Detective Agency* didn't it? Only you've taken the *Atkins* off. No, 'ang about, you've taken *Atkins* and that little comma thing off an' left the 's' on, so now it says *Sdetective Agency*! Haw, haw, haw!"

The man sauntered further into the room and sat himself down in the chair across the desk from Churchill. He wore a sleeveless jacket and his trousers were held up with a length of fraying rope. A trail of earth from his muddy hobnailed boots lay on the floor.

"Do I 'ave the pleasure of addressin' Mrs Churchill?" he asked, removing his cap deferentially.

"Yes," she replied, her nose wrinkling at the amount of dirt on the man. "And you are?"

"Mr Rumbold, that's me. Are thems jam tarts?" he asked, eying the plate on the desk.

"They are indeed." She paused before reluctantly adding, "Would you like one?"

"I wouldn't say no."

"Lovely jubbly." He picked one up with his fat, grimy fingers and took a large bite. "How's Atkins's widow?" he asked with his mouth full.

4

"I'm afraid I can't tell you, Mr Rumbold. I've never met the lady."

"Crocodile, weren't it? On some river in Africa, I 'eard."

"Yes, the Zambezi I believe."

"Cor! What a way to go!"

"You're not the first to say that. How may I help, Mr Rumbold?"

"I almost forgot why I've come 'ere for a moment!" He pushed the rest of the tart into his mouth and wiped his face with his sleeve. "That's a nice tart that is. Now where was I? Oh yeah, I'm 'ere 'cause someone's speared me onions."

"Your onions, Mr Rumbold?"

"Yep."

"Speared?"

"Yep."

"May I ask where your onions were when they were speared?"

"They was in the ground!"

"They were in the process of growing?"

"Yep, that's right. Enormous beauties they would've been too, only someone's put paid to that."

"And what were they speared with?"

"Prongs of a fork. Someone's dug 'em all up an' speared 'em with a fork."

"And then what did they do with them?"

"Just left 'em lyin' on the ground."

"How barbaric."

"Ruined! Me onion crop's ruined."

"And you'd like me to find the person responsible for this savage attack?"

"Yep. I'm worried me turnips'll be next."

"We can't let that happen."

"No, we can't. Someone's already 'ad a go at me marrows fortnight last."

"Oh dear, really?"

"Yep, but I still got three of 'em at a secret location." He tapped the side of his nose conspiratorially. "I've won the prize for the largest marrow in Wessex seven years on the trot."

"Congratulations, Mr Rumbold."

"Last year's was 'eavier than the missis."

"That's quite an achievement. It sounds as though someone is attempting to sabotage your winning streak."

"You've 'it the nail right on its 'ead. There's one thing people don't like in this village, Mrs Churchill. Do you know what it is?"

"Haggis?"

"Success. People can't abide success in others. An' there's nothin' what provokes another man's anger as much as an enormous marrow."

"Is that so, Mr Rumbold?"

"Yep. Mark me words."

"Consider them marked." Churchill picked up her notebook and pen. "Now, what have you got for me to go on? Any idea who could be behind this?"

"Could be Tubby Williams."

"Tubby?"

"Yep."

"Williams?"

"Yep."

"And why do you think Tubby Williams might wish to spear your onions?"

"He don't like me."

"Do you know why?"

"'Cause me onions do better than 'is."

"From what you've told me so far, Mr Rumbold, I have

managed to glean that your vegetable growing is of a competitive nature and that this Tubby Williams is a rival competitor. Am I correct?"

"You'd be right correct, Mrs Churchill."

"Good! I like it when I'm on the right track. Perhaps you can give me the names of any other rivals."

"Stropper 'Arris, Colin Sniffer Downs an' Barry Woolwell."

"Those are rather unusual names."

"What's wrong with Barry Woolwell?"

"I'm sure there's nothing wrong with him on a personal basis, and his name is fairly normal-sounding, I grant you that. But what's with this Sniffer Stropper Tubby business?"

"Them's just nicknames they've 'ad for so long we've all gone an' forgotten their real ones."

"I see. And of these four competitors you think Mr Tubby Williams is the one who's behind the vegetable attacks?"

"Yep."

"Have you asked him about it?"

"Oh, I've gone and asked him a lotta times what he means by 'avin' a go at me veg. I went an' slashed 'is gourds last year."

Churchill winced. "Oh dear, Mr Rumbold. It's disappointing to hear that you've sunk to the same unpleasant depths. This tit for tat has been going on for a while, has it?"

"Yep, it's been years now, it 'as."

"So why are you asking for my help now?"

"It's gettin' worse, an' there's the Compton Poppleford 'Orticultural Show comin' up. I want this sorted afore the show."

"You haven't been out slashing gourds or any other varieties of vegetable recently, have you?"

"Nope, the gourds is the last ones I done."

"Good. Well, do continue to rise above it and keep your nose clean, Mr Rumbold."

"All the slashin's be'ind me now, Mrs Churchill. I'm as straight as they come, haw haw haw!"

"As straight as your carrots, perhaps?"

He gave her a blank look. "Yer what?"

"Isn't that the ideal shape for a prize carrot, Mr Rumbold? Long and straight?"

"Yep, that's the best kind. I once grew a carrot what was 'eavier than a small pig."

"Good for you."

He lowered his voice to a mischievous whisper. "And I once grew one what looked exactly like a—"

"Thank you, Mr Rumbold!" Churchill held up her hand as she interrupted him. "I've heard quite enough."

"Looked exactly like a what?" asked Pemberley.

"It's entirely irrelevant to our investigation," replied Churchill.

"It might not be."

"Believe me, Pembers, it is."

"It looked exactly like a—"

"Tra la la! We can't hear you, Mr Rumbold," said Churchill loudly. "And the conversation has reached its natural conclusion. I think the next course of action would be for Miss Pemberley and me to visit the crime scene. Fancy a jaunt over to the vegetable patch, Miss Pemberley?" She picked up her handbag and rose to her feet.

"Not particularly."

"Oh, come on. It'll be fun."

Chapter 2

"YOU SHOULD HAVE WORN your walking shoes, Miss Pemberley," said Churchill as they followed Mr Rumbold up the muddy lane that led to the allotments. "Your little girl slippers are quite ruined."

"I hadn't anticipated a visit to a vegetable patch this afternoon."

"Surely you've learnt by now to expect anything. Your years working for Atkins must have prepared you for that."

"Atkins would never have taken on a case of vandalised vegetables," whispered Pemberley bitterly. "He would have shown Rumbold the door. Did you see how much dirt he trampled into our office? I'll have to brush that up when we get back. And he has a very odd smell about him, doesn't he? Like mouldy mushrooms."

Churchill pondered this as she marched her stocky frame around the puddles. She quietly agreed that this was a petty investigation to be getting involved in.

"I haven't actually confirmed to Rumbold that we'll be taking on his case," she whispered in reply. "I'm still weighing it up."

"It doesn't even merit any weighing up. It's a waste of our time."

"Ah, but it's money. We don't have many other cases on our books at the moment."

"We don't have any."

"Exactly, and therein lies my point. A simple, boring case is better than no case at all."

A feeling of despondency began to descend upon Churchill no matter how hard she tried to fend it off. Her detective agency had got off to a strong start with the solving of a high-profile murder case, but business had been quiet ever since.

Around her birds sang happily in blossoming apple trees and the scent of lilac lingered in the air. The distant bleats of sheep drifted on the summer breeze from the green rolling hills encircling the village. Churchill inhaled the fresh air and tried to reassure herself that she had made the right decision to move to Dorset from noisy, smoke-filled London.

"This is me kingdom," announced Rumbold as they reached an allotment surrounded by a fence covered in barbed wire.

"You take your security quite seriously, I see," said Churchill, looking askance at the eyesore. "It reminds me of a prisoner of war camp."

"Yep. Look, I've raised me toolshed up on stilts so I got a good view over everythin'."

The gardener took a large bunch of keys from his pocket and unlocked the three padlocks that held fast the gate.

"How on earth did the culprit get close to your onions?" asked Churchill.

"Wire cutters," replied Rumbold.

He proceeded to show Churchill and Pemberley the

hole in the fence and the damaged onions, which lay scattered about the allotment. One had even been placed on top of the scarecrow's hat.

"The culprit considers himself a bit of a joker, I see," said Churchill. "Take some photographs of the crime scene please, Miss Pemberley."

"But I didn't bring the camera with me."

"Why ever not?"

Pemberley replied with a whisper from the side of her mouth. "I didn't think we'd decided to take on the case yet."

"It's money though, isn't it?" whispered Churchill in return.

"Hullo there!" announced a loud, clipped voice. Startled, Churchill turned to see an elderly man with a grey, handlebar moustache standing on the other side of the barbed wire.

"Good afternoon, Rumbold," he continued. "And Miss Pemberley, how delightful! Don't believe I've had the pleasure of meeting you yet, madam," he said to Churchill. "However, I deduce that you're the esteemed Mrs Annabel Churchill I've heard so much about."

"The very same," she replied with the slightest hint of a blush.

"Marvellous! I hoped our paths would cross sooner or later, and lo and behold they have! Colonel Slingsby, retired officer of the British Indian Army. Delighted to make your acquaintance at last, Mrs Churchill."

"And yours too, Colonel. Are you visiting your allotment here this afternoon?"

"No need for an allotment, Mrs Churchill. I've twenty-seven acres down at Ashleigh Grange."

"Oh, of course." Churchill's face reddened further, realising that any upper-class gentleman worth his salt had stacks of acreage at his disposal. "Twenty-seven acres, eh? That must be a bind to maintain, Colonel."

"It is, but the staff do it all."

"I suppose they would. No use in one having twenty-seven acres if one doesn't have staff."

"Staff are more of a bind than the acres, but there's little use in complaining. It's all part and parcel of the family seat."

"If one inherits these things there's very little one can do about it, I suppose," said Churchill.

"Naturally, I was quite happy with the apartment in Chelsea, though. Wasn't the intended heir, you see, but then the older brother went and popped his clogs, leaving no legitimate heir. The darned estate now hangs around my neck like the proverbial millstone."

"It ain't all bad though, is it, Colonel, 'cause you're president of the Compton Poppleford 'Orticultural Society, ain't you?" said Rumbold. "And you gets to judge all the competitions. It's thanks to this man," Rumbold continued, turning to Churchill, "that I've won all them marrow competitions 'ands down for the past seven years."

"One of the many benefits of having friends in high places," said Churchill with a smile.

"The chap's a talented gardener, Mrs Churchill. He's earned every bit of his success," said the Colonel. "I've never known a man so dedicated to his vegetabilia. Makes the acts of vandalism inflicted upon them all the more disgraceful. The culprits should be rounded up and shot at dawn."

"That's rather a severe punishment for damaging a few onions, isn't it?" asked Churchill.

"Not a bit of it! In fact, shooting's too good for the likes of them! This isn't mere vandalism we're talking about, but a sustained campaign of malevolence and vindictiveness.

There's no place for it in polite society, I say. None at all! You can make some excuses for it in the Punjab, but not in Dorset. It simply won't do, and it ought to be stamped out at once. I'm afraid the only answer is to shoot those responsible and make an example of them in order to deter others."

"But what if you shoot the wrong people?" asked Pemberley.

"Shoot the wrong people?" shouted the Colonel incredulously. "A chap never shoots the wrong people. He only shoots those who deserve it!"

"Quite so," said Churchill. "Have you any idea who might have been behind the attack on Mr Rumbold's onions, Colonel?"

"One of the rival chaps, I imagine. Sniffer Tubby or someone like that."

"Which one?"

"Sniffer Tubby, I expect."

"Does such a person exist?"

"I believe so."

"I don't know no one called Sniffer Tubby," said Rumbold.

"Perhaps you could list the names of your rivals for the Colonel's benefit," suggested Churchill.

"Tubby Williams, Stropper Harris, Colin Sniffer Downs and Barry Woolwell."

"Oh, it'll be one of them for sure," said Colonel Slingsby.

"Do you know any of them personally, Colonel?" asked Churchill.

"Not quite man to man. I know Rumbold the best because of the beard. Had a beard like that myself during the Boer War. Takes me back."

"So to surmise then, Colonel, you have no idea who

might have carried out the attack on Mr Rumbold's vegetables," said Churchill.

"One of the rivals."

"And can you know that with any degree of certainty?"

"It must be, though, mustn't it? Any fool can see that. Round them up I say."

"And have them shot?" asked Pemberley.

"Good gracious no, woman! Round them up, and then only when you have found out which one did it do you shoot him. Unless all of them did it, in which case you would naturally shoot them all."

"Thank you, Colonel Slingsby," said Churchill. "You've been most helpful. I think we've seen all we need to here, haven't we, Miss Pemberley? It's time we toddled off to continue with our next case."

"Do we have another case, Mrs Churchill?" asked Pemberley.

"Yes, we do. Remember the one I told you about this morning?"

"No, I can't say that I do."

"How forgetful of you, Miss Pemberley. Anyway, we need to head off now to attend to it, don't we?" Churchill took her arm. "Come along; I'll jog your memory on the way."

Chapter 3

ON RETURNING TO THE OFFICE, Churchill and Pemberley found a small, round-faced woman waiting by the door.

"Mrs Bramley?" said Pemberley. "Is something up?"

"Oh you're 'ere at last. I was wond'rin' where you'd got to. The door was locked and even though I knocked at it there was no answer, so I stood 'ere for a while wond'rin' what to do next and—"

"We were out, Mrs Bramley," said Churchill impatiently, "but we have returned now, so do come and join us for a cup of something hot and strengthening."

As Mrs Bramley removed her felt hat and sat herself in front of Churchill's desk, Churchill hoped their visitor had an interesting case to present. She didn't want to waste all her time trying to solve the mystery of Rumbold's damaged onions.

"You proberly know I own the tea rooms what's on the 'igh street."

"And very fine tea rooms they are too, Mrs Bramley. I must commend you on your scones, in particular. Would you like a jam tart?" Churchill pointed to the plate on her desk, which now contained grains of soil from Mr Rumbold's dirty hands. "On second thoughts, don't touch those, Mrs Bramley. Miss Pemberley, would you mind fetching fresh supplies from the new baker downstairs? These jam tarts have been contaminated."

"I've just put the kettle on the ring," said Pemberley. "Listen out for it in case I'm not back in time."

"What d'you think o' the new baker?" asked Mrs Bramley. "Simpkins, ain't it?"

"Yes, that's right," replied Churchill. "He's certainly more likeable than Bodkin, but his produce isn't as well-risen. We had a very soggy batch of Eccles cakes from him yesterday."

"You should tell 'im."

"I will, but he's quite new, isn't he? And rather nervous and eager to please. I'll give him some time to bed down a little, then I'll hit him with it."

"I wouldn't go 'itting 'im."

"I won't actually hit him. I meant I would just tell him the hard truth. After all, Miss Pemberley and I are his biggest clients, being located, as we are, directly above his shop."

"I'd like to 'ave an office above a bakery."

"Why, Mrs Bramley? Your wonderful tea rooms are the talk of the village."

"Thank you, Mrs Churchill. I've run 'em for fifteen years and three months now, and I've always liked doin' it. Keeps me outta trouble 'cause I often thinks what I'd be doin' with me time if I weren't runnin' 'em, and I jus' dunno what I'd be doin'!"

"And how can I help you today, Mrs Bramley?" Churchill readied herself with her notebook and pen.

"Well, everythin' was going perfect till Mrs Cranster retired in January."

"Her departure caused a problem, did it?"

"Not 'er departure, as such; it were the arrival o' the one what replaced 'er."

Pemberley returned with a paper bag exuding the delicious aroma of baked goods.

"Oh, excellent, Miss Pemberley!" Churchill's stomach rumbled. "What did you get us?"

"Custard tarts."

"Perfect. Just hand the bag over, will you? We don't want to be putting them on that plate until it's been thoroughly disinfected. Custard tart, Mrs Bramley?"

"Thank 'ee."

"So Mrs Cranster retired in January," said Churchill, having finished a mouthful of tart. "Who's her replacement, then?"

"Young Kitty Flatboot from Cherrybrick Farm. 'Ave you come across the Flatboots, Mrs Churchill? There's 'undereds of 'em. Breed like rabbits, they do. Old Mr Samuel Flatboot's still alive, then 'e's got 'is seven sons and each of 'ems got—"

"The ins and outs of Mr Flatboot's progeny are possibly superfluous, Mrs Bramley," interrupted Churchill. "What's the problem with Kitty Flatboot?"

"She's got sticky 'ands."

"Sticky hands?"

"Yeah."

Churchill sighed. "I always despair at the way members of our lower classes fail to maintain simple habits of cleanliness."

"No, Mrs Churchill. Kitty washes 'er 'ands."

"Then why are they sticky?"

"It's a sayin'. Some o' the coins in the till gets stuck to 'er 'ands, like."

"Is this a rare and unusual form of magnetism?"

"I believe what Mrs Bramley is saying is that Kitty Flatboot is stealing from the till," stated Pemberley bluntly as she placed the tea tray on the desk.

"Is she? Well, why didn't you just say so, Mrs Bramley?" said Churchill. "You should dismiss the girl at once!"

"I can't be certain as it's 'er what's takin' the money."

"Who else could it be?"

"The only other person what uses the till is meself."

"In that case the thief is either Kitty or you, Mrs Bramley. And it doesn't take a genius to rule out you because you wouldn't steal from yourself, would you? So therefore it has to be Kitty."

"Yeah, 'owever I've never seen 'er do it."

"Well, the girl's hardly going to steal money from the till while you're watching, is she?"

"I s'pose not. I don't like to think it's 'er but I know as it must be. If someone could witness 'er doin' it I'd 'ave summat to go on."

"Have you confronted her about the thefts?"

"No, I'm waitin' till someone's seen 'er do it."

"And how much do you estimate that she's stolen from you so far?"

"Eight pounds, fourteen shillings and sixpence."

"That's a significant and surprisingly precise sum of money."

"I've got to watch the pennies. I'm a widow, see."

"In summary then, Mrs Bramley, you would like me to conduct some surveillance on this young Kitty Flatboot in order to confirm whether she does indeed have sticky hands or not."

"Yes please, Mrs Churchill. I feel bad for spyin' on the

girl, but it's me only 'ope now. She's stealin' from a poor widow, she is! I wonder what my Barney would say if 'e could see what was 'appenin' to me!"

"Barney?"

"Me late 'usband. 'E were a treasure, 'e were. Married for forty years, we was, and never a cross word."

"That's no insubstantial achievement."

"If only 'e could see what she's doin' ter me!"

"It's quite disgraceful," said Churchill. "The girl has no scruples at all. We'll sort her out, won't we, Miss Pemberley?"

Pemberley rolled her eyes and Churchill surmised that she was despairing over the prospect of yet another petty case.

"Come on, Miss Pemberley, it'll keep us out of trouble. And it's important to do our duty on the behalf of a poor widow who's being stolen from."

Pemberley looked far from convinced.

Chapter 4

"LOOK at the state of my knees," complained Pemberley, hitching up her skirt in the office the following morning.

"I can't say that I often look at a lady's knees, or anyone's knees for that matter, Pembers, but they don't look too bad for a lady of your years."

"I'm talking about the dirt on my stockings."

"Oh yes, they're in quite a mess. Which soap flakes do you use? I swear by Lux. You don't get grubby stockings with Lux."

"No, this happened just now! I was mown down by Inspector Mappin on his bicycle!"

"What on earth possessed him to do that?"

"I don't know. He was blowing his whistle as he pedalled like the clappers along the high street, but I didn't notice him initially because my mind was floating about elsewhere."

"Well, that'll teach you, Pembers. It always pays to be aware of your surroundings. Don't take your hat off, we're going out." Churchill grabbed her handbag and leapt up from her seat.

"But I've only just arrived!"

"We've got to go and see what Mappin's up to. The inspector rarely moves at any speed quicker than a sloth's pace. Something important must have happened."

Churchill and Pemberley left the office and marched over the cobbles, in the direction Inspector Mappin had been heading.

"Have you noticed that our destination seems rather popular with the other people on the high street, Pembers?" said Churchill. "Seems as though everyone's got wind of something. I wonder what could have happened."

After a short walk they reached the lane which led up to the allotments.

"Perhaps someone's attacked Mr Rumbold's vegetables again," said Pemberley.

"They might well have, mightn't they? Perhaps they cut them all up and cooked them in a summer vegetable stew. Though I can't imagine it would pull in this much of a crowd. Look, there's Mrs Thonnings from the haberdashery shop. I've never even seen the woman on her feet before. I had begun to doubt whether she possessed any."

"At least I wore my sensible shoes today," said Pemberley as they bustled up the muddy lane.

"Well done, Pembers. Now you're prepared for anything the day throws at us."

Just as she finished speaking, Churchill bumped into the owner of the haberdashery shop. "Oh, I do apologise, Mrs Thonnings." She looked up ahead to see that the lane was filled with people. "Goodness, is there some sort of blockage?"

"It certainly appears that way," replied Mrs Thonnings.

"What's happened up at the allotments?"

"I don't really know. I saw everyone walking in this

direction and decided to follow. We're just like a herd of sheep, aren't we?" she said with a giggle.

"Speak for yourself, Mrs Thonnings," replied Churchill. "Come on, Miss Pemberley, we need to get through this throng of onlookers. Make way for Churchill's Detective Agency!" she called out. A sea of disgruntled faces turned to glare at her. "Investigators coming through!"

Churchill used a combination of well-positioned handbag and elbows to fight her way through the crowd.

"No, you're not coming through, Mrs Churchill," said Inspector Mappin once she had battled her way to the front.

"Good morning, my respected arm of the law!" she said cheerily, admiring his bushy brown mutton-chop whiskers. "What's afoot?"

"There's been a murder," said an old man in a tweed jacket with his hands in his pockets and a pipe in his mouth.

"A *murder*?" said Churchill, stunned. "Who? Where?"

"Mr Williams," replied the man. "He's been murdered on his own allotment."

"Not Tubby!" said Churchill.

"Aye, that's him. Tubby Williams," the man confirmed.

Inspector Mappin rolled his eyes. "Stop giving this woman information, Mr Woolwell. I don't want her getting herself involved."

"I'm a detective, Inspector Mappin," corrected Churchill.

"An amateur sleuth."

"Who happened to be married to Detective Chief Inspector Churchill of Scotland Yard for more than forty years," added Churchill. "I know my onions, and I know what happened to Mr Rumbold's onions as well. Tubby

Williams was the prime suspect! Where's Mr Rumbold now?"

"How should I know?" said Inspector Mappin.

"You should make it your business to know. You should be rounding up suspects before they can start covering their tracks."

Inspector Mappin sighed. "See what you've started now, Woolwell?" he said. "Now Mrs Churchill is about to trample all over my case like a bull in a... on an allotment."

"You do say the silliest things, Inspector," retorted Churchill. "I have no intention of causing any disruption to the investigation; however, you would be foolish to turn down my offer of help. Let's not forget the murder I solved shortly after my arrival in Compton Poppleford, eh?"

"I don't suppose you'll ever allow me to forget it."

"Very good, Inspector, and may I also add that the chief suspect in the murder of Mr Williams just happens to be one of my clients."

"Suspect? What are you talking about? I only just found out there'd been a murder twenty minutes ago! It's enough of a job keeping the crowds out of here without trying to work out who's done it."

"You don't have enough personnel, Inspector Mappin. Mr Rumbold could be on his way to the nearest port by now."

"I've got two constables coming over from Bulchford and a chief inspector is on his way from Dorchester. That will be plenty enough assistance."

"My trusty assistant Miss Pemberley and I are also at your service, Inspector."

"Thank you, Mrs Churchill, but there's no need."

"You're turning away our considerable skill and expertise, Inspector Mappin."

"I think this lady's got a lot to offer, Inspector," Mr Woolwell chipped in. "Why not give 'er a go?"

"With all due respect, Mr Woolwell, you really don't have the first idea what this lady is like. She'd take over the police station if I gave her half a chance."

"No danger of that, Inspector," replied Churchill. "It's a rather dull and austere place. With quite a draught too, I might add."

"Do excuse me," said the inspector. "I have a murder case to solve."

"Very well. Come along, Miss Pemberley, we're not wanted here. Miss Pemberley? Where've you got to?" Churchill looked around but could see no sign of her trusty assistant.

"Have you seen Miss Pemberley?" she asked Mr Woolwell.

"The old, thin woman with spectacles and straggly hair?" he asked.

"Yes."

"No."

"How mysterious. I could have sworn she was standing just behind me."

Chapter 5

ASSUMING Pemberley had returned to the office, Churchill pushed her way back through the crowd and began walking back down the lane toward the high street. *Was it possible that Tubby Williams had been murdered by Mr Rumbold in revenge for the attack on his onions?* she wondered. *It seemed a rather heavy-handed response, but perhaps all the tit for tat had escalated out of control.*

The door to the office was still locked, suggesting that Pemberley hadn't yet turned up there. Churchill retrieved the key from her handbag, unlocked the door and stepped into the hallway. On the floor lay a folded piece of paper. She picked it up, unfolded it and read the scrawled handwriting:

Forget about onions, problem now resolved.
Mr Rumbold

. . .

Churchill gasped. *Surely this counted as a confession from Mr Rumbold?* She scurried up the narrow staircase to the office in the hope that Pemberley would somehow be present, but there was no sign of her. Churchill filled the kettle, placed it on the gas ring and sat down to reread Mr Rumbold's short note.

Problem now resolved.

He was guilty! And what's more, he was probably at Weymouth already, embarking on a ship bound for the continent.

Churchill got up from her chair and paced the floor. Then she glanced at the telephone on Pemberley's desk and wondered whether there was someone she should telephone about this unexpected turn of events. She realised Inspector Mappin would still be at the allotment, so there was no use trying to contact him.

What should she do?

At that moment the glass door opened and Pemberley stepped in.

"Oh, Pembers! How I've missed you!" Churchill waved the note at her secretary. "Read this! It's a confession from Rumbold, and he's on a ship bound for France!"

Pemberley frowned, took the note and read it.

"Confession?" she said quizzically. "This isn't a confession. It merely states that we should forget about the onions as the problem is now resolved. I assume the problem he refers to here is Tubby Williams."

"Of course it is," said Churchill, snatching back the note. "And Rumbold murdered him!"

"Mrs Churchill, it's quite unlike you to leap to conclusions. The note doesn't really tell us anything other than Mr Rumbold is aware of Mr Williams's death."

Churchill took a deep breath. "You're right. I think I've overexcited myself this morning, and Inspector Mappin was so terribly rude. Rudeness sits most uncomfortably with me, Pembers. It puts me utterly out of sorts."

"It doesn't necessarily mean that Rumbold is innocent, though," said Pemberley. "Why would he put a note through our door to tell us the problem is resolved?"

"Exactly!" said Churchill. "He's up to something, isn't he?"

"He might not be."

"But he might. I think we need to ask him, Pembers. That's the only way to set the matter straight. It'll be some time before Inspector Mappin gets to him, that's for sure. But what if he's already on his way to France?"

"Why are you so convinced he's heading there?"

"We're only spitting distance from the south coast, aren't we?"

"I see what you mean. He could have caught the train from Dorchester to Weymouth by now, couldn't he?"

"He could have, though we're overlooking the fact that the branch line to Dorchester takes about three days."

"How long?!"

"It's actually only about forty-five minutes, Pembers, but it feels like three days on those hard seats."

Pemberley checked her watch. "It's half-past nine, which means Rumbold could feasibly be on the boat to France by now."

"I knew it!"

"He could have arrived at Weymouth by nine, having reached Dorchester at about eight or eight thirty. I don't know what time the first branch line train is, but he may have driven to Dorchester instead."

"Yes, of course he could have! Perhaps he left his motor car at Dorchester station," said Churchill.

"Only I'm not sure Mr Rumbold has a motor car. He doesn't really look like the car-owning type, does he?"

"No, but we'll need to find out. And we need to find out quickly, because someone's going to have to chase him across the English Channel. Where does he live? Is he married?"

"I'm sure he lives in Spitalduck Lane, but I don't know which house, and I'm not sure about his marital status."

"I'm guessing he's a bachelor, Pembers. I can't imagine a wife tolerating his poor hygiene levels. Have you seen how filthy his fingernails are? I'm sure he could cultivate a row of miniature vegetables beneath them."

Their musings were interrupted by a knock at the door.

"Do come in!" chimed Churchill.

A dirty, bearded man walked in with his cap in his hand.

Churchill allowed a moment to pass in order to double-check the identity of the man standing before her, having expected him to be at least halfway to the continent by this point.

"Oh hello, Mr Rumbold," she said eventually. "You're here."

"You seem surprised, Mrs Churchill."

"Surprised? Me? No, I'm never surprised. Oh dear, what's that awful smell? It smells like something's burning."

"It smells like someone put the kettle on the gas ring and then forgot about it," said Pemberley, leaving the room to investigate.

"Thank you for your note, Mr Rumbold," said Churchill, taking a seat behind her desk. "It was most… er, informative."

"I'm glad to 'ear you've read it, Mrs Churchill. In light

of what we spoke about yesterday I didn't want you ter go investigatin' poor Tubby Williams when 'e's already dead."

"It's terrible news. There was a great kerfuffle at the allotments this morning."

"It's taken me by shock, it really 'as." Mr Rumbold slumped down into the chair opposite her. "It's no secret me an' 'im was rivals, but I loved 'im like 'e was me own brother, I really did. You can ask the wife. She knows 'ow much affection I 'ad fer the man. He proberly speared me onions an' I might of slashed 'is gourds, an' that ain't even the 'alf of it. But we shared the same great love, an' that were vegetables. We loved growin' 'em, an' the world's a sadder place today without 'im."

A tear trickled down Mr Rumbold's grimy cheek leaving a trail of clean skin. Churchill felt a pang of sympathy for the man.

"Miss Pemberley, could you make some tea for us all, please?" she called out.

"I would do, Mrs Churchill, if someone hadn't burnt the bottom off the kettle."

"Oh dear. Has someone?"

Churchill opened one of the drawers in her desk, exposing a paper bag filled with enticing treats.

"Would you like an emergency chocolate eclair, Mr Rumbold?"

"No thank'ee, Mrs Churchill. I've lost me appetite for today."

Churchill continued to look down at the bag, wondering whether it would be disrespectful to snaffle an emergency eclair herself. She thought better of it and reluctantly closed the drawer.

"When did you hear about Mr Williams's sad demise?" she asked Mr Rumbold.

"Stropper Harris come round this mornin' while I was eatin' me eggs on toast. 'E was the one what found 'im."

"Goodness! Mr Harris discovered the body?"

"Yep."

"And when did you last see Mr Williams?"

"I think I was proberly the last person to see 'im alive," sniffed Rumbold. "It were yesterday evenin' at the allotments."

"The last person to see him alive? Gosh." Churchill tried to calm the theories that were thrashing about wildly in her brain. "And what time might that have been?"

"It'd just got dark when I decided to go 'ome. We was the last two up there. After that I went to the Pig and Scythe for a few, then I went back an' it were just 'im 'angin' around."

"Did you converse with one another?"

"Oh yeah, we was conversin' an' that."

"About vegetables?"

"Of sorts. It was more o' the usual accusin', like. I was tellin' 'im I was gonna 'ave me revenge on 'is cabbages, an' 'e was goadin' me, sayin' as 'e knew where me secret marrows was."

"Oh dear. Not a particularly friendly conversation, then?"

"I don't see it like that; it's jus' 'ow it was. Like I said, I loved 'im like me brother. Then I went off 'ome an' he proberly stayed there guardin' 'is veg like he did some nights, an' then the murderer's gone up an' shot 'im."

"He was shot, was he?"

"Yep."

"And how did you come to know that?"

"Stropper told me."

"And how does Mr Stropper know that?"

"'E found 'im, Mrs Churchill. 'E seen him! I don't want

ter go into no details or nothin', but 'e told me as Tubby were shot."

"Oh dear, that's terrible. And to think that his murderer was likely to have been lurking around the allotments at about the same time you were there, Mr Rumbold."

"Yep. Well, I gotta get back to me wife now, 'cause she's all upset an' barricadin' the door so as the murderer don't get in." He rose to his feet.

"I think you should reassure your wife that the culprit isn't likely to be after her."

"Yep, I done all that, but I'm the last one she pays any 'eed to. And to be 'onest with yer, Mrs Churchill, I'm a bit scared meself. I don't tell the wife that 'cause it'd scare 'er even more, but there's a murderer out there carryin' a gun, and any one of us could be next!"

Chapter 6

AS MR RUMBOLD LEFT, Churchill sat back in her chair and sighed.

"I think Rumbold purposefully visited us to put us off the scent. What do you think, Pembers?"

"But why us?" replied her assistant, holding the burned-out kettle in one hand. "We're not even investigating the murder. That's down to Inspector Mappin."

"Unfortunately it is. I have to say that if I were ever murdered the last person I'd want investigating my death is that cack-handed inspector."

"I managed to get a good look at the crime scene."

"Really, Pembers? How on earth did you manage that?"

"I snuck up and had a peek while Inspector Mappin was single-handedly trying to control the crowd."

Churchill shivered. "You're a braver woman than I am. And what did you see?"

"I'd like to tell you over a nice cup of something, but our kettle's ruined."

"So it is, Pembers. Well, come on, let's go down to Mrs

Bramley's Tea Rooms. We can also start work on the case of Kitty's sticky hands while we're at it."

Mrs Bramley's Tea Rooms were located in a small white building on the high street with frilly curtains adorning the bay window. Inside, a dozen tables were covered in lace tablecloths, each with a little white vase filled with pink carnations. There was just enough space for Churchill to manoeuvre herself between the tables.

"I'd forgotten how bijou it is in here, Pemberley," she said as she wedged herself onto a chair and knocked into the disgruntled lady sitting behind her. Churchill felt slightly irritated by the manner in which her spindly secretary was able to slip into her chair with next to no effort. "The seats of these chairs are designed for people with no fleshy parts, have you noticed that Pembers? I shan't be able to sit here for long without something going numb. Despite the discomfort, I must say that tea rooms are my most favourite places to spend time in. I don't know what I'd do without them. Oh look, that must be our sticky Kitty," she gestured at a freckled girl serving tea at a nearby table. She had chubby cheeks and a prominent overbite. "Are all the Flatboots plain?"

"I can't say I've studied them in that way before," replied Pemberley. "Having never been a beauty myself I can't say I put much stock in looks."

"I must confess that I was," said Churchill proudly.

"A beauty?"

"Yes! Don't look so surprised, Pembers. My slim waist and well-turned ankles were the talk of Teddington when I was a spring chicken. Why else would Detective Chief Inspector Churchill have chosen me for his bride?"

"Your scintillating wit and conversation?"

"Oh yes of course, well that goes without saying. More important than the waist and ankles, really. But it's nice to be admired, Pemberley, and important to make the most of it while it lasts, don't you think?"

"I wouldn't know."

"Let's summon this Flatboot girl and get some tea. Yoo-hoo, Kitty! Over here!"

Kitty Flatboot scowled as she approached the table.

"What d'yer want?" she asked sulkily.

"Tea for two, please."

Kitty wrote the order in her notebook.

"Anythin' else?"

"And two slices of Mrs Bramley's delightful walnut cake as well, please."

Kitty Flatboot noted this down and took the order to the kitchen.

"Well, there goes a girl with few manners," commented Churchill. "I'm surprised Mrs Bramley chose to employ her at all."

"Perhaps it was because you said *yoo-hoo* to her."

"What's wrong with yoo-hoo?"

"I'm not entirely sure, but I know that I wouldn't like someone yoo-hooing me."

"That's because you're the sensitive type, Pembers. Anyway, tell me all about the crime scene at the allotment. What did you see?"

Pemberley shuddered. "Ugh, it was horrible."

"A murder scene is never pleasant."

"I was talking about the mud."

"The mud was horrible?"

"Yes, I hate it."

"But you're a country girl, Pemberley. You should be used to it."

"I've never liked mud and never will."

"So what about the murder scene?"

"Tubby Williams was lying on his back in the mud next to a row of broad beans."

"How did you know it was him?"

"I recognised the trousers. He always wore the same tweed trousers with leather patches on the knees."

"From what I'm learning about gardeners, they lack a certain sartorial elegance. And how did you know it was a row of broad beans he was lying next to?"

"They're not as tall as peas or runner beans; they're quite stocky plants with those pea-like leaves."

"You sound like you know your beans, Pemberley. Was there any obvious sign of injury to Tubby's body?"

"An injury to the chest. A rather nasty injury, in fact, with quite a lot of blood."

"Caused by?"

"Either a knife or a gunshot wound, I'd say."

"Oh dear."

"I'm more inclined to think it was a gunshot wound because there's usually more than one knife wound. When they have a knife they jab, jab, jab a few times don't they? It's because they're not quite sure if each jab is doing the job."

Churchill winced. "I suppose not."

"But with a simple shooting, just one shot can be enough to satisfy the culprit that his victim is dead."

"Indeed. And a gunshot wound is consistent with what Stropper told Rumbold."

"Mr Harris."

"No, it was Mr Stropper."

"His name is Stropper Harris."

"I see. Very well, carry on then. What else?"

"I'd say he'd been there a while. A few hours, perhaps.

Some of the blood looked quite dry and rigor mortis had begun to set in."

"How do you know that?"

"I poked him with a beanpole."

"You poked him?"

"Only gently. And just his arm. I didn't want to get too close."

"Understandable."

The conversation briefly paused when Kitty Flatboot arrived with their tea and cake.

"I think he was probably murdered late yesterday evening," said Pemberley.

"That makes sense. The murderer could have been lurking in the allotments at that time waiting for Rumbold to go home so he could get on with the business of murdering Tubby."

"Unless Mr Rumbold is the murderer."

"And he could well be, couldn't he? He suspected that Tubby had speared his onions, and was the last one to see him alive after a conversation in which they goaded each other about harming one another's vegetables. And he put that strange note through our letterbox."

"But he claims to love him like a brother."

"I have two words for you, Pembers. Cain and Abel."

"That's three words."

"But only two people. The long and the short of what I mean is that just because someone considers another person to be like a brother, it doesn't mean they wouldn't murder them."

"They're more likely to, in fact."

"Well, I wouldn't go that far."

"As in the case of Cain and Abel."

"Let's forget I mentioned them. I think Rumbold must

be considered a suspect. We can put him on our incident map when we return to the office."

"Does that mean we have a case now?"

"I'd say that we do, wouldn't you?"

"But isn't it actually Inspector Mappin's case?"

"Pfft. We can work on it secretly, Pembers. And it's sort of our case because we took on Rumbold's onion case, which has since grown into something rather larger and infinitely more sinister."

"We took on the onion case, did we?"

"Yes we did. Oh hello, Mrs Bramley!"

The proprietress waddled up to the table with a floral apron tied so tightly around her waist that her top half looked as though it was about to be separated from the bottom.

"Good mornin', ladies, and what a lovely fine mornin' it is!"

"Good morning, Mrs Bramley," said Churchill. "I'm not so sure about it being fine, though."

"'Ows that then? What's 'appened?"

"Have you not heard about the murder up at the allotments?"

"Oh yeah. Mr Williams, weren't it? Very sad. I didn't know 'im, though."

"Neither did I," replied Churchill. "But it's rather disconcerting all the same, wouldn't you say?"

"It's right sad." She lowered her voice to a whisper. "'Ave you seen 'er yet?"

"Kitty, you mean? Yes, we've seen her all right."

"With 'er hand in the till?"

"Well, no." Churchill realised she hadn't been watching Kitty closely at all. "Not yet, anyway. But we're keeping an eye on her."

"Soon as you see 'er do it, you let me know."

"I'm sure it's only a matter of time, Mrs Bramley, don't you worry. Anyway, I expect you've overheard a few conversations in your delightful tea rooms about the murder this morning. Has anyone been speculating on who might be behind it?"

"You know what it's like when these things 'appen. Ev'ryone's an expert, ain't they? One name keeps croppin' up, though."

"Ah yes, and whose name might that be?"

"Mr Rumbold's name."

"Really? Now that is interesting. Did they have any evidence to back it up?"

"'E were seen leaving the allotments late last night with a gun in 'is 'and."

"Well that's rather damning, isn't it? Who saw him with the gun?"

"It was… oh, erm. I can't remember 'is name now." Mrs Bramley glanced around her tea rooms. "And 'e's not in 'ere no more. Gah. The name'll come to me."

"Can you describe him to me?"

"Normal lookin'. Normal height. Normal weight. Square chin and spectacles. Brown 'air. What I likes to call a bit of a bore. Likes cricket. Orders egg sandwiches but never eats 'is crusts."

"Interesting. Thank you, Mrs Bramley."

Chapter 7

"ANY IDEA where we can find Mr Stropper, Pemberley?" asked Churchill as they left the tea rooms.

"I don't know where he lives, but I know where he is now."

"That's rather clever of you, Pembers. How do you know that?"

"He's over there." Pemberley pointed to the base of the clock tower, where a man was regaling a small crowd of people with what appeared to be an engaging story.

As they drew nearer Churchill could see that he had raised his height by standing on a crate and was putting on quite an animated display.

"There 'e lay, 'is eyes starin' up at the 'eavens!" announced Stropper Harris, re-enacting the victim's unblinking gaze. He was a lean man with pock-marked skin, and he wore a red-and-white plaid shirt.

"Did you run away?" someone called out.

"Not likely! The dead don't scare me!"

"I would of," said someone else.

"Me an' all," said another.

"Was there lots of blood?" called out another person.

"It was everywhere!" declared Stropper Harris.

The crowd responded with a collective gasp.

Stropper glanced at his watch. "Right, that's it. Ten minutes is up. The next recountin' is in fifteen minutes. A shillin' a listen, and don't be 'angin' round for it if you've already listened to one. It's a shillin' each time."

As the crowd began to disperse, Stropper Harris removed a hip flask from his pocket and took a large swig.

"It seems as though our friend Mr Stropper is capitalising on his role as the man who found the body," commented Churchill in a disapproving tone. "Mr Stropper!" she called out to him.

He acknowledged her with a raise of his hip flask.

"I'm Mrs Churchill of Churchill's Detective Agency, and this is my trusty assistant, Miss Pemberley. We're investigating the dreadful murder of Mr Williams at the allotments."

"It's a pleasure to meet you, ladies. Helpin' Mappin out, are you?"

"No. We were on the case before Mappin."

"'Ow d'you manage that, then?"

"We'd already taken on the case of Mr Rumbold's onions, in which the deceased was the prime suspect."

"'Ow d'you know Williams done it?"

"Mr Rumbold told us."

"Rumbold could of been mistaken."

"He could have been, and I suppose we'll never know now, given that the prime suspect is no longer with us. I understand you discovered his body."

"That I did," he said proudly.

"What time was that?"

Stropper Harris looked at his watch. "The next tellin's in thirteen minutes. A shillin' per person."

"I'm afraid we don't have time to wait about for the next telling; we have a busy day ahead of us. Can you just tell me what time you found the unfortunate Mr Williams?"

"I'll tell you in twelve and an 'alf minutes' time."

"And after we've both parted company with a shilling, presumably?"

"C'rect."

"Mr Stropper, my assistant and I are not your average members of the great unwashed, you know. We're private detectives. Your assistance is required in our investigation."

"That's no excuse to get round payin' the shillin', Mrs Churchill. You wouldn't believe some o' the excuses people 'ave been coming up with today. One fellow told me he deserved to listen fer free 'cause Williams was married to his wife's cousin's mother-in-law's sister."

"That seems like a fair excuse to me, Mr Stropper."

"The name's 'Arris. Stropper 'Arris."

"I think your charging of a fee to listen to some exaggerated tale of how you found Mr Williams shot dead on his allotment is an exploitation of the poor man's demise. Not to mention the fact that it's incredibly disrespectful."

Stropper Harris's eyes narrowed. "'Ave you ever discovered a body, Mrs Churchill?"

"No I haven't."

"So you've no idea what it's like to be followed around by 'alf the village askin' the same three questions over and over. They won't leave me alone! I decided it's better to situate meself on this vegetable crate beneath the clock tower and charge people for a regular tellin'. That way everyone gets to hear what 'appened and I gets paid for me time."

"That actually sounds like quite a sensible solution," said Pemberley.

Churchill glared at her, then turned back to face Mr Harris. "I take your point, Mr Stropper. But can you at least make allowances for myself and my assistant?"

"Sorry, no. Once I start makin' allowances for two people, everyone'll be wantin' allowances made for 'em. Then everyone's got an excuse for not adhering to me schedule of tellings or paying me a shillin'. Look at this fellow 'ere." He gestured at a large man with a red face who was loitering nearby. "'E's just waiting to try an' get a question in! And when I tell 'im 'e's got ter wait ten minutes and pay me a shillin' he's goin' to start askin' for allowances just like you two! Rules is rules, Mrs Churchill."

"Fine. I shall wait a further ten minutes and pay you a shilling if you will answer just one question for me, Mr Stropper. Do we have a deal?"

He took another swig from his hip flask. "All right," he said eventually. "But only 'cause you're a proper investigatin' detective."

"Thank you, Mr Stropper. I understand that you're a gardener yourself, and are therefore au fait with most members of the gardening community. Have you any idea who might have carried out this attack on Mr Williams?"

"Rumbold."

"Really? But you called at his house this morning to inform him of the incident. Did you believe he was responsible at that point? Did you ask him if he'd done it?"

"You said just one question, Mrs Churchill, and I've answered it. If there's time I'll take questions after the next tellin'."

Chapter 8

AFTER ENDURING A HEAVILY EMBELLISHED tale from Stropper Harris about the manner in which he had discovered Tubby Williams's body, Churchill and Pemberley were no wiser than they had been before.

"Well, that was a waste of a shilling apiece, wasn't it, Pembers?" said Churchill as they walked back along the high street toward their office. "And he didn't even have time to answer any questions afterwards!"

"I suppose he had to go to the little boys' room at some point."

"The call of nature could have waited a minute or two longer, I feel sure of that. However, I'm very much looking forward to populating our incident board again, Pembers. Do we have enough pins and string?"

"We do indeed."

"Oh good. You get started on the incident board, then, and I'll pop into this little cookshop here to buy us a new kettle."

· · ·

The shelves of the cookshop were stacked to the ceiling with pots, pans, serving bowls, plates, dishes and cups. There was barely room for Churchill to move without knocking something to the floor.

"Goodness, what a cluttered little place," she muttered to herself as she searched for a kettle. "It needs a proper sorting out. And how can one possibly reach anything on the top shelf?" She craned her neck to see what was perched on it. "I should think that quite a layer of dust has gathered up there by now. I can't say I'd like to pay full price for something with a layer of dust on it."

"What was that?" came a man's voice from the back of the shop.

"I was talking to myself," she replied, "but since you ask I was just commenting that I wouldn't pay full price for something that was covered in dust."

"What's covered in dust?"

"I don't know, but I imagine the items up on the top shelf there must be. How do you even see what's up there?"

"I have a stepladder."

"Good for you, but a stepladder won't do for me at all. I abhor heights. And how do you find anything in this place? Everything's piled on top of everything else with no sense of order to it at all."

"All you need do is ask, madam."

The man stepped into view from behind the shelving and Churchill felt her heart skip a beat. He had dark, twinkling eyes, a handsome square jaw and a head of silver hair. He wore a crisp white shirt beneath a tailored waistcoat, and was surprisingly broad-shouldered and trim-waisted for a man of his advanced years. Churchill found herself smiling.

"Oh, good morning, sir. I'm Mrs Churchill of

Churchill's Detective Agency; just a few doors along the high street from here in fact. Above the bakery. It used to be Bodkin's Bakery but it's Simpkins's now."

"It's a pleasure to meet you, Mrs Churchill, I've heard all about you."

"Oh goodness, have you really?" Churchill felt a rush of heat to her face. "I do hate it when people say that."

"Oh, I'm sorry, I meant no harm by it."

"No, I didn't mean *hate* it. I chose my words wrongly there. I quite *like* it, really, I suppose it makes me rather bashful as it suggests people have been talking about me without my being present, and that's always rather alarming to think of, wouldn't you say?"

"I suppose so. I'm Mr Harding, by the way."

"It's a pleasure to make your acquaintance, Mr Harding." Churchill smoothed her hair, wishing she'd had a shampoo and set before stepping inside the shop.

"Are you looking for anything in particular, Mrs Churchill?"

"I am indeed. We're in need of a new kettle. I rather ruined our previous one, I'm afraid. I put the gas ring on and then forgot all about it!"

"Oh dear. Though I should think it's fortunate that you didn't cause a fire."

"Isn't it? And may I just explain that the comment I made about this shop being cluttered was misplaced. I didn't really mean to use that word. What I actually meant was that you have a lot of stock here. In fact, your shop is so well-stocked that perhaps a less discerning customer might perceive it to be cluttered, but it does, in fact, have a certain order to it."

"No need to apologise, Mrs Churchill. It is cluttered, but at least I know where everything is. Organised chaos, I like to call it."

"Organised chaos!" Churchill found herself emitting a loud giggle. "Oh, I like that, Mr Harding. How funny! And I apologise for the comment about the dust. I'm quite sure there is no dust at all in your fine store."

"I give everything a good going over with my feather duster whenever business is quiet."

"Now there's a certain something about a man with a feather duster, Mr Harding. Quite a something indeed." Churchill adjusted her collar, feeling a little warm beneath her blouse.

"Is that so? Well, allow me to show you my range of kettles."

"Thank you, that would be wonderful."

Churchill spent an engaging fifteen minutes discussing the various kettles on offer with the store owner before choosing one.

"Thank you for devoting so much of your precious time to my mission, Mr Harding," she said as she paid for the kettle. "You must have so many other things to be getting on with."

"I'm not sure that I do," he replied, glancing around the shop. "We haven't been disturbed by any other customers, have we? They're all standing up at the allotments, goggle-mouthed, this morning. Murder isn't good for business."

"Rather a shocker, though, isn't it? Did you know the deceased?"

"Only in passing. I'm not much of a gardener, I'm afraid. To be honest, it doesn't really hold my interest, although a good friend of mine is president of the Compton Poppleford Horticultural Society."

"Colonel Slingsby?"

"The very same."

"He must be extremely shocked about the tragic loss of his friend."

"He is indeed. And there's something that's puzzling him rather."

"What's that?"

"One of the guns from his gunroom went missing shortly before the murder."

"Really? Was it used in the murder?"

"I don't know if it was the same one, but it's rather a coincidence, don't you think? I understand the police will be able to confirm which weapon was used in due course. I'm not quite sure how they do it; something to do with how a gun leaves unique markings on the bullet casings or similar."

"It's pretty much something like that. I was married to Detective Chief Inspector Churchill of Scotland Yard for many years."

"Were you indeed? So you know a good deal about sleuthing, do you?"

"I'm not one to blow my own trumpet, but yes, I should say so."

Mr Harding gave an impressed nod. "Perhaps Inspector Mappin might find you of some assistance with his enquiries in that case."

"You'd think so, wouldn't you? However, he has made it abundantly clear that he doesn't require my help."

"He doesn't know what he's missing out on," said Harding with a wink that made Churchill's spine tingle.

"Why, thank you, Mr Harding. That is praise indeed."

"Not at all, Mrs Churchill. I hope you enjoy the kettle."

"Oh, I will. Thank you, Mr Harding. I promise never to burn it on the gas ring. Never, ever."

Chapter 9

"THE INCIDENT BOARD is pure perfection, my second-in-command," said Churchill as she arrived back at the office.

"Thank you," replied Pemberley. "You seem in high spirits after your kettle purchase."

"Indeed I am, Pembers. They've been lifted by this incident board with all its lengths of string and pins and pictures and photographs. Goodness, is that Mr Rumbold?" She peered more closely at the board. "He looks quite youthful and so much better without all that face fungus. Where did you find this photograph?"

"In my mother's scrapbook."

"Why on earth did your mother have a picture of him?"

"I don't know. There are many things I have yet to understand about my mother."

"Let's not go into them now. What do you know of Mr Harding?"

"The cookshop man? Is he a suspect?"

"No, of course he isn't. He just sold me a kettle."

"I bet he did."

"What do you mean by that?"

"It's his job, isn't it?"

"Yes, I suppose it is. I just can't help but think there's something you're not explaining to me, Pembers."

"He doesn't seem to have any problem selling things to the ladies of Compton Poppleford."

"Good for him."

"He's rather too easy on the eye for them to turn him down."

"Is he? I hadn't noticed!" Churchill gave a loud laugh.

"Haven't you? Just about every other female in the village has; even me, and I don't usually pay much attention to these things, as you know."

"His wife must be rather irritated that all the ladies of Compton Poppleford have noticed her husband is visually unchallenging."

"His wife died a number of years ago."

"Oh dear, that is sad."

"Then he took up with a ballet dancer."

"Oh my! Really?"

"Then that ended."

"Good. Ballet dancers are rather self-obsessed, aren't they? I suspect that's why the relationship ended."

"No, no. It ended because he had a tryst with Mrs Thonnings."

"What?! She of the haberdashery shop?"

"The very same."

"But she's not his type!"

"How do you know what Mr Harding's type is?"

"I'm a good judge of character, Pembers, and I can tell you now that Mrs Thonnings is not his type. Have you noticed how cheap her blouses are? They're practically see-through."

"Perhaps that's what he liked about her."

"Nonsense, Pembers. Mr Harding has more class than that. Mrs Thonnings indeed! Well, I suppose we've all done things we're not proud of."

"What's wrong with Mrs Thonnings? I thought you liked her."

"I don't suppose there's anything much wrong with her, apart from the cheap blouses. I'm rather surprised that's all."

They were interrupted by a knock at the door.

"Do come in!" chimed Churchill.

A police officer stepped into the room.

"Inspector Mappin! To what do we owe this pleasure? I assumed you'd be too busy today to pay us a visit."

"I am," he said gruffly, "but the back-up from Bulchford has arrived now, as has the chief inspector from Dorchester."

"You must be glad of the assistance, Inspector."

"Indeed I am, Mrs Churchill. And it would be of even greater assistance to me if you could find your way to not getting involved."

"Getting involved with what, Inspector?"

"The murder case that has gripped the village of Compton Poppleford today."

"Oh that. No, I shan't get in your way, Inspector. I shall merely continue my work on the case I had already taken on before the tragic event occurred."

"Which is what?"

"The case of Mr Rumbold's onions."

"I see. As long as you stay well away from the Williams case that's fine by me."

"There may be a slight overlap, Inspector. You see, Williams was the prime suspect in the onion case."

"I assume the case is closed now that he's deceased."

"Not exactly closed, no. I may need to root around for further evidence."

"Please don't root around, Mrs Churchill. There really is no need."

"You'll hardly notice me, Inspector."

"With all due respect, Mrs Churchill, you're not the sort of person who moves about unnoticed."

"Is that intended as an insult or a compliment, Inspector?"

"It's more a statement of fact than anything else. Now please reassure me that there will be no *overlap*, as you put it, between your case and mine. I couldn't bear it if you began meddling again."

"Do I look like a meddler, Inspector?"

"Yes."

"How offensive to make such a suggestion!"

"If I'm wrong, how do you explain that large incident board on the wall over there?"

"Oh, that little thing. That's just something Miss Pemberley and I cobbled together for fun. In fact, Miss Pemberley did all of it, I didn't have anything to do with it at all because I was off buying a kettle at the time."

"You asked me to do it, Mrs Churchill," said Pemberley. "I think your exact words were, '*You get started on the incident board, then, and I'll pop into this little cookshop here to buy us a new kettle.*'"

"Whether those were my exact words or not is splitting hairs rather. The long and short of it is that we're not meddlers, are we? We're professional investigators and shall forge our own path, leaving you to forge yours, Inspector."

"I don't want our paths to cross again, Mrs Churchill."

"They won't even run parallel. They shall run forever in opposite directions."

"Until they meet on the other side of the world," added Pemberley.

"They won't even do that," corrected Churchill. "We shall take evasive action to avoid any possible collision."

"I do hope so," replied Mappin. "Otherwise we shall end up in a very sorry state of affairs indeed."

"Who's your chief suspect?" asked Churchill.

"There isn't one yet."

"Rumbold's name is being cast around. You might want to ensure that he doesn't go hopping off to the port any time soon. And I hear that one of Colonel Slingsby's guns went missing shortly before Williams was shot."

"Who told you that?"

"Oh, I couldn't possibly reveal my sources."

"You've been meddling!"

"The information was extended to me, Inspector. I didn't even ask for it."

The inspector tutted. "The gossipmongers in this village risk undermining a serious investigation. I shall have to give one of my strict talks at the village hall again."

"Goodness, that sounds rather serious."

"It is. Now stay out of this please, Mrs Churchill. That includes you and your secretary. Leave this case to the people who actually know what they're doing."

"And who might they be, Inspector?"

Inspector Mappin glowered at her as he left the room.

Chapter 10

"THERE'S one thing you can say about all officers of the law, Pemberley, and I know it from having been married to one for many years."

"And what's that?"

"They always assume they're in the right. Take Inspector Mappin as an example. He's completely convinced of his ability to solve the murder of Mr Williams while the likes of you and I are demoted to the role of mere meddlers."

"It's his job, I suppose."

"But it's our job too, Pembers! I'm going to make sure we solve this crime before he does."

"How will we do that?"

"We'll simply crack on with it. Now then, when we were investigating Rumbold's onions, didn't he mention the name Barry Woolwell?"

"I think so."

"I'm sure Woolwell is a member of the gardening gang. I happened to bump into him at the allotments this morning. Have you any idea where the chap resides?"

"I don't, but I've often seen him staggering out of the Wagon and Carrot."

"Right then, that's where we'll need to go if we want to find him. Hopefully we'll get to him before he reaches the staggering stage."

"Don't underestimate the staggering stage, Mrs Churchill, it can be quite useful. People are more talkative at that level of inebriation than they might otherwise be. Atkins invariably picked up golden nuggets of information from drunkards."

"Did he indeed?" Churchill checked her watch. "In that case, let's give Woolwell a bit longer in there. Another two tankards should do the trick. How long do you think that'll take him? About an hour?"

"I think that sounds like a good estimate."

"Excellent."

Churchill tapped her pen on the desk and hummed a tuneless ditty.

"I'll tell you what I noticed about Mrs Thonnings this morning, Pemberley."

"What did you notice?"

"That she uses a tawdry colour of hair dye. These things often reveal themselves in the harshness of daylight, don't they? When she's tucked up in the corner of her gloomy haberdashery shop, her hair appears, to all intents and purposes, to be a deep red. But out in the sunshine it has quite a tacky orange hue."

"Why has Mrs Thonnings become a candidate for your ire all of a sudden, Mrs Churchill?"

"There's no ire. It was just an observation I made this morning."

"Is it because of her romantic involvement with Mr Harding?"

"No!" Churchill spluttered. "That's simply by-the-by. I

can only assume the man likes orange hair dye as much as he likes see-through blouses. Anyway, what do you make of the colonel's missing gun?"

"It's suspicious."

"It is rather. We need to find out who might have gained access to his gunroom."

"Perhaps we could ask him."

"We could, Pembers, but it wouldn't do to turn up at Ashleigh Grange unannounced. We would need to invite ourselves via an acquaintance of the colonel's."

Churchill allowed Pemberley to give this some thought before chipping in with a suggestion. "Oh, I've just thought of someone! When I was purchasing the kettle this morning, Mr Harding mentioned that he was a friend of the old crumb."

"That'll give you an excuse to talk to Mr Harding again, then."

"It's not a case of having an excuse Pembers. This is an important part of our investigation. Why don't you come with me? We'll pop into the cookshop to speak to Harding, and by then Woolwell will hopefully have consumed enough scrumpy to be in a talkative mood over the road at the Wagon and Carrot."

Chapter 11

"OH DEAR," said Mr Harding as Churchill and Pemberley walked into his cookshop. "Is there something wrong with the kettle?"

"Oh no, Mr Harding, please do put yourself at ease." Churchill felt her face warming as his dark eyes met hers. "The kettle is a delight. In fact, my tea has never tasted so good!"

"Surely the taste is in the tea leaves rather than the kettle," suggested Pemberley.

"Not for those with a refined palette," snapped Churchill. "Every stage of the tea-making process plays its part in the quality of one's brew."

"The water makes a difference too," said Mr Harding.

"Oh, it does indeed. It makes an enormous difference," agreed Churchill.

"Unfortunately, the water here in Dorset has quite a high mineral content," continued Harding. "Travel west to Devon and you'll be blessed with lower mineral levels in the water, which makes for a softer, rounder-tasting cup with significantly less scum."

"I cannot abide scum," said Churchill.

"The water in Devon is so soft that sometimes I consider moving there for the quality of the H2O alone."

"Oh, please don't leave, Mr Harding!"

Churchill's loud appeal was met with a stunned silence.

She gave an awkward cough. "Don't leave now, is what I meant, Mr Harding. Don't go to Devon immediately because we came here to ask you a favour."

"I have no plans to leave for Devon at this moment, Mrs Churchill. I would have to find a buyer for my shop first."

"Of course. And you can hardly do that within a day, can you? In fact, it's such a faff moving from one place to another that it's not really worth considering it at all."

"You've just moved here from London haven't you, Mrs Churchill?" said Pemberley.

"Yes I have, and as I said it's a thorough faff. However, I am exceedingly pleased to have made the move because now I have met some lovely people, such as your good selves."

"You mentioned a favour, Mrs Churchill," Mr Harding said.

"That's right, I did. Thank you for reminding me. Miss Pemberley and I are visiting you this afternoon in our professional capacity as private detectives. We were wondering if you could somehow see your way to negotiating a little *tête-à-tête* between ourselves and your good friend Colonel Slingsby."

"But that's three people," said Pemberley.

"Congratulations on your counting ability, my trusty assistant."

"A tête-à-tête is only between two people," she continued. "Its meaning in French is 'head-to-head'."

"How about tête-à-têtes then, Pembers?"

"That means two head-to-heads, not one head to two heads."

"I think the thread of this conversation is straying a little now, and Mr Harding's time is precious."

"You'd like me to ask the colonel if he'd be happy to meet with you two fine ladies?" asked Harding.

"Why yes, that would be wonderful, thank you. We did meet him informally only yesterday, quite by accident, in fact, while we were at the allotments conducting an investigation."

"I'm sure he'd be delighted to speak with you. I can telephone to him now. What should I say it's regarding?"

"It's regarding the dreadful murder of Mr Williams, but please reassure the colonel that our questions will be brief and certainly not probing as we have full respect for his no doubt emotional state at this present time."

"Right ho. Excuse me then, ladies, while I step out the back and make the call."

"Thank you, Mr Harding. You're terribly helpful."

"Isn't he helpful, Pembers?" whispered Churchill once Mr Harding had disappeared into the room at the back of his shop.

"Yes, all the ladies say that."

"Do they indeed? You're lumping me in with *all the ladies* of Compton Poppleford now are you, Pemberley?"

"Well, it *is* what everyone says."

"Because he's a helpful man, that's why. There's no smoke without fire, you know. A man earns his reputation."

"So does a woman."

"She does indeed. Mrs Thonnings ought to be reminded of that."

"Why Mrs Thonnings again?"

"Not all ladies consider the potential blemishes on their

reputations before conducting themselves in a certain manner. Shush now, I can hear him coming back."

"The colonel would like to know what time he should send his motor car for you ladies?" said Mr Harding.

"Would he really do that? For us? Oh my, that's very kind of him. What do you think, Miss Pemberley?" Churchill checked her watch. "Shall we say four o'clock?"

"If I suggest four o'clock to the colonel I have no doubt he'll have a fine afternoon tea – or tiffin, as he likes to call it – awaiting you on your arrival," said Harding.

"Well, that sounds just perfect. Don't you agree that it sounds quite perfect, Miss Pemberley? Thank you, Mr Harding. How thoroughly agreeable."

Mr Harding stepped into the back room again.

"Why do you keep asking me questions without waiting for my reply?" whispered Pemberley.

"I don't think I asked you any questions, did I?"

"Yes, you did. You asked me what time I thought the car should pick us up and whether I agreed that afternoon tea sounded perfect."

"I suppose I was just being polite and that I was assuming you'd simply go along with whatever I suggested, Pembers."

"I wanted to say that we should leave enough time to speak to Barry Woolwell first."

"Oh dash it, you're right. We've only got twenty minutes. And what if we can't find him?"

"Exactly. I was going to mention that before you forged ahead with our plans."

"Well, nothing's stopping you from speaking up, Pembers."

"Only the loudness of your voice."

"Now you're just being a wallflower! My voice isn't the least bit loud. Shush now, he's coming back again."

"That's all arranged, then," said Harding. "The colonel's chauffeur will collect you from the high street at four o'clock. Keep your eyes peeled for a red and cream Daimler."

"Oh, they'll be peeled all right," said Churchill. "How can I ever thank you for your help this afternoon, Mr Harding? I'm most grateful, I truly am. If there's ever anything I can do for you in return you will let me know, won't you? We're practically neighbours on the high street, and I was commenting to Miss Pemberley just the other day that—"

"We have another appointment, Mrs Churchill," Pemberley interjected.

"Yes, thank you, Miss Pemberley. As I was commenting to Miss Pemberley just the other day, in fact the same Miss Pemberley who is standing right next to me now, funnily enough—"

"We only have twenty minutes," interrupted Pemberley again.

"Shush now, the grown-ups are talking. As I was—"

"Perhaps you can enlighten me during your next visit, Mrs Churchill," suggested Mr Harding. "Miss Pemberley is quite insistent that you have another appointment to get to. You can come and visit me any time you like."

"Oh, can I really, Mr Harding? I must say I could do with replacing some of my crockery—"

"I'll see you then, Mrs Churchill," he replied before she could finish her sentence.

"Yes indeed, see you then. Cheerio, Mr Harding!"

Chapter 12

"SO WE'VE JUST enough time to speak to Barry Woolwell before the colonel's motor car collects us," said Churchill as they strode toward the doorway of the Wagon and Carrot. "Oh dear, it seems we've missed the staggering stage."

Rolling down the steps of the Tudor-timbered pub was the tweed-jacketed form of Barry Woolwell. Behind him came a lean man with a hooked nose who picked Woolwell's cap up from the ground and dusted it off before proceeding to haul the old man to his feet.

"Goodness, the fellow's completely stewed to the gills," commented Churchill.

"No, not 'im; 'e's just tired," replied the hook-nosed man, plonking the cap back on Barry Woolwell's head.

Churchill introduced herself and Pemberley. "I was hoping we might be able to interview the chap about his good friend, the sadly deceased Tubby Williams."

"'E's too tired to speak," said the man, pulling one of Woolwell's arms across his shoulders.

"I can see that."

"What d'you want ter know?"

"We're after Mr Woolwell's version of events, but I think we'll have to try him tomorrow once he's sobered up."

"Who said anythin' about 'im bein' drunk? It's the shock what's 'it 'im."

"Shock?"

"Yeah, the shock of Tubby's death. It's 'it 'im all of a sudden."

"There's no doubt that he's been deeply affected by something," Churchill retorted. "Are you a member of the gardening fraternity?"

"I'm 'is mate, Sniffer."

"Mr Colin Sniffer Downs?"

"Yeah. What of it?"

"I recall Mr Rumbold mentioning your name."

"'E did, did 'e?"

"A few people have named him as the chief suspect."

"Oh no. Rumbold wouldn't shoot no one."

"Who do you think might have done it?"

"Dunno. It weren't 'im, though."

Barry Woolwell suddenly righted himself, fixed his eyes on Churchill and broke out into incomprehensible song.

"Good afternoon, Mr Woolwell. Are you with us again?" she said.

The old man continued to sing, his cap slightly askew on his head.

"What's that ditty he's singing?" Churchill asked.

"The Old Roast Beef of England," replied Mr Downs.

"I don't recognise his version."

"It's the official song of the Compton Poppleford 'Orticultural Society."

"Not the Old Roast *Leaf* of England, then?" suggested Churchill with a chortle.

"What's that?"

"It was a little joke. I thought you might prefer a more plant-themed song for the horticultural society."

Mr Downs gave Churchill a blank look. "I've got ter get 'im 'ome," he said.

"Yes, I think you should. Where is Mr Woolwell's home, exactly? We could call on him there tomorrow."

"'E's in one o' the Grubmill cottages. Can't remember the name of it off 'and."

"I'm sure we'll find it, Mr Sniffer. Thank you for your time. Oh look! Here comes our car, Pemberley."

Churchill was relieved to see the red and cream Daimler making its way along the cobbles toward them. She held out a hand and the expressionless chauffeur slowed the car to a standstill.

~

"This is the way to travel, isn't it, Pemberley?" said Churchill as they cruised through the outskirts of Compton Poppleford. She waved majestically to a small boy carrying a duck under his arm.

"It's quite comfortable," replied Pemberley, "though I prefer a Rolls Royce to a Daimler."

"When did you travel in a Rolls Royce?"

"When I was companion to a lady of international travel."

"Oh yes, I recall you mentioning her now. Your life experience isn't as limited as it might initially appear to the casual onlooker."

They drove past a long estate wall before stopping in front of some ornate stone gateposts. The chauffeur got out to open them before proceeding down the long drive.

"Oh look, the colonel has a deer park," said Churchill,

admiring the view from the window. "I've always fancied having a deer park. I occasionally pretended that Richmond Park was my own personal patch. In fact, I convinced myself of it to such an extent that I became quite annoyed whenever I saw an oik on a horse cantering through it."

The large sandstone manor house drew nearer, glowing gold in the afternoon sunshine.

"And the colonel doesn't have a mere porch, does he, Pembers? Look, it's a colonnade. That's another something I've always rather fancied."

The car pulled up on the sweeping gravel driveway and two footmen stepped out of the house to open the doors on either side of the car.

"There's something rather agreeable about making the acquaintance of someone with class, isn't there, Pembers?" said Churchill as they followed the footmen into the house. "I find it restores one's faith in human nature. I was beginning to doubt I'd come across anyone in Dorset with good breeding. There are so many rustics here, aren't there? You know, the Flatboots and the like; the sort who have to remind themselves to breathe."

"Ladies!" The colonel's voice echoed around the vast hallway, resplendent with its grand staircase and full-length portraits of men in military uniform. The colonel wore a brown plaid suit and a purple silk cravat. "Welcome to Ashleigh Grange," he continued. "Tiffin on the verandah? This way!"

"How could we refuse, Colonel?" replied Churchill with a jingling laugh. It was then that she caught sight of Pemberley's cardigan. "Oh, good grief, Pemberley," she whispered. "Can't you take that rag off and hide it somewhere? It's not good enough to wipe the floor with, let alone to take tiffin on the verandah with the colonel."

"If I'd known we were coming here I'd have dressed for the occasion!" hissed Pemberley in reply. "Do you think your stout walking shoes are suitable?"

Churchill glanced down at her footwear and gasped. "Goodness, you're right, Pembers! You'd only wear shoes like these to a place like this is if you were going out for a shoot. I should keep an emergency pair of dainty slippers in my handbag."

"I would say that the dreariness of my cardigan is nullified by your shoes."

"And vice versa."

"Quite."

The footmen opened a set of double doors, and the colonel stepped aside to allow the two women to walk out onto the verandah in front of him. A row of neat columns supported the roof above them and a lawn, bright green in the sunshine, sloped gently down to formal flower borders edged with topiary. Stone statues and urns were dotted about, and beyond the garden was the deer park and a spectacular view of Compton Poppleford with its church spire rising proudly from the huddle of houses.

A table had been laid on the verandah with a fresh white tablecloth, two teapots and an assortment of dainty sandwiches and cakes. Churchill felt embarrassed to find herself salivating like a dog.

"Oh, Colonel, you shouldn't have," she said.

"I didn't. It was my staff."

"You have wonderful staff, Colonel."

"No need to stand on ceremony. Take a seat and tuck in!"

Churchill and Pemberley did as they were told, and a maid poured out the tea. The Colonel tucked his serviette into his collar and sipped from his cup.

Silence ensued for a short while as the two ladies ate,

until Churchill noticed that the Colonel's plate remained empty. "Won't you have a sandwich, Colonel Slingsby?" she asked.

"Digestion's a little out of sorts today," he replied. "The shock of this murder business has rather got to one."

Churchill had momentarily forgotten why they were here. She glanced down guiltily at the sandwich and cake crumbs on her plate and wondered if it had been disrespectful to enjoy her food so heartily at such a tragic time.

"Of course." She placed her serviette on her lap and tried to resist eating anything more. "You must be rather shaken by the terrible news concerning Mr Williams."

"It's always a sad day when we find ourselves a man down," he replied sombrely.

Churchill noticed that Pemberley was busily working her way through the iced fancies she had been planning to tackle next.

"Any idea who—?"

"You're about to ask me who did it, aren't you? Truth is I have no idea, Mrs Churchill. None at all."

"Some people have suggested Mr Rumbold as a possible suspect."

"Some people are ignorant fools."

"Then you don't think he did it?"

"You've met the man, Mrs Churchill. Wouldn't hurt a fly even if it stuck its proboscis into his mother's eye."

"That's a rather unpleasant-sounding fly," commented Pemberley. "They have flies like that in the Punjab, do they?"

"They certainly do. Awful buzzy things the size of teacups."

Churchill shuddered.

"Snakes as long as ten men lying end to end," continued the colonel. "Cockroaches the size of cats and tigers that creep into your bedroom in the dark of night to chew off your leg and eat your face."

Churchill shuddered again. "I shan't be hurrying over to the Punjab any time soon."

"Dreadful diseases that make a man's flesh fall off," added the colonel. "And a race of pygmies that would boil your brain and eat it while you're still alive."

Churchill let out a shriek and upset her tea over her bosom.

"Always gets the ladies going, that one!" he cackled.

"Oh Colonel!" said Churchill, wiping her blouse with her serviette. "Was that last one a joke?"

"It was. No such thing as the brain-eating pygmies. I haven't come across them, anyway. Might exist for all I know."

Churchill managed to snatch the last iced fancy before Pemberley got to it.

"Colonel, may I ask you a question about the death of Mr Williams, tragic though it is?"

"Fire away, my good woman."

"I happened to hear that you're missing a gun."

"Oh yes, that's rather a puzzle."

"The gun went missing yesterday, did it?"

"Certainly did. Have you finished eating? I'll show you the gunroom."

Churchill crammed the iced fancy into her mouth as they got up from their chairs. Colonel Slingsby led them back into the house, along a plush carpeted corridor and into one of the many rooms in the eastern wing of the house.

Chapter 13

"HERE WE ARE," said the colonel. "The old family arsenal."

The gunroom was lined with cases containing a range of well-polished firearms.

"You have an extremely large arsenal, Colonel," said Churchill. "I'm surprised you even realised one was missing."

"Easy to spot, all right. There's an empty space just over there." He pointed to one of the cabinets, which contained a number of pistols and revolvers. The empty set of hooks jumped out at them.

"It is pretty sizeable in here," he continued. "Good range of shotguns and some antique firearms knocking about. Here's a musket one of my old ancestor Slingsbys used to shoot the Duke of Middleford during the English Civil War. Knocked his block clean off! Story goes that the duke took another ten steps before he even realised what had happened."

"Without a head?" asked Churchill, looking at him askance.

"No bean to speak of at all. The old Slingsbys have always had a knack for a good shot. Got a few trophies in here as well." He pointed at several stag heads mounted on the walls. "There's a whole host more in the trophy room, including tigers from the Punjab. My brother and I enjoyed some good shooting back in the day. Reckon we once emptied Poppleford Wood of every living creature!" He gave a cackle.

"How terribly sad," said Pemberley.

"They all breed again like the clappers," he replied with a dismissive wave.

"But how can they breed again if there are none left?" asked Pemberley.

"Let's not get into that now, Pembers," whispered Churchill from the corner of her mouth.

"We must have left a few quaking behind the tree trunks," said the colonel.

"Tell us about the gun that has gone missing, Colonel," said Churchill in a bid to distract him.

"Oh yes, that. My Webley Mark IV. A solid workhorse of a revolver, it was. Will be much missed."

"Don't you think you'll ever find it again?"

"Sadly, no. Someone's snaffled it, haven't they? Sold it down at Dorchester market for a tidy sum by now I'll bet."

"The thief didn't murder Mr Williams with it, then?" asked Pemberley.

"Goodness *no*, woman! Why on earth would someone do that?"

"It's rather a coincidence, don't you think, Colonel?" asked Churchill. "Your revolver goes missing and later that night Mr Williams is shot dead."

"Good grief!" The colonel's mouth hung open. "You think the murderer stole my weapon?"

"It's a possibility, don't you think?"

"But that means the murderer has been in my home! Haven't seen any murdering sorts around here! Unless the chap broke in without my knowledge, of course, and made a clean getaway."

"When did you notice that your gun was missing, Colonel?"

"About eight o'clock yesterday evening. Was in here having a puff on the old pipe and surveying the arsenal, as you do."

"Indeed."

"That's when I saw it."

"Saw what?"

"I mean, I didn't see it."

"I'm sorry?"

"It wasn't there!"

"So you didn't see it?"

"No! It was gone!"

"Eight o'clock yesterday evening was when you noticed that your Webley Mark IV revolver was missing, Colonel?" clarified Churchill.

"Got it in one, woman. Got it in one."

"And the revolver had been present yesterday morning?"

"Oh, yes. I got it out and gave it a little buff shortly before breakfast. Mind if I smoke?"

"Not at all, Colonel. Did you have any visitors here yesterday?"

"Let's see now." Colonel Slingsby lit his pipe, rested one hand on the mantelpiece and puffed a plume of smoke into the air.

"Harding popped round about half past eight when I was just finishing breakfast."

"Mr Harding from the cookshop, you mean?"

"The very same. Then Woolwell showed his face for a

little while. And later on Downs dropped by."

"Barry Woolwell and Colin Downs, whom I believe they call Sniffer?"

"Yes, those two. Then I took a constitutional to the allotments and back; a four-mile round trip from here."

"And that's when Miss Pemberley and I met you, Colonel."

"I do believe it was. Shortly after I returned home Williams pitched up."

"The murder victim?"

"That's the one. Last time I saw the man. Had a spot of lunch together. Not long after that Harris popped his head around the door."

"Colonel, may I ask why you had so many visitors from the gardening fraternity?"

"Quite simple, Mrs Churchill. They were currying favour."

"For what?"

"The Compton Poppleford Horticultural Society's Annual Show. They all wanted me to pick out their produce for the prizes. Attempts are made to bribe me with all sorts: potatoes, scrumpy, liquor and even straightforward spondulix."

"Straightforward what now?"

"Stuff, Mrs Churchill. Funds, you might call it. Chips, chinkers, root-of-all-evil, tin, slugs or even the filthy."

"I'm afraid you've completely lost me, Colonel."

"He means cash," said Pemberley.

"Thank you for the translation, Pembers. Why ever didn't you say that to begin with, Colonel?"

He shrugged and took another puff on his pipe. "Oh, and Rumbold visited me about six," he added.

"Any other visitors?"

"Those are the only ones I'm aware of. And while I

was busy entertaining them some muttonhead must have broken into my gunroom and stole my Webley."

"I suppose what needs to be ascertained now is whether your Webley was used in the murder of Mr Williams. I do believe there's a method of matching a gun to a crime by analysing the unique markings a firearm leaves on the bullet casings."

"You're on the ball, woman. That would indeed ascertain it."

"Have you kept any spent casings from your Webley revolver, Colonel?"

"Can't say I'm in the habit of keeping them. Might be a few knocking about in the garden."

"What would they be doing out there?"

"Left over from target practice on Bertrand. Valet usually picks them up, but let's have a look out there, shall we?"

"Who's Bertrand?" asked Churchill as she and Pemberley followed Colonel Slingsby out of the gunroom, along a corridor and into a drawing room with doors that opened out into the garden.

"Bertrand's pig ugly. Can't stand the sight of him," replied the colonel, unlocking the drawing room doors.

"Poor man!" said Pemberley. "Or boy!"

"He's a boy, all right," replied the colonel as he stepped out onto the terrace and then strode across the lawn.

"Colonel, do you mean to tell us that you use an ugly boy for shooting practice?" asked Churchill, striding alongside him.

"Afraid so. I keep him out here."

Churchill shook her head, while Pemberley's expression was one of abject horror.

"I don't think I want to see him," Pemberley said, her step slowing.

"Come on, Pembers, we'll help each other out," whispered Churchill. "I don't think I can cope with seeing the poor lad either, but hopefully this will give us a chance to rescue him and have him put in a home."

As they followed the colonel around a yew hedge the sound of trickling water grew louder.

"You keep him by a pond, do you Colonel?" asked Churchill.

"He looks after it for me."

"And you repay him by shooting at him?"

"Exactly."

They rounded the hedge to find a circular pond with a fountain at the centre of it. At the far side of the pond stood a pock-marked stone cherub missing both arms and part of one leg.

"There he is," said the colonel.

Churchill felt an enormous sense of relief. "So *that's* Bertrand," she said. "I was terrified he might be a real boy."

"Goodness no, woman. Do I look like someone who'd take a potshot at a real boy? I'd fire a warning shot past his ear if I caught him stealing apples from my orchard, mind."

"Poor Bertrand!" Pemberley cried out, walking around the pond toward the cherub. "He's not that ugly!"

"Have a look around on the ground over there for spent casings," the colonel hollered. "I only use my Webley on him. Prefer to use the shotguns for live quarry."

Churchill joined Pemberley, and together they began examining the grass around the stone cherub.

"What a relief that someone's stolen the colonel's revolver," said Pemberley. "He won't be able to shoot at poor Bertrand any more."

"He's only a lump of stone, Pembers."

"I know he is, but don't you find that when an inanimate object has been fashioned into the image of a person or animal you develop feelings for it?"

"Can't say that I do, Pemberley. I think you ought to get yourself a pet or a husband." Churchill surveyed the ground around her and sighed. "It looks as though the colonel's valet is rather efficient at scooping up the bullet casings. I can't see any at all."

"Look, there's a hole in the lawn here," said Pemberley.

"Very good. A little home for a worm, perhaps?"

"No, a bullet hole. And when I put my finger in it I feel some metal."

"Oh! A casing, perhaps?"

"I hope so. I can't get it out, though."

"Let me have a go at it, Pembers. I'm known for my strong fingers."

Churchill sank onto her knees beside the hole in the lawn and poked her finger inside.

"By whom?" asked Pemberley.

"By whom what? What do you mean?"

"Who knows you for your strong fingers?"

"You ask such odd things at such odd times, Pemberley. Can't you see I'm trying to get this bullet casing out of the colonel's lawn?"

"Find something, ladies?" he called over from the other side of the pond.

"Yes, I think so, Colonel!" Churchill called back, cutting her finger on the casing. "Oh, darn it." She dabbed at the blood with her handkerchief. "You'd think the old fellow would come and help, wouldn't you?" she muttered. "It's his bullet casing and his lawn, after all. What we need is a long, hard implement with a little hook at the end to extract the blasted thing. Ah! I know what would work,

Pembers. My crochet hook! Be a love and rummage around in my handbag for it, will you?"

Pemberley located the crochet hook and handed it to Churchill.

"Easy does it," she said, inserting the hook into the hole. "That's got it... Now, out we come. There we go... Ah ha! Hello, sailor!" Churchill held up the soil-encrusted piece of metal casing.

"We've got it, Colonel!" she called over to him.

"Marvellous," came the reply.

"It's amazing how useful this crochet hook is," said Churchill. "I think I've used it for just about everything except crochet. Never could get the hang of that craft. Managed to tie my fingers up in knots instead of the wool." Churchill placed the bullet casing in her handbag. "Now, help me up, please, Pembers. The old knees have gone numb."

Chapter 14

"I'M RATHER reluctant to share our precious bullet casing with Inspector Mappin," said Churchill as they approached the small white police station at the bottom of Compton Poppleford high street. "He'll claim the credit for all our hard work."

"I think we're doing the honourable thing," replied Pemberley. "It might help him with the case."

"I sometimes grow tired of being honourable, don't you, Pembers? I quite fancy being dishonourable for a change."

"But then you'd be ever so disappointed in yourself, Mrs Churchill. And you'd have to live with that disappointment for the remainder of your days."

"Oh look, there's a nice shiny car parked outside the police station. It must belong to the chief inspector from Dorchester."

Churchill and Pemberley stepped into the station to find Inspector Mappin and the chief inspector sharing a pot of tea.

"Busy day, gentlemen?" asked Churchill.

"We're conducting a briefing," said the chief inspector through his thick red moustache. He rose to his feet and Mappin followed suit.

"I thought you'd be busy tracking down the murderer, Inspector Mappin," said Churchill.

"That's what I've been doing all day," he replied defensively. "This is the first opportunity I've had to sit down."

"And the hard work is continuing as we speak," added the chief inspector. "We've got our men out crawling all over Compton Poppleford."

"Have they not learnt to walk yet, Chief Inspector?"

"Who are these women?" the chief inspector barked at Mappin.

"How rude of us not to introduce ourselves, Chief Inspector," said Churchill. "I'm Mrs Annabel Churchill of the eponymous Churchill's Detective Agency, and this is my *aide-de-camp* Miss Doris Pemberley."

"Private detectives?" asked the chief inspector with a sceptical expression.

"Indeed, and you are Chief Inspector who?"

"Llewellyn-Dalrymple."

"Try saying that with your mouth full!"

"I beg your pardon?"

"Just a little quip to lighten the mood, Chief Inspector. We won't detain you for long. Miss Pemberley and I have some evidence to present."

"Oh yes?"

Churchill removed the bullet casing from her handbag. "This was retrieved from the lawn at Ashleigh Grange using a crochet hook. It's a spent casing from Colonel Slingsby's Webley Mark IV. The gun was stolen from his gunroom yesterday at some time between breakfast and eight o'clock in the evening. This casing may help you find out whether the colonel's revolver was used in the shooting of Mr Williams last night. Have you retrieved any casings from the murder scene?"

The chief inspector gave an impressed nod. "Yes, we have," he said, "and it is my belief that they came from a Webley. Analysis of this casing you've found will enable us to establish whether the same gun was used."

"I thought as much," said Churchill proudly as she handed him the casing.

"It's from a Webley all right," he said, examining it closely. "I've got a ballistics chap over at Bovington who can take a look at this along with the other casings we've gathered from the murder scene."

"If it's the same gun the culprit must have stolen it from the colonel's home yesterday," said Churchill. "Perhaps you'd like a list of the people who visited him."

"I'll say," replied the chief inspector, picking up his notebook and pencil. "What have you got for me?"

"Mr Rumbold, Mr Downs, Mr Woolwell, Mr Harris and Mr Williams, our tragic victim."

"And Mr Harding," added Pemberley.

"Well, he didn't have anything to do with it, did he?" Churchill said scornfully.

"You never know," said Pemberley. "The chief inspector should write his name down anyway. As well as Colonel Slingsby's name, as a matter of course."

"All written down," announced the chief inspector, flicking his notebook shut. "I'm assuming you know where to find all these chaps, Mappin?"

The inspector nodded sheepishly.

"I have to say that Mrs Churchill's work from today knocks the socks off yours, doesn't it?" continued the Chief Inspector. "How does it feel to be outwitted by two old ladies?"

"Less of the *old*, please, Chief Inspector," said Churchill.

"They even dug a bullet casing out of the lawn with a knitting needle," he continued. "Can't say I've seen you do anything nearly as enterprising today, Mappin."

"It was a crochet hook," corrected Churchill.

"Never mind the details."

"On the contrary, Chief Inspector, details are extremely important when you're trying to solve a crime. They often make the difference between solving it and... er... not solving it."

"Who are you, exactly?" asked the chief inspector, folding his arms.

"I've already told you. I'm—"

"A private detective. Yes, I heard that. But where does your expertise come from?"

"Well, since you ask, I was married for over forty years to Detective Chief Inspector Churchill of the Metropolitan Police."

"I see. Solved a few cases himself, did he?"

"He did indeed. In fact, he cut his teeth on the Jack the Ripper case when he was just a fledgling constable."

"Fledglings don't have teeth," said Pemberley.

"Perhaps not, but my husband certainly did."

"It's probably best not to describe him as a fledgling if you're mentioning teeth."

"Thank you, Miss Pemberley. The comment was only intended to serve as an illustration to the Chief Inspector of my late husband's policing pedigree."

"Jack the Ripper, eh?" said Chief Inspector Llewellyn-Dalrymple. "Fat lot of luck they had catching him."

"You can't win 'em all, Chief Inspector."

"You're right, Mrs Churchill. That's a motto I like to use

myself. Poor Mappin here doesn't seem to win any at all, do you, Mappin? And now you've been thoroughly shown up by two elderly biddies. Inspector Mappin nil, Women's Institute one!" The Chief Inspector gave a booming laugh.

"We are *not* members of the Women's Institute," Churchill insisted.

"I was a member briefly," said Pemberley, "but there was a horrible lady there who kept flicking jam at me."

"You'll let us know if your ballistics fellow confirms that the colonel's gun was used in the murder, won't you, Chief Inspector?" said Churchill.

"Absolutely," he replied. "And thank you for all your help, ladies. Go and take a well-earned rest in your armchairs, and allow the strong arm of the law to take it from here."

Chapter 15

"THE DAY I take a well-earned rest in my armchair is the day I die, Pemberley," said Churchill back at the office.

"Oh, you mustn't mention your death."

"Why not? We'll all die some day."

"That's what everyone says, but I like to believe there's a possibility that I might not."

"You're going to be the first immortal being, are you, Pembers? Well, good luck."

"It's a nice thought."

"You comfort yourself with that, then, while I admire the incident board. Doesn't it look good now? Although I don't know why on earth you've put Mr Harding's photograph up there. That's a mistake."

"No, don't take him down!"

"But he's not a suspect, Pemberley."

"He visited the colonel's home yesterday."

"That's because he's the colonel's friend."

"He could have taken the gun."

"Don't be ridiculous! Why would he do that?"

"To shoot Mr Williams with it."

"Nonsense. He has no motive whatsoever."

"How do you know that? You only met him for the first time today!"

"Was it really only this morning? I feel like I've known him for years."

"Everyone who visited the colonel's home yesterday must be considered a suspect," said Pemberley.

"Only if Chief Inspector Loonybin-Dullpimple confirms that the colonel's gun was used in the murder."

"Let's jump the gun and assume it was," said Pemberley. "Did you notice my little joke there, Mrs Churchill? I said *jump the gun* while discussing the colonel's Webley."

"Leave the jokes to me, Pembers."

"The colonel is also a suspect."

"I suppose he must be considered. Do you have a photograph of him handy to add to our incident board?"

"There's a picture of him here in full military regalia. It was printed in the *Compton Poppleford Gazette* last year."

"Perfect, Pembers." Churchill surveyed the picture. "What a fine moustache. Doesn't he look imperial?"

"And imperious."

"A perfectly charming gentleman. He's what my mother would have called an *old fool*."

"I suspect many other people would call him that too."

"But his heart's in the right place, isn't it?"

"Is it? I don't like the man. I can easily imagine him shooting Mr Williams. Did you see the damage he'd done to poor Bertrand the cherub?"

"There's a marked difference between killing a man and shooting at a lump of stone that resembles a chubby, winged infant."

"He's not just a lump of stone!"

"Now, now, Pembers. Let's make a nice cup of tea with

Mr Harding's kettle and then everything will seem a little better."

"We mustn't forget the staff," said Pemberley.

"But we don't have staff. If we did, it wouldn't be me making the tea, would it?"

"No, I mean the colonel's staff. He has at least two footmen and a minimum of three maids and a valet. And there must be a butler milling about somewhere."

Churchill sighed. "And a housekeeper to boot."

"Not to mention the chauffeur."

Churchill felt her shoulders slump. "And what's the betting a tradesperson visited the place yesterday as well? You know the sort, don't you? One of those chaps in overalls and a flat cap who enters the place whistling nonchalantly with a toolbag in one hand and a list of jobs in the other. No one pays him the slightest heed because they assume he's there to tighten a nut or loosen a bolt or paint the ceiling."

"I know just the sort."

"I should think about three of them visited Ashleigh Grange yesterday. People like that are always coming and going at these ancestral seats."

"Our incident board isn't big enough to accommodate them all," said Pemberley despondently.

"I'm sure we can make room," said Churchill. "We could begin by removing Mr Harding. There's no need—"

"He stays!"

Churchill startled. "Goodness, Pemberley, you can be quite formidable when rattled. I'll leave him up there for now, just for the sake of completeness, but there's no need to waste any time contemplating him as a suspect."

. . .

Pemberley bought some lemon cake from the baker while Churchill made a pot of tea.

"Lovely," she said as she placed her teacup back on its saucer. "And only slightly impaired by the water's high mineral content. Isn't it nice to have a conversation with someone who really knows what they're talking about, Pemberley? Mr Harding strikes me as the sort of man who always has something knowledgeable to say, whatever the topic."

"Perhaps during our next conversation with him he can enlighten us regarding the whereabouts of the colonel's missing revolver?"

"Pemberley! I won't have you slandering Mr Harding in that manner."

"It's not slander. I'm merely entertaining him as a suspect along with all the others."

"Well, stop entertaining him this minute." Churchill picked up her pen and hovered it over a sheet of paper. "Now then, Pembers, what we need is a plan for solving this murder. I think we should visit each member of the gardening gang tomorrow and see what he has to say for himself. Let's start with Barry Woolwell so we can catch him before he overindulges at the Wagon and Carrot again. After Barry we should check on our bearded friend, Rumbold. He's the most suspicious of the lot. Then we'll move swiftly on to Mr Sniffer Downs, as we haven't really probed him yet. Finally, we'll have to take the bit between the teeth and tackle Mr Stropper, the annoying one."

"He might try and charge us a shilling again."

"So be it; we can't escape speaking to the fellow. Now, following this plan will mean that by teatime tomorrow we should have a good overview of events. What do you think?"

"I think it's an excellent plan, Mrs Churchill. By then we should have a perfectly passable conspectus."

"Well, I'm not sure what you said just then, but it sounds good. I'll tell you what else I'd like to discover, and that's the location of Mr Rumbold's secret marrows. Don't you recall him telling us that he had three of them hidden at a secret location? We need to find out where that is. Now, I think it's time we both went home, had a hearty supper and turned in for the night. We need plenty of beauty sleep before our busy day tomorrow."

"I'm not a good sleeper, Mrs Churchill."

"Try, Pembers, you might surprise yourself."

Churchill had just risen from her seat, picked up her handbag and put on her hat when the door was swung open aggressively.

"Goodness, that's a strong wind!" she gasped.

"It's not wind!" came a growl. "It's Inspector Mappin!"

"Inspector!" Churchill said cheerily as he marched in through the door. "We're just knocking off for the day. Oh dear, you look a little hot under the collar. Is something the matter?"

"It certainly is, Mrs Churchill! *You're* the matter!"

"Me, Inspector? I don't understand."

"You and your interfering, meddlesome ways," he said, spitting angrily. "Embarrassing me in front of Chief Inspector Llewellyn-Dalrymple in that manner!"

"Oh dear! I thought we were being helpful." Churchill brushed down her blouse in case some of the police officer's spittle had landed on it. "I must admit I was in two minds, wasn't I, Miss Pemberley? I even paused outside the police station and questioned whether we were doing the right thing bringing the bullet casing in. Miss Pemberley here assured me we were, and that we'd only be disappointed in ourselves if we didn't help out. I wish we hadn't bothered now."

"So do I! Now the chief inspector thinks I'm an incapable fool!"

"Oh, I wouldn't listen to anything Loopywelly-Dimple says. He strikes me as the sort of man who's never happy unless he's brusquely admonishing someone. It's probably the only reason he became a chief inspector, to be quite frank. You find that sort in the army, too. They spend all day shouting at people, then retire to bed sucking their thumbs with a mug of hot milk."

"What on earth are you talking about, woman?" fumed Mappin.

"Never mind, Inspector. Would you care to leave the premises now? Miss Pemberley and I were just about to head off to our respective homes. We have a busy day ahead of us tomorrow."

"Oh no you don't!"

"I beg your pardon?"

"I'll have none of that *busy day* business, Mrs Churchill. You stay well away from this murder case!"

"But I took this case on before the murder was even committed, Inspector. Miss Pemberley and I were called upon to investigate the damage done to Mr Rumbold's onions."

"Onions have nothing to do with this. It's cold-blooded murder, and it's my job to get to the bottom of it! I am ordering you to stay away."

"And what happens if we don't?"

"The pair of you will be arrested for interfering with a police investigation!"

"Is that an arrestable offence, Inspector?"

"It'll have a more official sounding name to it, which momentarily escapes me, but *yes, it is!*"

"Well, that is a shame."

Mappin pointed a thick forefinger at Churchill. "If I see you speaking to any one of those men who visited Colonel Slingsby yesterday there'll be trouble."

Churchill's heart sank. "Which ones in particular, Inspector?"

"Woolwell, Sniffer Downs, Stropper Harris and Rumbold."

Churchill felt silently relieved that he hadn't mentioned the name Harding.

"What about Mr Harding?" chipped in Pemberley.

"Oh, but he's entirely innocent!" protested Churchill.

"Ah yes, Harding and the colonel himself," said Mappin.

Churchill felt her teeth clench with anger.

"And what about the staff?" asked Pemberley.

"Eh?"

"Mrs Churchill and I realised that the staff at Ashleigh Grange also have access to the gunroom. The colonel has at least two footmen, a minimum of three maids and a valet—"

"Yes, yes, woman, I get the picture."

"Not to mention visiting tradespersons," continued Pemberley.

"Were there any yesterday?" asked Mappin with a furrowed brow.

"We don't know yet," retorted Churchill, "but you'll have to find out all by yourself, Inspector, seeing as you clearly don't want our help."

"I have the constables from Bulchford to assist me, Mrs Churchill, as well as the chief inspector."

Churchill gave a derisory snort. "Loopywelly's not going to do any of the legwork, is he? He just busies himself with ordering everyone else about."

"Leave this matter to the police, Mrs Churchill. That's my final warning."

"Of course. Are you going to leave us in peace now, Inspector?"

Mappin glanced around the room. "And take that incident board down."

Churchill felt her grip tighten around the handle of her handbag.

"We can put what we like on our office walls, Inspector," she snarled. "Now get out of here. Shoo!"

Mappin sneered as he left the room, and Churchill felt her heart pound with rage as he descended the stairs.

"Well, tomorrow's going to be a quiet day for us, isn't it, Mrs Churchill?" said Pemberley sadly.

"No, it isn't, Pembers. Not one little bit of it. The original plan remains in force. Go home, have some supper and turn in early—"

"But we're banned from speaking to everyone!"

"Not everyone, Pembers. Old Churchy's going to come up with another little plan."

Chapter 16

"MURDER IN COLD BLOOD," said Pemberley grimly, as she read the headline from the Compton Poppleford Gazette the following morning.

"Murder in cold mud, more like," replied Churchill.

"Those allotments are always muddy, even at the height of summer. By the way, thank you for the invitation to cocktails this evening, Mrs Churchill."

"Ah, excellent. You received it then."

"I did, yes, but why did you have that Flatboot boy bring it round? You could have merely given me the invitation yourself."

"I was testing him out, Pemberley. He's a Flatboot, is he?"

"Yes, Timmy Flatboot."

"I knew he was a Timmy. I found him catapulting snails into Farmer Drumhead's slurry pit yesterday evening. I told him I had a shiny farthing for a boy who was willing to do a spot of work. If you received your invitation that hopefully means everyone else has got theirs too."

"Who's everyone else?"

"The wives, Pemberley."

"Wives?"

"Yes, the wives of the gardening gang. Mappin has banned us from speaking to the men, but he didn't mention the women, did he?"

"Oh, I don't know about this. What if he finds out?"

"So what if he finds out? We'll simply tell him it's a ladies' social gathering and he'll have no further interest in it."

"Maybe you could invite some other ladies just so that Inspector Mappin doesn't find an excuse to accuse us of anything."

"That's a good idea, Pembers. Who else shall we ask?"

"Mrs Higginbath?"

"Not her. She still won't allow me to have a library ticket."

"Mrs Thonnings?"

"Definitely not Mrs Thonnings."

"Mrs Bramley?"

"Good idea. Let's have her as our dummy guest."

"I don't think she'd like to be called a dummy guest."

"No, she wouldn't, so don't go telling her, Pemberley. Perhaps as you've still got your hat on you could pop down to the tea rooms and invite her."

The small, rustic cottage Churchill rented from Farmer Drumhead was a little dreary for entertaining. There were two rickety wooden chairs, two drab armchairs and a sofa with springs that had a habit of poking through the upholstery without warning. In a bid to brighten the place up,

Churchill draped a colourful scarf from Liberty's over the table and placed some candles in a lopsided candelabra she had found in the cupboard under the stairs.

Churchill then proceeded to brighten herself up by changing into a green satin cocktail dress and applying a generous layer of scarlet lipstick.

Pemberley arrived ten minutes before everyone else, as instructed.

"Good evening, Pembers. Is that a new cardigan?"

"No, it's an old thing."

"Well, it looks newer than your usual fare."

"Thank you. What a lovely dress, Mrs Churchill."

"Oh, this old thing? It'll pass for this evening, I suppose. It's shrunk quite considerably since I wore it to the Richmond-upon-Thames Ladies' Lawn Tennis Club Benefit Gala Evening. Would you like a cocktail?"

"Yes please."

Churchill went over to the table and began mixing a drink.

"This is a lovely cottage," said Pemberley, admiring the room.

"Nonsense, Pembers. It's at times like this where I regret leaving my worldly goods in storage at Sunbury," replied Churchill, pouring a large measure of gin into her cocktail shaker.

"Why?"

"Well, look at the place, it's positively dismal. I should have considered another venue. The wives are going to be singularly unimpressed."

"It's nicer than my home," said Pemberley.

"I doubt that! Your chairs are surely more comfortable." Churchill added a large swig of cherry liquor to the cocktail shaker, followed by a dash of crème de violette.

"They're not. They're so dreadful, in fact, that I spend most of my time in bed when I'm at home."

"I see, well perhaps I needn't worry after all. People in the provinces probably have inferior living standards to those in the Capital."

They were interrupted by a knock at the door.

"Our first guest has arrived, Pembers! Go and see who it is."

Pemberley went to answer the door and returned a short while later with a tall, large-nosed lady with a notice-able squint.

"Mrs Rumbold," announced Pemberley.

"Mrs Churchill!" said Mrs Rumbold shrilly. "And what a lovely cottage. Thank you so much for inviting me. I don't often get invited places, so how nice to come out for a change, away from all the talk of gardening and murder."

"It's a delight to meet you, Mrs Rumbold," said Churchill, silently wondering what she made of her husband's possible involvement in the murder of Tubby Williams. "Would you care for a drink?"

"Oh yes, I'd care very much for one. Thank you."

Churchill poured a drink from the cocktail shaker, popped a cherry on a cocktail stick into the glass and handed it to Mrs Rumbold.

"A favourite cocktail of mine called The Aviator," said Churchill. "My good friend Lady Worthington introduced me to it following a flight she took from Croydon Airport to Paris."

"With Imperial Airways?" asked Pemberley.

"I imagine so."

"I flew many times with them from Croydon to Paris," continued Pemberley. "And to Cairo, Athens, Alexandria and occasionally the Emirate of Sharjah."

"You were companion to a lady of international travel weren't you, Miss Pemberley?" asked Mrs Rumbold.

"Yes, I was."

"*Chin chin,* as they say in Italy," interrupted Churchill, thrusting a glass into Pemberley's hand. "How's your husband, Mrs Rumbold?" she asked, her eyes watering from the strength of her drink.

"He's rather miserable, if truth be told," she replied, her squinting eyes also watering. "The death of his friend has shaken him a little."

"It's shaken the entire village," said Churchill. "Dreadful business, and to think it was only two days ago that we were talking to him about his onions."

Mrs Rumbold groaned. "Those dratted onions. I wish he'd never planted them. Anyway, that's enough about him. I'm looking forward to an evening with no talk of gardening or murder. May I say again how lovely it is of you to invite me here, Mrs Churchill?"

"You may. Is that someone at the door, Pembers?"

Pemberley went to answer the door and returned with a squat lady with a squashed nose and a wide chin. Churchill decided that her appearance wasn't too dissimilar to that of a bulldog.

"Mrs Downs," announced Pemberley.

"Wife of Mr Sniffer?" asked Churchill.

The squat lady nodded.

"Drink, Mrs Downs?"

The squat lady nodded again.

"I last saw your husband yesterday as he escorted Mr Woolwell out of the Wagon and Carrot," said Churchill.

Mrs Downs rolled her eyes and Churchill waited for her to say something further, but nothing was forthcoming.

"Hello?" said a woman with a headful of blonde curls and protruding teeth.

Churchill jumped. "Goodness, who are you?"

"Mrs Harris. I hope you don't mind me wandering in like this, the door was open."

"No, not at all, Mrs Harris. Wife of Mr Stropper? How lovely of you to join us. Drink?"

"Thank you."

"Isn't this nice?" said Mrs Rumbold. "Isn't it lovely of Mrs Churchill to invite us to her delightful little cottage?"

"Very nice," said Mrs Harris, spluttering slightly at the strength of her drink.

"Your husband must have made quite a bit of money charging everyone a shilling to listen to him yesterday," commented Churchill.

"Oh yes. I think he made about fifty pounds."

"Really?"

"He even charged me a shilling!" laughed Mrs Harris.

"Men, eh?" chuckled Churchill.

"Not all men. Mr Rumbold would never do that," said Mrs Rumbold.

"He's the noble type, is he?" said Churchill.

"He's a gentleman."

"Who else have you invited, Mrs Churchill?" asked Mrs Harris.

"I think we're just waiting for Mrs Woolwell and Mrs Bramley now."

"Oh, how lovely," replied Mrs Harris. "I'm looking forward to having a nice chat with them both. I'm keen to find out how marriage is treating Mrs Woolwell. There's quite a mismatch between her and her husband. One wonders what they have to talk about. And I haven't seen Mrs Bramley for a while; she works ever so hard. I think she finds life difficult being widowed. Actually, I don't think she found life much easier when she was married. Barney

Bramley always seemed to be suffering some misfortune or other."

"Oh dear. Can you give us an example?"

"He could never get his carrots to do anything. He was always asking Stropper for advice but nothing seemed to work. And he once tried growing a marrow, but it stopped at courgette size."

"Poor Mr Bramley. There goes the door knocker again, Miss Pemberley."

Two more guests had arrived: Mrs Bramley and a slightly built, pale-faced woman dressed in black.

"Good evenin', Mrs Churchill," said Mrs Bramley. "I brought Mrs Williams along. She'd 'eard about the cocktails and said she 'ad an 'ankering for one."

"Mrs Williams!" said Churchill, trying her best to combine solemnity and joviality in respectful measure. "Of course you're welcome to join us. Please do accept my apology for not sending you an invitation; I thought it would be disrespectful under the circumstances. And do please accept my condolences on the sad passing of your husband."

"Thank you," she said quietly. "I need a drink."

"Of course!"

Churchill poured out another cocktail and thrust it into Mrs Williams's hand. She suspected it would be quite difficult to find out who might have murdered Tubby Williams with his widow present.

Churchill forced a grin onto her face as a young, pretty, dark-haired woman was ushered into the room by Pemberley.

"I'm Mrs Woolwell!" said the woman, smiling to reveal a neat row of white teeth. She had sparkling violet eyes and wore a yellow cocktail dress made of silk.

"You're Barry Woolwell's wife?" asked Churchill

incredulously, trying to marry up the woman who stood in front of her with the old man dressed in shabby tweed stumbling drunkenly out of the pub.

"That's right!"

Rendered uncharacteristically speechless, Churchill handed her a cocktail.

Chapter 17

"LOVELY EVENING FOR IT, isn't it?" said Mrs Woolwell.

"For what?" asked Mrs Rumbold.

"For a cocktail in this delightful cottage!"

"Oh yes," said Mrs Rumbold. "I've already told Mrs Churchill how lovely it is to be invited somewhere. I don't often get invited out any more."

"I invited you to my birthday party last week," said Mrs Harris, her blonde curls trembling indignantly.

"Oh yes, so you did. Unfortunately, I was unable to attend," said Mrs Rumbold, her squint becoming more pronounced as she struggled to find a viable excuse. "The cat was sick."

"Is that Boffy?" asked Mrs Bramley.

"No, Boffy died last year," replied Mrs Rumbold.

Churchill startled as Mrs Williams emitted a loud sob.

"But your current cat has recovered from its sickness, has it?" asked Churchill hopefully.

"Yes, she did, although her tail still doesn't work," said Mrs Rumbold. "It won't go up when it's supposed to."

"Well, you missed a good party," said Mrs Harris. "Wasn't it good, Mrs Bramley?"

"Yeah, it were, and I 'ad no idea Mrs Downs 'ad a voice like that," said Mrs Bramley.

Bulldog-faced Mrs Downs smiled and rolled her eyes again.

"So what's the occasion, Mrs Churchill?" asked Mrs Woolwell. "Is it your birthday, too?"

"Oh no, I try not to acknowledge my birthdays too often these days. I like to think that if I ignore them I won't grow any older."

"Oh, how funny, Mrs Churchill!" laughed Mrs Woolwell.

"Does that actually work?" asked Mrs Harris earnestly.

"I like to think it does," replied Churchill. "Anyway let's raise a toast to the ladies of Compton Poppleford. How lovely to meet you all!"

Everyone raised their glasses and Churchill noticed that Mrs Williams's was already empty.

"But we're not all the ladies of Compton Poppleford," said Mrs Rumbold. "Mrs Higginbath and Mrs Thonnings aren't here, for starters."

"Oh yes, and Mrs Thonnings is simply wonderful!" enthused Mrs Woolwell. "What a refined, clever lady she is. And witty too!"

"My cottage only has room for a select number," said Churchill, refilling Mrs Williams's glass.

"Oh, but you must invite her next time!" said Mrs Woolwell. "She's the life and soul of every party. She was at Mrs Harris's birthday party last week, wasn't she, Mrs Harris? That story she told about the pepper pot and the long johns had everybody in stitches."

"Good," said Churchill curtly. "Now, Colonel Slingsby was telling me yesterday that your husbands all visited him at Ashleigh Grange on the same day. I believe they wished to curry favour so their vegetables might have a better chance of winning the top prizes at the horticultural show."

"They always do that," said Mrs Harris coldly.

"Constantly competing to be the colonel's favourite," added Mrs Woolwell with a sigh.

"It's got a bit too much," said Mrs Rumbold. "I'm so fed up with it all that I've even considered getting a divorce. Have you seen my husband's allotment?"

"He showed us around it," said Churchill. "It's certainly well fortified. But someone still managed to sabotage his onions despite that."

"And it wasn't Tubby!" Mrs Williams cried out. "He kept accusing him and wouldn't let up. It drove poor Tubby half mad."

"Only because he couldn't think of anyone but Tubby," said Mrs Rumbold. "But he didn't shoot him, if that's what everyone thinks. He had nothing to do with that."

"Yet he was the only other person up at the allotment with him that evening," said Mrs Williams.

"Mr Harris found him," added Churchill.

"What's that supposed to mean?" snapped Mrs Harris.

"It doesn't mean anything," replied Churchill awkwardly. "Other than that, in many cases, the last person to see the deceased alive and the first person to discover them dead are quite often the police's main suspects." She shrank back from the glares of Mrs Rumbold and Mrs Harris, quickly explaining herself. "Although that is in many cases and not all cases, of course, and doesn't mean at all that your respective husbands had anything to do with it. I think the real suspect must be the man who took the gun from the colonel's gunroom on the day your husbands all visited him."

"It wasn't my husband," said Mrs Rumbold.

"Nor mine," said Mrs Woolwell.

"Or mine!" added Mrs Harris.

Mrs Downs shook her head.

"And I weren't there neither," added Mrs Bramley. "I ain't never set foot in Ashleigh Grange, and me poor Barney ain't never been there neither, God rest 'is soul."

"Why are we talking about gardening and murder again?" Mrs Rumbold cried out. "I came here this evening with the express wish of talking about neither of them!"

"Tubby took it," said Mrs Williams quietly.

"Pardon me?" said Churchill. "Are you saying, Mrs Williams, that *your* husband stole the gun from the colonel's gunroom?"

"Yes," she replied before draining her drink.

"Where is it now?" asked Churchill.

"I don't know," replied Mrs Williams. "I've not seen it since he was…"

"It's all right, Mrs Williams, you don't need to say anything more," said Churchill. "Miss Pemberley, can you please help me with the jelly in the kitchen?"

"Oh lovely, where's the jelly?" asked Pemberley, looking around the kitchen for it.

"There isn't one, Pembers," whispered Churchill, "I just used it as an excuse. Did I hear correctly just then? Did Mrs Williams just say that her husband, the murder victim, stole the gun which was probably the murder weapon from Colonel Slingsby's gunroom?"

"Yes, I believe so. Rather strange, isn't it?"

"Incredibly strange. And it completely ruins our

chances of narrowing down the suspects. If Tubby Williams stole the gun we still have no idea who the murderer is. Or why he stole it."

Pemberley shrugged.

"There is much that baffles me here, Pembers," said Churchill as she opened the biscuit barrel and helped herself to a handful of custard creams. "Why on earth does Barry Woolwell's wife look like a Hollywood actress?"

"Why wouldn't she?"

"You've seen the man, Pembers! He's an old, grubby-looking gardening type with dirty fingernails. What does she see in him? Is he excessively rich?"

"No, not at all. He lives in one of the Grubmill Cottages."

"But he must have something about him to appeal to such a charmingly beautiful young lady. The other gardening wives are what you'd expect with their bulldog faces, buck teeth and so on."

"I think it must be down to Barry Woolwell's sparkling personality."

"Really, Pembers?" asked Churchill through a mouthful of biscuit crumbs.

"Yes, I've heard he can be quite the charmer."

"Well, it takes one to know one, I suppose. The evening is quite ruined now. I was hoping we could ply these ladies with alcohol over the course of it and carefully draw out a suspect from their careless chatter, but instead we've already reached a dead end. The last time I felt this floored was when I got lost in the maze at Hampton Court."

"I wouldn't be too downcast, Mrs Churchill. We can cheer ourselves up with the jelly."

"There isn't one, Pembers. Remember?"

"Oh yes, that's a shame. Please may I have a custard cream instead?"

"Yes." Churchill handed her one. "Now we just have to get all these women out of my house. They're a tiresome lot, aren't they?"

"It was your idea, Mrs Churchill."

"Thank you for reminding me, Pemberley."

"You can't throw them out yet. Surely we could have a game of charades first."

"I detest charades, Pembers, but it's a good suggestion."

"My Love is Like a Red, Red Rose!" said Mrs Woolwell. "How did you not get it?"

"A Red, Red Rose," said Pemberley.

"Yes. Lovely, isn't it?"

"The title of the poem is 'A Red, Red Rose'," corrected Pemberley. "It doesn't have the '*My Love is Like a*' bit before it.

"But he says it in the poem," said Mrs Woolwell, looking deflated.

"I thought you meant a red nose," said Mrs Rumbold.

Churchill sighed and glanced at the clock, wondering if half past seven was too early to ask everyone to leave.

"Wasn't there supposed to be a jelly?" asked Mrs Williams.

"There was, but we dropped it on the floor while transferring it from its mould," replied Churchill. "Sorry about that."

"What about another drink?" asked Mrs Williams.

Churchill would have made a sharp retort if Mrs Williams hadn't been so recently widowed. Instead, she got up to fetch a decanter filled with cheap sherry a friend had gifted her.

"This is the only alcohol left in the house," she lied as

she filled up Mrs Williams's glass. "Did your late husband explain why he stole the colonel's gun?"

"He told me someone was planning to do him some mischief."

Churchill's eyes widened. "Did he say who?"

"Not exactly. I recall that he showed me the gun. He was quite proud that he'd stolen it without being detected. And then he said something like, '*I'm going to put a stop to this once and for all.*'"

"Really? And did you ask him to elaborate?"

"No, because we were interrupted by the vicar. He always calls at the back door without warning, have you noticed that? Before you know it, he's getting himself comfortable at the kitchen table and making that smacking noise with his lips to signify that he wants a cup of tea."

"How irritating," said Churchill. "So the vicar saw the gun?"

"No, Tubby swiftly shoved it down his trousers."

"Was there an opportunity for Tubby to explain himself further once the vicar had left?"

"No, because he went out to his allotment then. He always left the house when the vicar turned up. He hated him."

"So that was the last time you saw your husband?"

"Yes."

Mrs Williams's face crumpled, so Churchill quickly topped up her glass. "There, there, Mrs Williams. We'll find the man who did this and make sure he gets his just desserts."

As Churchill said this she noticed Mrs Rumbold scratching uneasily at her neck.

Chapter 18

"I'VE REACHED A CONCLUSION, PEMBERLEY," said Churchill in the office the following morning. She had lain awake during the night thinking about the conversation at her cocktail party and a few things puzzled her still.

"What's your conclusion Mrs Churchill?"

"That Mr Williams wasn't murdered after all."

"Really? But how on earth could he not have been? How come he's dead?"

"The answer, Pembers, is that he took his own life."

"Oh no, he would never have done that. He was too cheerful to do such a thing."

"Never fall into the trap of judging a man's innermost thoughts by his demeanour, Pemberley. It's usually the cheerful ones who do this sort of thing."

"I refuse to believe it. Someone must have shot him."

"What makes you say that?"

"I visited the scene, didn't I? It didn't look like the man had caused the mischief by his own hand."

"What makes you say that?"

"I don't know the specifics, but the police will. You could say that I'm basing it on a hunch."

"There's no harm in having a hunch, Pembers, but we know the man stole the colonel's gun, and we've a good idea that it was the same gun that shot him. Therefore, I think he shot himself."

"No, I don't like that theory at all. And if he did shoot himself, how has the gun gone missing? I think Tubby stole the colonel's revolver because he wanted to challenge Rumbold, who had accused him of spearing his onions. Perhaps he didn't intend to cause Rumbold any harm, but he went to the allotment that evening to threaten him. Then there was a tussle and Rumbold managed to snatch the gun from him and shot the poor man. It was probably all done in the heat of the moment, and Rumbold probably didn't mean to kill him, but you know how it is when you get all cross about something and lose your temper. And if you've snatched a loaded gun from someone who's lost their rag with you it might accidentally go off and kill them."

Churchill gave this some thought. "Pembers, I could kiss you. Your theory is so much better than mine! I think that's exactly what happened. Williams stole the gun but Rumbold tussled with him and it all went wrong. He admits they were calling each other names, doesn't he? It clearly escalated to something more than that. How frustrating that we've pretty much solved this case when we're not supposed to have anything to do with it."

"I think we should write Inspector Mappin an anonymous note explaining our theory."

"Another good idea, Pemberley. And then we need to get back to Mrs Bramley's tea rooms and catch Kitty Flatboot with her hand in the till."

"That reminds me. I saw your Mr Harding in there

yesterday when I went round to invite Mrs Bramley to the cocktail party."

"*My* Mr Harding, Pembers? Don't be so silly. He's not *my* Mr Harding." Churchill felt her cheeks heating up. "What was he doing in there?"

"Drinking tea. He had put a 'back in fifteen minutes' sign on the door of his cookshop. Those signs always confuse me."

"Why?"

"Because it's not fifteen minutes, is it? It's fifteen minutes minus the time since the shopkeeper left it there."

"I'm not following you."

"So if Mr Harding puts his 'back in fifteen minutes' sign on the door at two o'clock and you turn up at ten minutes past two, you'll think you need to wait fifteen minutes for him to return, when actually it would only be five minutes."

"Ah yes, I see what you mean. But then one would be pleasantly surprised when Mr Harding arrived a mere five minutes later."

"No, because one would have decided that one had enough time to do something else with the fifteen minutes, such as pay a visit to the tea rooms or pop into the library, and do that instead."

"And if one went to the tea rooms, one would find Mr Harding in there. Where's the problem in that?"

"It's misleading. I can't bear a misleading sign."

"Let's return to what you were telling me before, Pembers. I hope you didn't converse with Mr Harding in the tea rooms, seeing as he's on the list of people Inspector Mappin expressly banned us from speaking to."

"No, I didn't speak to him. But I observed some confusion at the till between Mr Harding and Kitty Flatboot. It appears she had short-changed him."

"The minx! Fancy short-changing Mr Harding! What a dreadful thing to do to such a delightful man."

"It appeared to be a genuine mistake, and Mr Harding was perfectly charming and forgiving about it all."

"Well, he would be, you see. That's the sort of man he is. I believe you may have witnessed Kitty's sticky hands in action, however."

"I didn't actually see her take anything and pocket it; I only witnessed the conversation about pennies and something about him having given her a shilling rather than a sixpence, or something along those lines. It became confusing terribly quickly."

"Hmm, we shall have to keep an eye on that one, Pembers. Let's pay the tea rooms another visit today, and in the meantime please type an anonymous letter to Inspector Mappin informing him of our suspicions. But don't say they're *our* suspicions because then he'll realise the letter's from us. Make it as impersonal as possible."

"I think he'll guess it's from us anyway," said Pemberley. "And he might even brush the envelope and letter for fingerprints."

"Then put some gloves on, and I'll make us a nice cup of tea."

"But he's still going to guess it's from us, isn't he?"

"Send it to that Lupin-Winkle chap instead, then. He's even more hapless."

"It's rather difficult to write with all that racket going on outside the window."

"What racket, Pembers? I can't hear a thing."

"All that chatter and noise out on the street. You come to expect it on market day, but not on a nothing day like today."

"If you think that's noisy you wouldn't survive five minutes in London, Pemberley. All those motor vehicles, trams and trains, and the shouting market traders and cockneys. Cockneys are incapable of saying anything without shouting it."

"Presumably they need to shout over all the noise."

"Yes, but not that loud. They're deafening! Now, get on with that letter."

"Something's going on outside," said Pemberley, peering out of the window. "And I'm sure I just saw Inspector Mappin racing past on his bicycle again."

"Then something must have happened," said Churchill, grabbing her hat and handbag. "Let's go!"

Chapter 19

"THERE APPEARS to be something of a palaver up at the duck pond, Pembers," said Churchill as they followed the crowd turning off the high street and down a narrow lane.

"Make way for Churchill's Detective Agency!" she called out, elbowing her way through the crowd.

"You want to be careful saying that sort of thing," said Pemberley. "Inspector Mappin will think we're interfering again."

"You're not wrong, Pemberley," said Churchill. "I'll keep my voice down for now, but it's rather difficult to get through the crowd otherwise."

"Looks like we're about to become a herd of sheep again!" laughed a lady with orange-tinged hair.

Churchill felt a pang of anger as she noticed Mrs Thonnings standing beside her. "There's nothing sheepish about me," she retorted.

"Then why are you in the herd?" asked Mrs Thonnings.

"I'm investigating," said Churchill. "Do please excuse

me." She pushed on past the people in front of her in a bid to get away as quickly as possible.

"What are you doing here, Mrs Churchill?" asked Inspector Mappin once she reached the front of the crowd. "I thought I told you to stay away."

"Why don't you say that to all the other people gathered here?"

"Because they're not here to meddle."

"And neither am I, Inspector. It would be terribly foolish of me not to heed your advice wouldn't it?"

"Yes, it would."

"I'm merely here to find out what's going on, just like the rest of the village."

Inspector Mappin acknowledged this with a herumphing sound.

"So what is going on, Inspector?" she asked.

"I'll have more of an idea when I don't have to control the crowd and can get on with investigating. But I'm here responding to a report of a man in the duck pond."

Churchill raised herself up onto her tiptoes to see past the inspector but she couldn't make out much of the duck pond.

"Oh dear. Is someone trying to get him out?"

"The constables from Bulchford are doing that, but I fear we've lost him."

"Oh no! How dreadful, Inspector. Is it a drowning?"

"I fear so. But no more questions, Mrs Churchill, otherwise I'll begin to suspect that you're meddling again."

"It sounds very serious, Inspector. You need to get Inspector Doolally-Whatisname up here in a jiffy."

"Llewellyn-Dalrymple, if you please. He's just finishing his breakfast at the Piddleton Hotel. Now, will you allow me to get on with my job?"

"Of course, Inspector. You have my blessing."

"Does anyone know who it is in the duck pond?" Churchill asked the people around her. She received blank expressions and shaking heads in response.

Churchill pushed her way back through the crowd, ignoring another cheerful acknowledgement from Mrs Thonnings. As she rejoined the high street she was pleased to bump into Pemberley.

"Where've you been?" she whispered.

"Up at the duck pond. I went up Camp Lane and snuck through Mrs Sidebottom's garden."

"Pembers!" Churchill grinned with admiration. "Pray, what did you see?"

Pemberley's face grew sombre. "The constables from Bulchford have pulled him out, poor fellow."

"And?"

"It's him."

"Who?"

"Rumbold."

Churchill gasped. "No, Pembers!"

"Yes!"

"Are you sure?"

"I recognised the beard."

"No! And is he —?"

"Yes," said Pemberley sadly.

"But why? How? Oh goodness, the guilt of murder must have led him to take his own life."

"He didn't do that."

"How do you know?"

"Because his arms and legs were bound with rope."

"Good grief, Pembers! Another murder?"

"It looks that way."

"I'm shocked. In fact, I'm beyond shocked. And what of poor Mrs Rumbold? We only saw her yesterday evening at my dreadful cocktail party, and now she's a widow. Gosh, I wonder if she even knows yet."

"I don't think we should tell her. I can't bear to tell people bad news."

"I'm sure Inspector Mappin is able to manage these things delicately."

"I'm sure he's not."

"You may be right, Pembers, but we should try not to concern ourselves with it. It's not our job to worry, is it? In the meantime, we need to go and update our incident board."

Chapter 20

"SO IF MR RUMBOLD murdered Mr Williams, who murdered Mr Rumbold?" asked Pemberley as she and Churchill surveyed their updated incident board.

"How should I know, Pemberley? It's quite baffling."

"It could have been someone who wished to avenge Tubby Williams's murder," said Pemberley. "It might have been Mrs Williams."

"But she was with us yesterday evening, wasn't she?" said Churchill. "We can rule out all those ladies as we have unwittingly provided an alibi for them. Besides, I can't imagine Mrs Williams tying up Rumbold's arms and legs and tipping him into the duck pond."

"The colonel, perhaps?"

"He's getting on a bit. I think Rumbold could have overpowered him."

"Barry Woolwell?"

"He's not too young either. And he'd have to have done it before drinking his normal quota at the Wagon and Carrot."

"Sniffer Downs?"

"It could have been him, I suppose."

"Stropper Harris?"

"And him. Let's put those two at the top of our incident board Pemberley so we can treat them as our chief suspects."

"What about Mr Harding?"

"Oh, leave him out of it. He has nothing to do with any of this."

"How do you know that?"

"I just know, Pembers. He has better things to do than go around murdering people."

"So we're certain that Mr Rumbold murdered Mr Williams, are we?"

"I think so, Pembers. After all, he was the last man to see Tubby Williams alive."

"Or perhaps he was the only person who *owned up* to seeing Tubby Williams shortly before he died. Surely the actual murderer would have kept quiet about it?"

"Oh, I see what you're saying there. Yes, that's a good point. Perhaps Rumbold was happy to admit that he was at the allotments with Tubby because the man was entirely innocent of his murder. And that leads us to the possibility that Tubby and Rumbold were killed by the same man."

"Perhaps that man was with both of them at the allotment that fateful night."

"Yes, he could have been! And naturally he kept quiet about it."

"But Rumbold didn't mention there being anyone else at the allotment that evening. He said it was just him and Tubby."

"Good point. So our third man could have been hiding in the shrubbery somewhere, waiting for his moment. Perhaps Rumbold left and then our man struck."

"But if it's the same culprit, why didn't he kill both of the men at the same time if he wanted them dead?"

"Another good point, Pembers. I think our murderous chap must have gone up there after Rumbold had left because Tubby was in possession of the gun, wasn't he? Our murderer somehow had to wrestle the gun away from Tubby and shoot him with it. That could only have happened after Rumbold had left, otherwise he'd have got involved too, wouldn't he?"

"Perhaps Rumbold witnessed the murderer and that's why he also had to be killed."

"Oh yes! But why didn't Rumbold tell anyone who the murderer was in that case?"

"Perhaps he didn't really see who it was, but the murderer was so worried Rumbold might recall something that he decided to do away with him anyway."

"Yes, yes, yes, Pembers! That is surely what happened. We're good at this, aren't we? My poor little brain is beginning to ache rather. Do you think you could see your way to making a cup of tea with Mr Harding's kettle?"

"Do we have to keep calling it that? It doesn't belong to him any more, seeing as you purchased it from him."

"We can simply refer to it as *the kettle* from now on if you wish."

"Thank you. Because if Mr Harding turns out to be the murderer it would be an unfortunate association indeed."

"I shall excommunicate you if you slander that kind man again, Pemberley. Now get on with the tea because we've got some investigating to do this morning. Do you know where we might find Mrs Harris and Mrs Downs?"

Chapter 21

"OH HELLO, Mrs Harris. I didn't realise you worked at the greengrocer's," said Churchill. "What a pleasant surprise!"

"Mrs Churchill! Miss Pemberley!" Mrs Harris's blonde curls bounced cheerily. "Thank you so much for hosting such a wonderful party yesterday evening. I must apologise that my charade for *Gone with the Wind* was a little crude, I blame the drink."

"One must always blame the drink on such occasions, Mrs Harris. And I confess that my cocktails were rather strong."

"Strong but extremely quaffable, Mrs Churchill. You must tell us when the next party will be!"

"Indeed. But I'm afraid I cannot find myself in party mood this morning. You have heard the sad news, I presume?"

"Yes." Mrs Harris's teeth protruded from her down-turned mouth. "I've been trying not to think about it too much. Mr Perret the greengrocer told me to put on a happy face and not depress the customers, but now that you've reminded me I feel rather sombre."

"Oh dear. I've no doubt that you are a professional, Mrs Harris, and will be able to resume your cheery manner at the flick of a switch."

Mrs Harris smiled. "Oh, thank you. Yes, I do pride myself on being professional in my work. What can I help you with?"

"I'll have half a pound of onions please, Mrs Harris," said Churchill. She suddenly felt a lump in her throat as she glanced at the brown-skinned globes and was reminded of Mr Rumbold's allotment.

"Have you spoken to Mrs Rumbold since the, er… tragic event?" ventured Churchill.

"No, not yet," replied Mrs Harris sadly as she popped the onions into a paper bag. "I never know what to say to someone when their husband's been murdered."

"It's rather a test of one's etiquette, isn't it?"

"I shall go and see her later with some gooseberries."

"What a nice idea. Presumably, your husband is desperately upset about the loss of his friend."

"Devastated." Mrs Harris's shoulders slumped. "They were drinking together at the Pig and Scythe just last night."

"Really? That must have been shortly before Mr Rumbold was so tragically murdered."

"It was! They left the Pig and Scythe at eleven o'clock and Stropper got home about ten minutes after that. I had already returned home after your delightful party. Stropper parted ways with Rumbold on Barncock Lane, and then Rumbold walked off in the direction of the duck pond. It was on his way home, you see. Only he never made it!"

Tears streaked with black mascara started trickling down Mrs Harris's face.

"Oh dear. You need a handkerchief, Mrs Harris," said

Churchill, rummaging around in her handbag for one. "Not that old one, Pembers. You've used it!"

"Only on one side," said Pemberley.

"Put it away. I have a clean one in here somewhere."

"So your husband, Stropper, was the last man to see Mr Rumbold alive?" Pemberley asked Mrs Harris.

The woman nodded sadly.

"Here's a clean handkerchief," said Churchill. "Hold onto it for now and return it at your leisure."

"That Stropper Harris is a suspicious one, isn't he, Pembers?" said Churchill after they had left the green-grocer's.

"He was the last one to see Rumbold alive," said Pemberley, "and don't forget that he was also the first one to find Tubby Williams."

"Yes, indeed he was! I bet he's charging people a shilling to listen to his story about the last sighting of Rumbold now. The man is a disgrace."

"Oh hello, Mrs Downs. I didn't realise you worked at the butcher's," said Churchill. "What a pleasant surprise!"

Mrs Downs's bulldog face smiled.

"It was lovely to see you at the party yesterday evening," continued Churchill, "but what sad news we've woken up to this morning."

Mrs Downs rolled her eyes.

"Your husband must be extremely upset about the sad death of his friend."

Mrs Downs rolled her eyes again and Churchill felt her teeth clench with annoyance.

"Half a pound of sausages please, Mrs Downs."

As the woman fetched the sausages Mrs Churchill whispered to Pemberley from the side of her mouth. "Any idea how we can get this woman to talk, Pembers?"

"I think she's just shy."

"I'd call her uncooperative."

Mrs Downs placed the sausages on the counter and held out her hand for the money.

"Fourpence, please," she said.

"Of course, Mrs Downs. Now that we've commenced a conversation, I'm wondering whether your good husband had seen the recently deceased Mr Rumbold in the last few days?" Churchill said, handing her the money.

"Last night," said Mrs Downs.

Churchill was startled that the woman had finally answered one of her questions. "Last night? Really? Was that at the Pig and Scythe?"

"Wagon and Carrot."

"I see. So your husband saw Mr Rumbold at the Wagon and Carrot shortly before he went to the Pig and Scythe with Mr Harris, did he?"

Mrs Downs rolled her eyes.

"Is that a yes or a no, Mrs Downs?"

The woman shrugged.

"Or a *don't know*, perhaps? I see. Well, thank you for your help and the sausages."

"It seems that both of our chief suspects saw Mr Rumbold yesterday evening, Pembers," said Churchill as they walked back along the high street to their office.

"Perhaps they carried out the deed together," suggested Pemberley.

"In tandem? It's possible, isn't it? Oh, look. That chief inspector with the pompous name is heading our way."

Chief Inspector Llewellyn-Dalrymple doffed his hat as he approached them.

"Good morning, ladies, and quite a morning it is, too."

"Have you just come from your breakfast at the Piddleton Hotel?" asked Churchill.

"How on earth do you know about that?"

"News travels fast in villages, Chief Inspector."

"It certainly does. It's quite alarming! So, another murder, eh? Thank you for your help with the bullet case. My ballistics fellow examined it and has confirmed that the colonel's missing revolver was indeed used in the murder of Mr Tubby Williams."

"That's marvellous," said Churchill.

"It's not really marvellous," said Pemberley. "The man got shot. It's rather grisly."

"But marvellous that it's been confirmed," said Churchill.

"You two ladies showed great presence of mind with that piece of investigating. You should be detectives."

"We are, Chief Inspector."

"Oh yes. You have some sort of private detective agency thingummy, don't you? Keeps you out of trouble, I'll bet."

"On the contrary, Chief Inspector, it keeps us *in* trouble."

"Does it, by Jove? Goodness me!"

"There was no murder weapon in this second murder though, was there? It was a straightforward drowning, I believe," said Churchill.

"Oh no, there was a weapon all right. One of the Bulchford constables briefed me while I ate my eggs and bacon. He informed me that the chap had suffered a blow to the head."

"But I thought he drowned?"

"He was deposited into the duck pond after being hit on the bonce. We'll have the police surgeon look him over, but it sounds like a drowning while unconscious as a result of a knock to the head."

"Poor Mr Rumbold!" cried out Pemberley. "And he had his wrists and ankles bound, too!"

"How do you know that?" asked the chief inspector.

"I happened to peer out from Mrs Sidebottom's garden, which has a commanding view of the duck pond," said Pemberley.

"You need to be careful about what you're viewing. You'll give yourself bad dreams," warned the policeman.

"I get those anyway."

"Righty-ho. Well, I'll be on my way now. These murders won't solve themselves, you know!"

"Wouldn't life be dreadfully boring if they did, Chief Inspector? Do let us know if you need any help at all. We have our ears to the ground, you see. Apparently, Mr Harris and Mr Downs were with Mr Rumbold yesterday evening."

"Were they indeed? Those names sound familiar."

"Probably because I mentioned them to you the other day. Both men also visited the colonel's home the day before Mr Williams's death. You might also be interested to know that it was Mr Williams who took the colonel's revolver."

"Just a moment. Are you telling me that the murder victim stole the murder weapon that was used to murder him?"

"Yes. Confusing, isn't it? You might want to have a word with Mrs Williams. She says that her deccased husband showed her the gun he'd stolen from the colonel and said he planned to do someone some mischief. If you ask me, I think the mischief plan got out of hand and was inflicted on him instead."

"And how do you know all this?"

"It just happened to be mentioned during a social event."

"By Mr Williams's widow?"

"The very same."

The chief inspector retrieved his notebook from his pocket and made some hasty notes.

"I see," he said as he flicked the notebook shut. "Well, I think it's a spot of good luck that I bumped into you two ladies this morning. You've certainly enlightened me on one or two points."

"It's our pleasure, sir. At this rate we'll have the case solved before you do!"

The chief inspector gave a hearty laugh. "How funny! Two old ladies beating the police at their own game. That would really be something, wouldn't it? Ho, ho!"

Chapter 22

"I THINK we've done enough sniffing about for this morning, Pemberley," said Churchill once they had updated their incident board in the office. "It won't be long before we're accused of interfering and all the rest of it. I don't want to give Mappin any more grist to his mill. It's a funny expression that, isn't it? I have no idea what grist is."

"It's a grain that's been separated from its chaff and is ready for milling."

"Oh, I see. You know what it is, do you? I wasn't actually asking for an explanation just then. I know what I mean when I say it, and that's the important thing. Now, why don't we have a nice cup of tea and I'll settle down to read a few more of Atkins's cases. He really did have some fascinating ones, didn't he? I recall I got halfway through a case in which he was visited by a mysterious masked man who turned out to be a Bohemian prince. I should like to find that one again."

"I remember it well. There was an adventuress involved."

"Isn't there always? I'm beginning to suspect that Mrs

Thonnings is one of those. I can't for the life of me think how a story about a pepper pot and a pair of long johns could be amusing. Mrs Harris is clearly one of those people who is easily entertained."

"Ah, but there's no denying that Mrs Thonnings is refined and clever. And witty, too."

"Don't you start, Pembers! Compared with the average citizen of Compton Poppleford – a town of predominantly rustic stock – Mrs Thonnings could perhaps be considered to have some degree of refinement. But that's not saying much. She'd be eaten alive in the drawing rooms of Richmond-upon-Thames."

"Really? Do they do that sort of thing there?"

"They'd wash her down with an aperitif, Pemberley."

"Ugh!"

"She's probably unaware that an entire world exists beyond Dorset. I shouldn't think she's ever been east of Blandford Forum."

"She and Mr Harding once took a trip to London together. They went to Harrods. They showed us all the photographs when they returned."

"I can't think of anything I wish to hear about less, Pembers. Please put the kettle on while I proceed with some work."

They were interrupted by a knock at the door, and in strode Inspector Mappin.

Churchill sighed. "If you're here to tear us off a strip again, Inspector, you can do an about-turn and toddle back down the stairs. I'm in no mood for it. Miss Pemberley and I have stayed well away from your suspects."

"I've no plans to tear anything off anyone, Mrs Churchill," he replied, removing his hat and placing it on the hatstand. "I'm here to make enquiries."

"I see. You need our help now you have a second murder on your hands, do you?"

"No, just enquiries, as I've already said. Merely routine." He withdrew a notebook from his pocket and scratched at his brown mutton-chop whiskers with the tip of his pencil. "I believe you hosted a social gathering at your home yesterday evening."

"Indeed I did, Inspector. Do sit down; you're making the place look untidy. Would you like a cup of tea?"

"On this occasion, yes I would. Thank you, Mrs Churchill." He lowered himself into the chair on the opposite side of her desk.

"I confess there was a little soirée *chez moi* yesterday evening," said Churchill. "What of it?"

"Who was in attendance, Mrs Churchill?"

"There was myself, Miss Pemberley, Mrs Rumbold, Mrs Harris, Mrs Downs, Mrs Bramley, Mrs Williams and Mrs Woolwell."

"Not Mrs Higginbath or Mrs Thonnings?"

"No. Why does everyone always mention those two? *No.* They were *not* there."

"And what time did Mrs Rumbold arrive?"

"She was the first one there. I do believe it was about half past five. Do you recall it being around that time, Miss Pemberley?"

"I do indeed," Pemberley replied, placing the tea tray on Churchill's desk.

"And what time did Mrs Rumbold leave your house?" asked Inspector Mappin.

"About a quarter past eight. I began eviction proceedings at eight o'clock, and she was the last to depart. She's quite a talkative lady after a few drinks."

"So you can vouch for Mrs Rumbold being on the

premises between the hours of half past five and a quarter past eight yesterday evening?"

"Yes, I can vouch for that. Do you think she murdered her husband?"

"Merely routine enquiries, Mrs Churchill."

"Oh, come on, Inspector. That's what police officers say when they're trying to make something interesting sound incredibly dull because they don't want anyone else to get excited by it. What's going on? Is there any evidence that she did it?"

"It's not for me to say at this stage. Did she mention any sort of grievance with her husband while she was at your party?"

"Not that I can remember."

"She said she'd got so fed up with competitive gardening she'd considered getting a divorce," said Pemberley.

"Oh, that's right. Yes, she said that," added Churchill.

Mappin wrote this down. "She mentioned divorce but nothing to suggest violent intent? Murder?"

"Inspector, if she was planning to murder her husband she was hardly going to mention it at my cocktail party, was she?"

"Probably not. But it's worth asking the question as you can never quite predict what women find themselves talking about at these sorts of gatherings."

"None of them are stupid enough to admit they're about to do away with their husbands, if that's what you're thinking. Does our alibi put her in the clear?"

"I don't think it does. She left your home at a quarter past eight, when Mr Rumbold was still at the Wagon and Carrot."

"After which he moved on to the Pig and Scythe."

"I won't bother asking how you know that, Mrs

Churchill, but yes he did. He left the Pig and Scythe shortly before half past eleven and we estimate that the time of death was around a quarter to midnight."

"When Mrs Rumbold was presumably tucked up in bed at home."

"That's what she'd have us believe."

"You don't seriously think she's the culprit do you, Inspector? I know she mentioned divorce at my party, but I think it was half-said in jest."

"Or said in half-jest," added Pemberley.

"What's the difference?" asked Churchill.

"I don't know, but there'll be one."

Inspector Mappin put away his notebook, finished his cup of tea and retrieved his hat from the hatstand.

"Thank you for your time, ladies," he said. "Now, I must remind you not to—"

"Meddle? I believe that's a word you unfairly associate with our work, Inspector. Please don't worry. We shall merely trip on by with the delicacy and grace of two ballerinas, shan't we, Miss Pemberley?"

"I don't know any ballet moves."

"Maybe not, Pembers, but if you did I'm sure you would manage a plié with great aplomb. As for myself, I did a fair bit of ballerinaring in my youth."

An astonished snort erupted from Inspector Mappin.

"Yes, it's true, Inspector. I haven't always been the size of a brick outhouse, you know. I once had a twenty-four-inch waist. And I can still pirouette when I've had enough gin to numb the old knees. My tutu is in storage back in London, though it would merely suffice as a garter these days. Inspector, your face has turned the colour of an angry tomato. Are you embarrassed by my mention of the word *garter*?"

"No, not at all, Mrs Churchill. I'm not the type to

embarrass easily. It's just that all this talk of waists and pirouetting is confounding me a little. I need to get on with solving these murders."

"Absolutely, Inspector. And if you need us to be alibis for anyone else at the party do please let us know."

Inspector Mappin put his hat on and left the office.

Pemberley emitted a loud shriek as she returned to her desk.

Churchill startled. "Good grief, trusty assistant! Why on earth are you making that horrible noise?"

Pemberley gave a sob and pointed to a scrap of paper on her desk.

"It's the note Mr Rumbold put through our door! And now he's dead!" She pulled a balled-up handkerchief from the sleeve of her colourless cardigan and squashed it into her eyes.

Churchill walked over to Pemberley's desk and put an arm around her thin frame. She glanced down at the note and felt a lump in her throat as she read the words Rumbold had written just a few days before:

Forget about onions, problem now resolved.
  Mr Rumbold

"Come now, Pemberley, it won't do to get upset. He was quite an annoying man with exceptionally poor personal hygiene. It's sad that he's dead, but crying about it won't bring him back. The best we can do now is find the chap who murdered him."

"But how can we do that without meddling?" wailed Pemberley.

"Churchy always finds a way, Pembers."

Chapter 23

"A NICE CAKE will cheer you up, Pemberley," said Churchill as she squeezed herself onto a flimsy chair in Mrs Bramley's tea rooms. "And hopefully we'll catch that Flatboot girl with her hand in the till while we're at it. Don't you ever pause to think how lucky we are to have a profession where we can enjoy a little tea and cake while we're working?" She rearranged the lace tablecloth, which had become dislodged during her struggle to sit down.

"We're very lucky indeed. Mr Atkins enjoyed it, too. He once had an important case to investigate at Raffles Hotel in Singapore. He stayed there for three weeks and it didn't cost him a bean."

"Is that so? Well, I'm the modest type, so I'm quite content with the Dorset tea rooms. I don't go in for all that showy Raffles business."

"But it's a wonderful hotel."

"I'm sure it is, Pembers," said Churchill, purposefully distracting herself by trying to summon Kitty Flatboot.

"I stayed there a few times while I was—"

"*A companion to a lady of international travel.* Yes, I think you've told me about it a few times now. This Flatboot waitress is rather slow off the mark, isn't she? Oh, here she comes."

Kitty Flatboot sulkily took Churchill's order and ambled off to the kitchen.

"It always amazes me how so many members of the lower classes take no pride in their work," commented Churchill. "That sticky Kitty acts as if she's here under sufferance."

"Perhaps she is."

"Nonsense. She should be grateful for any decent paid employment. She's far better off working as a waitress here than as a scullery maid elsewhere. Or as a chamber maid, for that matter. She should be happy that a girl like herself – with, dare I say it, a minimal level of education – doesn't have to empty slops from other people's chamber pots."

"I think we should all be grateful we don't have to do that."

"I don't know why Mrs Bramley wants us to take the time to spot the girl with her hand in the till. She should just dismiss her and be done with it."

"Perhaps Mrs Bramley is more tolerant than your good self, Mrs Churchill."

"*Soft* is what I call it. She's another person who wouldn't last five minutes in the Home Counties."

"Would she be eaten alive by the ladies of Richmond-upon-Thames?"

"Most definitely. But she'd be lucky if she even got past Weybridge; they're very particular in that part of the world."

Kitty Flatboot returned with a pot of tea and a heavily laden cake stand.

"What a wonderful display of cakes," said Churchill.

"With that array I could almost forgive you for refusing to smile, Miss Flatboot."

The waitress glared at her. "Why d'you keep starin' at me?"

"Staring?" Churchill felt her cheeks flush. "I don't stare, young lady."

"You've been starin' at me as if you've been talkin' about me."

"I don't talk about people either."

"I feel as if you're talkin' and starin', and I don't like it."

"Well, perhaps you wrongly assume that people are taking an interest in you when they're not. This is the problem with young people these days, isn't it, Miss Pemberley? They're terribly self-absorbed."

Kitty glared at her again and walked away.

"I think subtlety might be the best approach here, Mrs Churchill," whispered Pemberley.

"There's no need to remind me how to do my job," hissed Churchill as she poured out the tea.

"But she knew you were talking about her. How can you carry out effective surveillance when you keep drawing attention to yourself?"

"It just happens to be fairly quiet in here, Pembers, and without many other customers about the Flatboot girl has simply assumed we're watching her."

"And she's right. You're sitting there gawking at her and making loud comments, which I'm sure half the clientele can hear."

"Fine," said Churchill through clenched teeth. "If you think you'll do better at this surveillance business you can take over the case while I look after the more important business of solving murders."

Churchill noticed her chair felt lop-sided.

"I'm probably no better at it—"

"No, I'm sure you will be, Pembers. You handle it all and inform Mrs Bramley next time you see that girl with her hand in the till. Have you told her about the incident when Kitty short-changed poor Mr Harding? No? I expected as much. It's down to me to do all the work as usual."

"Please don't take offence, Mrs Churchill, I merely suggested a little subtlety. And the name of the company is Churchill's Detective Agency, which means—"

"That I must do most of the work. Yes, yes. I get it." Churchill took a gulp of tea and winced as she burnt her tongue. "Ouch!" she exclaimed, quickly changing her tone when she noticed Pemberley's crestfallen face. "Oh no, Pembers, please don't cry."

Pemberley dabbed at her eyes with her handkerchief and Churchill felt her chair wobble.

"Pembers, I'm sorry. I didn't mean to be snappy. I suppose I took offence at the suggestion that I'm not as subtle as I'd like to be with my surveillance."

"You're not," sobbed Pemberley.

"Yes, all right, I admit it. Subtlety has never been my strong point, which I suppose is quite a drawback when it comes to detective work. Now, let's get those eyes dried and crack on with solving our cases. That's why we're here, isn't it?"

There was a sudden crack and Churchill suddenly found herself on the floor with a sharp pain in her lower back.

"My chair… Help Pemberley!"

All she could see was the underside of the table and the edge of the lace tablecloth.

"Mrs Churchill! Are you all right?" Pemberley's

concerned face appeared above her. "My goodness! What happened to your chair?"

Churchill glanced at the chair legs lying beside her on the floor.

"It gave up the ghost, that's what. Please can you help me up?"

Pemberley, Mrs Bramley and Kitty Flatboot managed to lift Churchill up from the floor and seat her on a sturdier chair which Mrs Bramley brought out from the kitchen.

"Oh Mrs Churchill, I'm sorry. I should've got the chair fixed," she said.

"There weren't nothin' wrong with it," said Kitty with a smile.

Churchill ignored the waitress's barbed comment, keen to forget about the episode as quickly as possible.

"Please don't worry Mrs Bramley, it's merely one of those things."

"But you hurt yerself."

"Merely a bump, Mrs Bramley. Think nothing of it. With Battenberg as good as this, I have quite forgotten about it already."

She pretended not to notice as Kitty Flatboot walked away, failing to stifle a laugh.

"Oh, good." Mrs Bramley gave a bashful grin. "It were Barney's favourite. He liked it so much 'e even went there."

"Went where?"

"Ter Battenberg. In Germany."

"Good grief. What a long way to travel just for some cake."

"And there weren't none there!"

"No cake?"

"No *Battenberg* cake."

"Because it's not actually a German cake," Pemberley chipped in. "The Victorians named it so to honour the marriage of Princess Victoria and Prince Louis of Battenberg."

"If only you could somehow travel back in time and inform Mr Bramley of that, Pembers. It would have saved him a completely futile journey."

"Perhaps I will one day."

"'E loved carrot cake too," said Mrs Bramley. "It was 'is dream for me to make carrot cake wiv carrots 'e'd growed 'imself. Trouble was they never came to nuffink."

"I'm sorry to hear it, Mrs Bramley. Carrots are not an easy vegetable to grow."

"So 'ave yer caught 'er yet?" she whispered, nodding in Kitty's direction.

"Not yet, Mrs Bramley, and I'm afraid to say that she appears to be on to us this morning. She asked me to stop staring at her."

"Oh, well p'raps you should then?"

"It won't be easy to catch her with her hand in the till without looking at her."

"I don't s'pose it will. And she's lookin' over at us now."

"I'd say that our cover has been blown for today. We're going to have to take a different tack."

"I'm sure you'll come up wiv summat, Mrs Churchill."

"Rotten luck about old Rumbold, isn't it?"

"Awful." Mrs Bramley's face sank. "I'm strugglin' ter believe it. And that poor Mrs Rumbold. I'll pay 'er a visit after I've finished up 'ere for the day."

"Has there been any gossip in here about who might be behind it?"

"All sorts o' names 'ave been discussed, but ev'ryone's baffled."

"Didn't you mention that one of your customers saw

Rumbold leaving the allotments with a gun in his hand following the murder of Mr Williams?"

"Oh 'im, yeah."

"Has he speculated on this latest tragedy at all?"

"Funny you should ask. He said 'e 'eard footsteps runnin' down the 'igh street late last night, an' the sound of a man laughin'."

"Laughing?"

"Yeah, almost like an evil cackle, 'e said."

"Goodness me. Can you recall the witness's name yet?"

"It's Mr... Oh, I keep forgettin' it. It'll come ter me in a minute. Square chin and spectacles. Brown 'air. Orders egg sandwiches but never eats 'is crusts."

"I recall that description, Mrs Bramley, thank you. We'll keep an eye out for him, won't we, Miss Pemberley? In the meantime, our work here is done for the day as Miss Flatboot has become too suspicious of us. I think a stroll is in order." She winced at the pain in her back. "A bit of fresh air will do us good."

Chapter 24

CHURCHILL ENSURED that their steps took them in the direction of the duck pond at the heart of the village green. The crowds had departed and two police constables appeared to be carrying out a detailed search of the area. The long, graceful fronds of a weeping willow swung gently in the breeze, and at the centre of the pond sat a small island that was home to a lively duck house.

The larger of the two constables waded around the island in a pair of oilcloth fishing waders. The other stood on the bank of the pond surrounded by ducks and holding a frying pan.

"Good afternoon, Constables," said Churchill. "How goes it?"

"It would go better if the ducks left me alone," replied the officer holding the frying pan.

"Perhaps they're trying to stop you frying their fish," said Churchill.

"Ducks don't eat fish," said Pemberley.

"So they don't, silly me," said Churchill. "Some fowl species consume them, though, don't they? I'm surprised you haven't been attacked by an angry heron, yet Constable."

"He gave them some of his sandwiches, that's what," the large officer in waders called over.

"Oh dear, always a mistake," said Churchill.

"I was once harassed by a squirrel for three long weeks," said Pemberley.

"All because you gave it a bit of food, eh? It should never be done."

"I didn't even feed it."

"Well, you must have done something."

"I did nothing at all. It just took a shine to me."

"That makes sense. Now then, Constable, perhaps you can explain to us what you're doing with the frying pan."

"I found it."

"Clearly, but where?"

"PC Gussage found it," replied the constable, pointing to his colleague in waders.

"Yeah, I found it," said PC Gussage.

"Where?"

"In this pond."

"Really? Someone dropped their frying pan into the duck pond?" Churchill chuckled. "I wonder how on earth that came about. It looks like a rather fine frying pan, too. Cast iron, I shouldn't wonder. And it doesn't appear to have been in the duck pond for long, it's not rusty at all... Oh, Pembers! Oh my goodness!"

Churchill grasped her secretary's arm to steady herself.

"Are you all right, Mrs Churchill?" asked Pemberley.

Churchill pointed at the frying pan in the constable's hand, her mouth opening and closing like that of a fish as she tried to articulate the words. "Th-th-that's it, Pembers," she gasped. "The weapon! Didn't Chief

Inspector Long-Surname mention that Rumbold had suffered a blow to the head?"

Pemberley paled. "My goodness, yes, he did!"

"A frying pan, Pembers. That's what the poor chap's bonce was bashed with. And once the murderer was done with it he tossed it into the duck pond."

"Along with Mr Rumbold."

"Exactly. How awful!"

Pemberley shook her head sadly. "If only ducks could speak," she said.

"Talking ducks? What on earth are you on about woman?" Churchill demanded.

"They must have witnessed it! They were probably roosting on that little island of theirs. Perhaps a duck was sitting on top of the duck house at the time, as one of them is right now."

Churchill glanced at the female mallard squatting on the duck house roof.

"I see what you mean, Pemberley. If only they could, eh? How frustrating. Have you tried interviewing the ducks, Constables?"

Her question was met with a blank stare from the two policemen.

"Just a little joke of mine," continued Churchill. "Did you realise you'd found the murder weapon?"

The constables both surveyed the frying pan.

"We suspected as much," replied PC Gussage, "but it ain't got a dent in it."

"It's got a cast-iron bottom," said Churchill. "An elephant couldn't make a dent in that."

"It probably wouldn't even try," added Pemberley.

"No, it probably wouldn't, my trusty assistant. But I think the lack of dent by no means rules out the frying pan as a tool in Rumbold's murder. He died from drowning, didn't he? All that was required from that formidable piece of cookware was a glancing blow to the back of the head to stun him."

"Oh dear. Poor Mr Rumbold," said Pemberley tearily.

"I take it you're going to present the frying pan weapon to your superiors?" Churchill asked the constables.

"Yes, but we'll dust it for fingerprints first."

"Don't you think the prints might have washed off while the frying pan lay submerged in the duck pond?"

PC Gussage pondered this. "They might have done, I suppose. It depends how greasy they were."

"No harm in trying, I suppose. I can imagine that most murderers have greasy fingers, can't you, Pembers?"

"They might have worn gloves."

"If he was a well-organised murderer he might have. If no fingerprints can be retrieved from the frying pan I don't suppose we're any closer to identifying the culprit."

"But we can find out who owned a frying pan like this," said PC Gussage. "And if we keep its existence top secret we can make seemingly innocuous enquiries about it among the populace of Compton Poppleford."

"I like your thinking, PC Gussage," said Churchill. "I'd say that you're more on the ball than Inspector Mappin."

"We'll need you to keep quiet about the frying pan," replied the constable. "Don't go shouting about it."

"Do we look like the sort of ladies who go around shouting about things?" asked Churchill.

An awkward silence ensued.

"You can be assured of our utmost discretion, Constables," said Pemberley.

Chapter 25

"DOWNS AND HARRIS. Those are our chief suspects now, Pemberley," said Churchill as they walked along the high street toward their office.

"They were both with Rumbold on the night he died," replied Pemberley, "but how on earth could one of them have secreted that enormous frying pan about his person?"

"Down his trousers?"

"The handle could slide down a trouser leg, I suppose, but what of the round pan section?"

"In the seat of his trousers? It could be managed as long as one didn't sit down," suggested Churchill.

"You'd need to have a large pair of buttocks to hide the round pan section."

"Posterior if you please, Pemberley! I quite agree. And as one would be unable to sit down, we'd need to find out which of them remained standing all evening."

"And how do we do that?"

There was a pause as both women considered this.

"Never mind that," said Churchill. "On reflection, I think that walking about with a frying pan secreted down the back of one's trousers would create an awkward gait; a sort of frying-pan-trouser-hiding-induced-waddle that would draw too much attention to the culprit."

"Perhaps one of the men walked freely about with it in his hand," suggested Pemberley. "He might have come up with a suitable excuse for having it with him."

"Such as what?"

"That he had bought it that day from the cookshop?"

"Now there's a thought," said Churchill. "Look, here we are outside Mr Harding's cookshop. Why don't we pop in and ask him which of the two men bought a frying pan from him yesterday?"

"What a good idea," said Pemberley. "But aren't we forbidden to speak to him?"

"Oh, pfft to that idea, Pembers. We'll only be two shakes of a lamb's tail. Mappin won't find out."

"Let's hope not."

The two women stepped inside the cookshop.

"What a wonderful arrangement of jelly moulds in the window," commented Churchill. "Mr Harding has such an eye for displaying things."

She felt a flush of warmth in her face as the man himself appeared from behind a display of casserole dishes, his eyes twinkling. The collar of his shirt was so crisp and white that Churchill was tempted to ask who had ironed it for him.

"What a pleasant surprise!" said Mr Harding with a grin.

"Is it really?" replied a flustered Churchill, smoothing down her jacket. "Are you truly pleased to see us?"

"Of course." He beamed. "How can I be of service to you today?"

"We have just a little simple question to ask you, Mr Harding."

"Ask away, ladies."

Churchill cleared her throat and rearranged her pearls. "Thank you for being so obliging."

"Not at all. It's my pleasure."

"How kind."

"Anything to help."

"How lovely of you, Mr Harding."

"Did Mr Downs or Mr Harris buy a frying pan from you yesterday?" asked Pemberley impatiently.

"No, I didn't sell any frying pans yesterday."

"The day before?"

"I sold one the day before yesterday, but it was Mrs Higginbath who bought that one."

"Have either Mr Downs or Mr Harris bought any cookware from you recently, Mr Harding?" asked Churchill.

"No. I don't recall either of them ever having set foot in my shop before."

"Oh."

"Why do you ask?"

"Well, a frying pan was... *Ouch*, Pembers! What was *that* for?" Churchill clasped her arm, with which Pemberley's sharp elbow had just made painful contact.

"We're not supposed to say anything, remember?" hissed Pemberley.

"What? Not even to Mr Harding?"

"Not to anyone."

Harding's brow lowered. "What's going on here?" he asked.

"Oh, I am sorry about this, Mr Harding," said Churchill. "I would dearly love to explain everything to you properly, but my aide-de-camp here has reminded me – in the starkest of manners – that I have been sworn to secrecy by the robust arm of the law."

"Goodness! Have you indeed? This all sounds rather important."

"It is, Mr Harding, it is. Perhaps when all this sorry business is concluded we can discuss it at length."

"I hope we can do just that. You have certainly piqued my curiosity, Mrs Churchill."

"I'm sorry to leave the matter unconcluded."

"I can be patient, Mrs Churchill. In the meantime my mind shall boggle over what could possibly connect the robust arm of the law with a frying pan. And actually it's quite interesting that you should mention the names of Mr Downs and Mr Harris."

"Is it? Why's that then?"

Mr Harding leant in closer and lowered his voice. "I hear that the pair of them are regular visitors to the grounds of Ashleigh Grange."

"The colonel's place?"

"The very same."

"And what do they do there?"

"I don't know, but it might be illegal."

"Really?" Churchill's eyes widened. "And does the Colonel know about their visits?" she whispered.

"Again, I don't know. If it's illegal I should imagine he doesn't, seeing as he's a thoroughly above-board sort of chap."

"Absolutely," replied Churchill. "And how did you hear about this?"

"I have also been sworn to secrecy, Mrs Churchill." Harding tapped the side of his nose with his forefinger.

"Have you? By whom?"

"It's a secret."

"But why?"

Harding grinned. "You won't get it out of me, you know. Or maybe you will once this sorry business is over."

"Oh, I see, Mr Harding." Churchill gave him a wink. "Well, thank you very much for your tip-off. The colonel has twenty-seven acres of land. Do you happen to know which area, within his vast acreage, the two gardeners frequent?"

"Close to the orangery, I'm told," replied Harding. "That's all I know."

"I am much obliged for the information," said Churchill. "You have been a marvellous help to us today, Mr Harding. If there is ever anything I can do to repay you then you'll let me know, won't you?"

"No need for repayment, Mrs Churchill. I am simply delighted to be of assistance."

"Oh, how refreshing! Don't you find that everyone is terribly intent on having favours repaid these days? I do so adore the traditional approach of helping one's fellow man, or woman, out of the goodness of one's heart. You're a true gentleman, Mr Harding. Thank you again."

Pemberley made a spluttering noise.

"Are you all right, Pembers?"

"Fine. There's just something stuck at the back of my throat. Can we go now?"

"Of course. We won't detain you a moment longer, Mr Harding. Adieu."

Chapter 26

"GIVE ME A HAND, will you Pemberley? I can't possibly get out of here all by myself." The ditch within which Churchill was lying felt damp and prickly. "Where are you, Pembers?" she cried. "You haven't deserted me, have you?"

"No, I'm here," came the secretary's voice. "Just switching on my torch."

As the light came on, a gloved hand loomed out of the darkness and grasped hold of Churchill's arm.

"You're quite strong for someone with such a spindly frame," commented Churchill.

"That's because I practise strength training with tins of beans."

"It's clearly paying off, and fortunately means that I won't have to spend the night in this ditch."

Pemberley heaved Churchill up, and the plump detective somehow managed to right herself on the road.

"You can stop blinding me with that torchlight now, Pembers."

"You've got some mud on your face Mrs Churchill."

"Oh dear, have I? Where?"

"Everywhere."

Churchill took off her gloves and rubbed at her face.

"Better?" she asked the torchlight.

"No, worse."

"What? How can it be worse?"

Churchill rubbed again.

"Now it looks very bad," said Pemberley sombrely.

"How? Oh this is ridiculous Pembers, get that detestable torch off me now. It's too dark for anyone to see my face tonight anyway, so we'll leave it as it is. Now I've been partially blinded by torchlight and the seat of my breeches is completely soaked through. I can't possibly get back on that bicycle again."

"But you'll have to," said Pemberley. "How else can we stealthily travel to Ashleigh Grange under the cover of night?"

"Couldn't we walk?"

"We'd never get there and back in time on one of these short summer nights. Bicycling is our only option."

Churchill groaned. "But my posterior is completely sodden!"

"It's quite possible to cycle with damp haunches."

"This is more than damp, Pemberley; I'm completely soaked through to the peachy skin of my—"

"You can still cycle, Mrs Churchill," interrupted Pemberley, "and we must push on. We don't have a lot of time."

"I can't ride that thing," said Churchill, pointing at the dark silhouette of her bicycle, which lay pitifully in the road. "Its balance is all wrong. You saw how it threw me off just now, didn't you?"

"The balance is provided by the cyclist."

"Some of it, perhaps, but not all of it. A bicycle with no balance is impossible to ride."

"You told me you were an accomplished cyclist."

"So I am! And you'll recall me telling you that my youth was spent bicycling around London. I only encountered one incident, and that was the milk cart's fault, not mine. And besides, the bicycles are better in London. They have proper balance and the handlebars don't have a habit of suddenly veering to the left. Your friend Mrs Frosling has lent us inferior models."

"Mrs Churchill, we must press on. We want to find out what Downs and Harris have been getting up to in the Colonel's back garden, don't we?"

"Yes, we do." Churchill sighed as she picked up her bicycle. "But I'm only getting back on this hopeless contraption because I'm a determined detective who soldiers on regardless of the obstacles in her path."

"Quite right. A determined detective who doesn't allow herself to be defeated by a velocipede."

"Indeed. I don't hold much affection for insects, Pemberley. I think a few of those velothingies were crawling over me in that ditch back there. Horrible things."

"Velocipede is an old-fashioned word for a bicycle."

"Less chat, more action, Pembers. We can't be standing around wasting any more time. Let's get on with our investigations."

A little while later the ladies' torches picked up the stone wall surrounding the Ashleigh Grange estate, and shortly after they reached the imposing iron entrance gates. Churchill removed her handbag from the basket on the front of her bicycle and happily left the contraption propped up against the wall as Pemberley walked over to the gates.

"Darn it, they're padlocked!" she hissed. "We won't be able to ride our bicycles along the driveway."

"Oh, never mind," whispered Churchill. "I've always preferred walking to bicycling, anyway. We can easily vault over this low wall. Fancy locking the gates when any old Tom, Dick and Harry can just hop over the wall!"

Churchill rested a hand on the wall, swung a leg over it and gently eased herself over. She was horrified to discover that the drop on the other side was much deeper than she had expected.

"Good grief!" she cried out from the bottom of another ditch, her left leg bent painfully beneath her. "Why on earth did the colonel put this dip here?"

"I shouldn't have thought he'd put it there himself," replied Pemberley as she carefully lowered herself down on the other side of the wall. "It must have been one of his forebears."

"Well, curse the colonel's forebears! The upper classes have such a loathsome habit of trying to keep people out."

Pemberley helped Churchill up from the second ditch and they began to walk along the driveway. Churchill hobbled as best she could given the pain in her left ankle from her latest fall.

"When do you think we should put out our torches?" asked Pemberley.

"When it's daylight."

"But someone will see our lights from the house when we get closer."

"Do you think so? It's only the colonel in there, isn't it? Just him and that enormous house. He must rattle around it like a dried pea in a tea chest."

"What about his staff?"

"Oh yes, I suppose we have to consider them, though I

suspect they're all asleep. All sensible people are asleep at this hour, and if they're not they are surely up to no good."

"I think we should put out our torches now. We should just be able to see the driveway in the moonlight."

"If you insist, Pembers. I pride myself on my excellent night vision. I'll guide the way."

It was a while before the dark outline of the house loomed into view.

"The problem with damp breeches is the chafing," whispered Churchill. "I'm not looking forward to seeing the state of my thighs when I pull them off."

"Please don't pull them off yet, Mrs Churchill."

"I might have to if this chafing doesn't subside! This evening's expedition has caused me a great deal of physical discomfort."

Pemberley grabbed Churchill's arm and gasped.

"What is it?" asked Churchill.

"A light! Look! Can you see it? It's either in one of the downstairs windows or somewhere in the grounds."

Churchill felt her heart thud in her ears. "Is it moving?" she asked.

"I don't think so."

They held their breath and watched, but the light remained steady.

"Let's proceed," whispered Churchill. "I think it's coming from inside the house; it's probably one of the maids awake with toothache. Don't you find that with maids? They're so often up in the night with toothache."

"I can't say I've noticed."

The women continued to walk cautiously along the driveway.

"She's probably trying to find the laudanum," whispered Churchill, "and it's likely she can't find it anywhere. Essential things have a habit of going missing in the dead of night, don't they? Especially bed jackets. One wakes in the night feeling a chill and can one find one's bed jacket anywhere? Not a bit of it, even though it had been hanging from the bed knob when one went to sleep. And where is the bed jacket in the end? In the place one would least expect to find it, of course. I once discovered my favourite bed jacket in the dog's bed. Have you ever attempted to retrieve a bed jacket from beneath a foul-tempered Jack Russell terrier, Pembers? I wouldn't recommend it, especially at three o'clock in the morning. Dogs do not take kindly to being woken at that hour."

"The light's gone out again!" exclaimed Pemberley.

Churchill sighed with relief. "Hurrah, the laudanum has been found! Now, how about we skirt around the east wing of the house? The orangery is probably at the back somewhere."

"Which one is the east wing?"

"The right one."

"That's the west wing."

"The left one, then, although I think the right one might be more promising."

"The west wing, you mean?"

"Oh, I don't know. This way, anyway," replied Churchill giving Pemberley a nudge. "Ouch! What on earth?"

"What's the matter?"

"A prickly shrub, that's what the matter is. It just leapt out at me."

"You must have walked into it."

"No, I didn't. I can see perfectly well in the dark and it wasn't there a moment ago. And what on earth is that tripping me up now?"

"It's a low wall. Can't you see it there by your feet? I think we may be nearing the kitchen garden."

"Lead the way then, Pembers, if you're so sure of where we are."

"Ouch!" exclaimed Pemberley.

"Did you bump into something by any chance?"

"A piece of statuary."

"What, that urn, which was visible from several feet away? Tsk, Pembers."

"We're going to wake the colonel up, I feel sure of it."

"That dry old pea is dead to the world, Pembers. He won't know anything until his valet brings him his tea at nine o'clock, and we'll be long gone by then. I can imagine him being quite the snorer. Does he strike you as a snorer?"

"I hadn't really considered it."

"You can see it in the noses of men his age with their enlarged nasal cavities."

"Is that a fact?"

"I should think so. Oh look, Pembers, is that the orangery over there?"

Churchill pointed at a section of building that appeared to reflect the night sky.

"It looks like glass. It could be."

"I wonder if it has any oranges in it. I have to say that it irks me when I come across an orangery without oranges in it."

"I suppose the word orangery is just another name for a tropical hothouse, so in theory it could house a whole range of flora."

"I suppose it could. But it should still contain oranges."

"By the sounds of it, Downs and Harris have been up to something next to the orangery."

"I can't imagine what."

"Hopefully we shall find out in just a moment."

The two ladies walked carefully along a winding gravel

path. Churchill repeatedly glanced up at the huge dark shadow of the house, fearful that another light would flicker on at any moment.

"What if the colonel discovers us here? What will our explanation be?" asked Pemberley.

"He won't, and if, by any chance, he does we shall simply say that we wished to see the beauty of Ashleigh Grange by night."

"Without his invitation?"

"We can add that we had no wish to disturb him."

"I can't see him accepting such an explanation without any argument."

"He won't find us here, Pembers, don't you worry."

They reached the orangery and began to walk slowly around it.

"I don't really know what we're looking for," said Churchill. "There are a few boulders lying about but nothing else of note. I do hope Mr Harding was correct. He wouldn't have led us on a wild goose chase, would he?"

Pemberley stooped down. "These aren't boulders," she said. "They're a cylindrical shape. Have a feel."

Churchill tentatively reached down with her hand and quickly leapt back.

"Good grief!" She smothered a shriek and her blood ran cold. "It's a human head!"

"That's *my* head, Mrs Churchill," said Pemberley. "I'm just going to quickly switch on my torch so we can see what's lying on the ground here. I'll do a quick on-and-off, and hopefully that won't cause any problems for us."

"Make it a quick on-and-off, Pembers. Very quick indeed."

The brief flash of light told them everything they needed to know.

"Marrows," said Pemberley.

Chapter 27

"IMPOSSIBLE," said Churchill. "Marrows don't grow to that size. Give us another quick on-and-off, Pembers."

Pemberley gave another flash of the torch.

"Goodness! Are they really marrows?" said Churchill. "I've seen hippos smaller than those things."

"Have you really?"

"No, not really, but the comparison gives you an idea of my great astonishment."

"Don't forget that Mr Rumbold told us his largest marrow from last year was heavier than his wife."

"Oh yes, I remember now… That's it Pembers!"

"What is?"

"These marrows must be the ones Rumbold was keeping secret! How many are there? It looks like three to me. Pemberley, I do believe that Mr Harding has led us straight to Rumbold's secret marrows."

"They can't be all that secret if Downs and Harris know about them."

"They may know about them *now*, but perhaps they didn't when Rumbold informed us of their existence."

"Or perhaps they did know, but Rumbold didn't realise they knew," suggested Pemberley.

"That may be true. I'm beginning to feel rather confused."

"So who knew about the secret marrows? And why are they secret?"

"Two pertinent questions, my trusty assistant," replied Churchill, "and I have no immediate answers to offer. There's no doubt the colonel knows about them. One could hardly miss these gargantuan vegetables plonked next to one's orangery."

"I'm surprised he wasn't tempted to ask his cook to whip one of them up into a stew."

"Have you ever eaten marrow, Pembers? It's the most tasteless substance known to man. It's like eating water, only with a slightly chewy consistency. And with pips in. Marrows are only useful for one thing, and that's being nurtured into oversized vegetabilia by men with dirty fingernails."

"They could be useful for storing things in," added Pemberley.

"Storing things? Why would anyone put something inside a marrow instead of using an item designed specifi-cally for storage, such as a box, cupboard or drawer?"

"To hide something, perhaps."

"If you had something to hide, you'd hide it in a marrow, would you?"

"No, but someone has."

"Who?"

"I don't know. I'll do a quick on-and-off again, and while I do so take a look at the marrow on the far right. It has some ribbon tied around it as if it's holding the vegetable together. I think someone has sliced it open, scooped out the innards, placed something inside and tied it back up."

"Goodness, Pembers, you have such a fertile imagination. Go on, then, give us another flash."

In the brief wink of light Churchill observed some wide green ribbon wrapped around one of the marrows, just as Pemberley had described.

"You're right, Pembers! I wonder what's going on there. Let's undo the ribbon and find out."

"Can we be sure we'll be able to wrap it back up again just as it was?"

"I've bandaged a few arms in my time, I'm sure we'll manage."

The two ladies shuffled carefully toward the tied-up marrow in the dark and stooped down to feel for the ribbon with their fingers.

"I've got it, Pembers. I can feel a knot of some sort, and I think it should come undone quite easily. There we go… Oh no, that's pulled it tighter now. Is there another knot somewhere? Here we are… No, that's not doing anything."

"We could cut it with my penknife."

"Yes, let's just do that. My patience is beginning to wear thin in these damp breeches."

There was a lot of fumbling about in the dark as Pemberley tried to find her penknife in her pocket, then attempted to cut the ribbon around the marrow. She was eventually successful.

"The marrow is open!" she whispered.

"So what's inside it?"

After a little more fumbling, Churchill's question was answered with a jingling sound.

"Coins!" exclaimed Pemberley in a loud whisper. "And lots of them!"

"Really?" said Churchill. "I'll do a quick on-and-off with my torch so we can get a quick look."

She turned it on and was dazzled by a hoard of glinting gold.

She gasped. "Are those sovereigns?"

"Yes," said Pemberley. "Now turn your light off."

Churchill fidgeted about with her torch. "I can't. It won't."

"Let me do it, then."

Pemberley reached over and tried to flip the switch. "Darn it! It's jammed."

"I know it is. Why do you think I couldn't turn it off?"

"You'll have to cover it up with your hands."

Churchill did so, and a faint pink-tinged light was all that remained.

"Good," said Pemberley. "Now, let me have a look at these coins."

"Do you need more light?"

"A tiny bit."

"Watch how, with a careful adjustment of my hand, I'm able to control the direction and intensity of light."

"That's very good," replied Pemberley, inspecting the coins. "There must be a fortune here! Let's count it."

"Oh, must we? Can't we just agree that it's a lot?"

"It'll help us work out roughly how much is here. I think it could be around two hundred pounds."

"Good grief, Pembers! Really?"

"Just a smidgen more light, please, and then I'll be able to count."

"I can't. It appears to have expired." Churchill fidgeted with the switch on her torch. "Nope, it's gone. What a contrary thing. You'll have to use yours."

"I think I'll manage without it. It's too risky turning all these lights on and off."

Churchill leant up against the orangery for a little while, listening to the faint jingle of coins.

"Finished yet, Pembers?"

"Almost."

Churchill asked the same question twice more and received the same response.

"It's no good," she said with a sigh. "These breeches are much too uncomfortable now. I'm sure the damp has caused them to shrink. I can tell by the tone in your voice that you're going to be a while yet, and as it's a mild night I'm just going to remove them and give them an airing."

"No, please don't."

"It's pitch black, Pembers! No one will be able to tell whether I'm wearing them or not. If it's any consolation to you – and there is no need for consolation, but I shall provide it anyway – my undergarments are both substantially sized and supportive. They're the ones I always wear when there's a brisk wind with a cold nip."

"You're giving me too much information and now I've lost count."

Churchill tutted. "These are coming off, then."

She lay her wet breeches out on one of the marrows to dry and sauntered a few steps to and fro.

"That feels better. Sometimes a nice airing is all that's needed. It really is a pleasant night, isn't it, Pemberley? I was about to recite a poem about the night just then, but I can't remember it now. Some poetic words dropped into my mind, but just as I tried to put them together they disappeared again. Do you ever find that?"

"Eighty-nine, ninety. Do I ever find what?"

"That you struggle to remember poetry?"

"Sometimes. Where did I get to? Ninety, was it?"

"Yes."

"'Twas a warm, dark night and all the stars—"

"Ninety-three. Sorry, what?"

"The stars, Pembers."

"Stars?"

Just then, the crack of a gunshot rang out, its ear-splitting sound echoing in the darkness.

Chapter 28

"COLONEL SLINGSBY, I wish to emphatically state that it is not a habit of mine to be sitting about in the drawing rooms of stately homes with little more than a humble travel blanket covering my nether regions," said Churchill.

The colonel stood in the centre of the room with a shotgun under his arm. He wore a quilted silk dressing gown and an elasticated moustache protector around his scowling face. Pemberley sat in a cane chair next to Churchill, her hands fidgeting nervously in her lap.

A large tiger head snarled down at them from above the fireplace and a cheetah skin covered the hearthrug. A portrait of a military man with an enormous moustache hung over a heavy wooden sideboard carved with elephants.

"There's a perfectly simple explanation for all this, Colonel," ventured Churchill.

"Good. I feared it would be a long-winded one," he replied.

"Yes, it's perfectly simple, you see, and it's all Inspector Mappin's fault."

The colonel raised an eyebrow. "Mappin? What's he got to do with it?"

"He prohibited us from speaking to you; therefore, it was quite impossible to politely request that we carry out some reconnaissance on your land."

"What the devil were you looking for?"

"Well, for some time now rumours have abounded in Compton Poppleford about Mr Rumbold's secret marrows. My trusty assistant and I had no idea where to begin looking for them, but then we received a tip-off that there was an item of interest located close to your orangery. Having no idea what that item might be, we were whole-heartedly surprised to discover the legendary marrows there."

"Legendary, are they?"

"Indeed, Colonel. You have been harbouring one of the village's greatest secrets."

"And about two hundred gold sovereigns," added Pemberley.

"It's two hundred this time, is it?"

"What do you mean by *this time*, Colonel?" asked Churchill.

"It's the bribes those gardeners keep leaving for me. I'm quite tired of it, to be honest with you. Wish they'd leave me alone. Who tipped you off?"

"I cannot reveal my source."

"Bet it was Harding. Man can't keep anything to himself."

"No, it wasn't him," replied Churchill in an odd, strangulated voice that didn't sound like her own.

"It was definitely Harding."

A tall, sombre butler entered the room with three glasses of whiskey on a salver and presented each of them with a glass. Churchill took one, astonished that the man was up and working at such an ungodly hour.

"Thank you, Higgs," said the colonel.

"Anyway, Colonel Slingsby," said Churchill. "We'd be extremely grateful if you'd agree not to mention this little night-time visit to anyone, and in return we won't mention that you almost blew our heads off with your shotgun."

"Nonsense."

"I beg your pardon?"

"I didn't fire anywhere near your heads. I fired into the sky."

"And without a bullet, no doubt," said Pemberley. "I assume you were firing blanks."

"No, there was a bullet all right," replied the Colonel. "Went right up into the sky."

"But presumably it had to come down again?"

"Wouldn't do anyone any harm if it did."

"I'd say that it would!" replied Pemberley. "It's terribly dangerous, Colonel!"

"But the outcome would be well deserved for anyone found trampling over my land in the dead of night. Dangerous business in itself. A chap's entitled to defend his property. Fire first, ask questions second. Did it in the Punjab all the time."

"Well, I suppose it worked," said Churchill. "It certainly frightened me out of my wits. I don't think I'll ever get back into them again."

"It was terribly heavy-handed," said Pemberley. "A quiet word would have sufficed."

The colonel snorted. "If a chap hears trespassers on his land in the middle of the night he's perfectly entitled to fire off a few rounds. He doesn't know who he's dealing with! A quiet word would hardly suffice if he's facing a crowd of hooligans armed with shovels and pickaxes! In fact, if a chap hears trespassers on his land in the middle of the night he comes to expect that he'll be faced with a few hooligans. What he doesn't expect to find is two old ladies, one of whom only has half her clothes on!"

Churchill felt her face redden. "I had suffered some dreadful chafing, Colonel, caused by an unfortunate incident in a wet ditch. You must have experienced similar levels of discomfort, especially in the Punjab with all that heat and perspiration."

"Never!"

"I see. Well, the most pressing question now, I suppose, is what do the marrows and the money have to do with Mr Rumbold's sad demise?"

"Blowed if I know. Nothing, probably."

"But what do you know about the marrows, Colonel?"

"Rumbold planted them and told me he didn't want anyone else to know they were there. But Stropper Harris spotted them from the window of the library and Tubby Williams happened upon them one day when he and I went out shooting. You can't keep giant marrows secret for long, can you? No one pays much attention to them when they're those little courgette things, they're harmless then. But once they're larger than the average family dog there's no hiding them."

"Who put the money in them? And what's it for?"

"Don't know who, but it'll be a bribe, like I said. Another whiskey, please, Higgs. And bring me my pipe, too. Would you like another whiskey, Mrs Churchill? Miss Pemberley?"

"No, we're fine, thank you, Colonel. I should put my breeches back on and then we can be on our way."

"And wash your face too," muttered Pemberley.

"Oh I'd forgotten about that," whispered Churchill. "Is it still covered in mud?"

"Yes."

"I do believe my valet is putting your breeches through the wringer, Mrs Churchill," said the Colonel. "Higgs will bring them in when they're done. I'll wake Pattison the chauffeur up and ask him to drive you both home."

"Oh no, please don't wake him. We can bicycle back. It's no trouble at all."

"Actually, it is," said Pemberley. "Remember the difficulties you had staying on it?"

"It was the bicycle, Miss Pemberley, and I shall be able to cope with the homeward journey with no trouble at all. It's mostly downhill."

"No it's not!" protested Pemberley. "It's mostly uphill!"

"Please stop disagreeing with me, Miss Pemberley. I don't want to trouble the colonel any further this evening. It's important that his chauffeur has a good night's sleep."

"Don't worry about him," replied the colonel. "I often wake him in the middle of the night and ask him to take me somewhere. Rarely get a good night's sleep myself. Must admit that I'm still at a loss as to why two fine, genteel ladies such as yourselves were trespassing on my land in the dead of night. Trespassing is the sort of thing that drives a chap wild with anger until he realises he's dealing with two harmless old ladies. Then it quite deflates a man and leaves him out of sorts."

"I apologise once again, Colonel," said Mrs Churchill. "With hindsight it was a rather foolish venture."

"Usually when a chap gets fired up he can take it out on the reprobate who caused the upset in the first place. But there is no outlet for a man's ire when faced with two members of the fairer sex. One feels rather pent up."

"Would you have preferred to box our ears, Colonel?"

"Well, I would have done, truth be told. Ah, thank you, Higgs." The colonel took his pipe and whiskey from the butler's salver. "But a fellow can't go around boxing a lady's ears. That would be quite unthinkable!"

"I'd say you'd be quite justified in doing so," said Churchill. "We were rather silly, weren't we, Miss Pemberley?"

"We were carrying out an investigation," replied Pemberley sulkily.

"You won't do it again, will you, ladies?"

"We promise, Colonel Slingsby. Never again," said Churchill earnestly.

"Suppose that's sorted then. All rather confuddling, if I may say so, but what else is there to add? On with the day, I reckon. I quite like breakfasting early. Tell you what, Mrs Churchill, how about I do what I can to help you with your investigation into these gardener sorts? I don't quite understand what you're looking for, but I do admire a chap – or occasionally a woman – who takes his or her initiative in such matters. I'll assist where I can. How about I have the minutes of the meetings for the Compton Poppleford Horticultural Society sent down to you? There may be a nugget or two in there, or there may be nothing at all."

"Thank you, Colonel, how helpful of you."

Higgs returned to the room carrying something on top of his salver.

"Your breeches, ma'am," he said to Churchill, lowering the salver so that she could see her neatly folded trousers lying on top of it.

"Thank you," she replied with a blush. "How politely presented."

"Please wake Miss Flint so she can escort Mrs Churchill to my mother's dressing room to change," the colonel said to his butler.

"Of course, sir."

"My housekeeper will help you look presentable again, Mrs Churchill."

"Oh, don't wake her on my account, Colonel!"

"She usually rises at two o'clock in the morning anyway," replied the colonel. "It's only an hour earlier than usual."

Chapter 29

"I THINK I'll lie low for a couple of days, Pembers," said Churchill as she nursed a cup of tea at her desk the following morning. "That was a rather mortifying situation to find ourselves in. Thank goodness I have a nice plate of iced fancies to comfort me."

"It wouldn't have been so bad if you'd kept your breeches on," replied Pemberley.

"Despite my best attempts to explain it to you, my trusty assistant, you fail to understand how unbearable chafing can become. I thought I would be quite safe in the dark in the middle of the night. How did I know the colonel was about to blast us with his shotgun?"

"We should have guessed that it was at least a possibility."

"We thought he was asleep, Pembers! I don't think we could have predicted any of last night's events, and they've left me feeling rather red-faced. The only consolation, I suppose, is that the colonel has agreed not to breathe a word of it to anyone, and especially not to that dreadful Inspector Mappin."

They heard the door open downstairs, followed by heavy footsteps on the staircase.

"It sounds like we have a new client," she said hopefully. "I quite fancy taking on a new case, don't you? I'm tired of grubby gardeners and marrows and saucepans and gun-toting colonels. I think a nice quiet murder in a vicarage would suit me perfectly. In the library with a dagger, which is actually a letter opener but can also make for an effective murder weapon."

"Morning, ladies!" Inspector Mappin tapped on the open door as he cheerfully stepped into the room.

Churchill felt her heart sink.

"And how are you both this morning?" he added with a grin.

"You're unusually frolicsome today, Inspector," commented Churchill sourly. "Has there been a development in the case?"

"No. No development at all," he replied, removing his hat and sitting down on the chair opposite Churchill.

"So what then?"

"Feeling tired, Mrs Churchill?"

"No, I'm fine. Why?"

"I heard you were engaged in some interesting antics up at Ashleigh Grange last night," said Mappin with a wink.

"Oh, damn and blast it!" retorted Churchill, slamming her tea cup down onto its saucer. "I should never have trusted the colonel not to say anything!"

"Oh no, I didn't hear it from him," replied the Inspector. "It wouldn't be right for a gentleman to gad about town talking about partially clad ladies finding their way into his home in the dead of night."

"Then who? Where did you hear about it? Not that

I'm admitting there's any truth in what you've heard. It's little more than back-fence talk."

"The colonel's housekeeper, Miss Flint, told the wife at the greengrocer's this morning."

"Whose wife?"

"My wife."

Churchill gave an angry snort. "The housekeeper should know better! In fact, she should be sworn to secrecy! The colonel will hear about this and have her fired."

"I doubt it. Miss Flint has worked at Ashleigh Grange since the colonel was in short trousers."

"Surely she's not that old, is she?" said Pemberley.

"Oh, she is, Pembers," said Churchill. "A doddery old biddy with a half-working brain to boot. They should have put her out to pasture years ago."

"I've always had the greatest respect for Miss Flint," said Inspector Mappin. "She's the keystone of Compton Poppleford."

"Is that so? Well, in that case the village is doomed. Why did I ever leave London to live here, Pembers?"

"The purpose of my visit to you this morning, Mrs Churchill, is to find out what the devil you and Miss Pemberley were up to in the grounds of Ashleigh Grange in the dead of night."

"We were achieving far more than you and your men, Inspector, that's for sure."

"What did you achieve exactly?"

"It's a secret."

"Mrs Churchill, I'm sure you don't need me to inform you that deliberately withholding information which would assist a police investigation is a crime in itself?"

"I couldn't say whether it would assist you or not, Inspector."

"Let me be the judge of that. Now, what were you doing there? You cannot expect me to believe that it was a little nocturnal perambulation to soothe the senses."

"That's exactly what it was, Inspector! You have an excellent nose for sniffing out people's motives. I can tell."

"I do indeed, which is why I happen to know that a nocturnal perambulation was not the reason for your hanging about in the colonel's marrow patch."

"Ah now, you've touched on a pertinent point there, Inspector. They're not the colonel's marrows."

"Whose are they, then?"

"They're Rumbold's secret marrows, Inspector."

"How did you know they were there?"

"We were tipped off that there was something of note there, but we didn't know exactly what it was."

"And how does this fit in with the murders of Rumbold and Williams?"

"We have no idea, Inspector. Do you?"

"No. None."

"Perhaps it's little more than a red herring, Inspector," conjectured Churchill.

"In the shape of a green marrow," added Pemberley.

"It could be indeed," said Inspector Mappin. "The next time you receive such a tip-off, why don't you simply consult me or one of my men? It would be preferable to you trespassing across the colonel's land in a state of undress."

"I wouldn't have dared mention it to you, Inspector, given that you are always accusing me of meddling."

"I don't *always*—"

"Ah, but you do. Poor little old me! I'm fearful of mentioning anything to you at all these days seeing as you're so determined to embark on that meddling speech every time we meet." Churchill pushed out her lower lip as though her feelings were hurt.

"Come now, Mrs Churchill, I'm always interested in hearing intriguing tip-offs. The only thing that bothers me is when you get yourself too involved."

"Have you ever known me to get too involved in something I shouldn't, Inspector?"

"Well yes, actually."

"There you go again! It's no wonder I try to keep things to myself."

"Mrs Churchill, I'm sure a balance can be struck between you passing on useful information and trampling all over my cases like a bull let loose in a paddock."

"Are you likening me to a loose bull, Inspector?"

"Not at all, Mrs Churchill."

"Well, it sounded very much like you were. And in the case of Rumbold's marrows, I don't think there is anything relevant to report. It's completely irrelevant, in fact."

"I think you may be right, Mrs Churchill. You must understand that I needed to visit you to find out more once I'd heard about the trespassing incident."

"Has the colonel reported it to you?"

"No, I only heard about it from the wife."

"If the good man himself hasn't reported it, and I doubt he will, then no charges will be brought and you really have no business stepping in here and snooping about."

"Mrs Churchill, I was merely visiting you to find out what had happened."

"Nothing of any interest to you, Inspector, and we've already ascertained that Rumbold's marrows are irrelevant to your investigation, so there's no need for you to pry any further."

Inspector Mappin scratched his head. "Well no, I don't suppose there is."

"Have you found out who the owner of the frying pan is, Inspector?"

"How do you know about the frying pan?"

"We saw one of the Bulchford constables with it shortly after they'd fished it out of the duck pond."

"We're still trying to establish who the owner of that particular piece of cookware might be."

"It has to be the murder weapon, doesn't it?"

"Not necessarily."

"Why else would someone throw their frying pan into the duck pond if they weren't trying to cover up the fact that they'd whacked a gardener on the bonce with it?"

"That's a good question, Mrs Churchill, but there may well be a logical explanation for that."

"Pfft. I sincerely doubt it. The frying pan was clearly used to clonk Mr Rumbold over the head. You need to find out who it belongs to as a matter of urgency."

"Yes, thank you for pointing that out, Mrs Churchill. We're working on it."

"Good. Now don't let us detain you a moment longer, Inspector. We know you're a busy man."

"Indeed I am, Mrs Churchill." He stood and put his hat on. "We have a murderer to catch, after all."

"So you do. Now toddle off and get on with it."

The two women waited for the Inspector to walk down the staircase before speaking again.

"Why didn't you tell Inspector Mappin about the money in the marrow?" Pemberley asked.

"Oh, you know what he's like. He'd get himself over-excited and in a bother about it all. The marrow money can be our little secret, Pembers."

"And the colonel's."

"Oh yes, and his as well. I shouldn't think he'll go shouting about it around town."

"Miss Flint will probably do that for him."

"No doubt she will. Dreadful woman. She's almost as bad as Mrs Thonnings."

"What's wrong with Mrs Thonnings?"

"Everything, Pembers. Now let's update our incident board and decide what we should do next."

"I thought you wished to lie low for a few days."

"What's the point? With Miss Flint telling everyone about our antics last night the whole village will know by lunchtime. I may as well get on with it and hold my head high."

"That's the spirit, Mrs Churchill."

"Delivery!" came a shout up the stairs.

"Come on up!"

"It's too 'eavy!"

"Let's go and help the delivery boy, Pembers. I suspect he's brought the minutes from the meetings of the Compton Poppleford Horticultural Society. No doubt they'll provide the perfect read for whenever we have trouble sleeping."

Chapter 30

AFTER SPENDING a pleasant morning updating the incident board and case file, Churchill and Pemberley repaired to Mrs Bramley's Tea Rooms for a sandwich.

"Hopefully we'll catch that Flatboot girl once and for all," said Churchill as she inspected the chair for sturdiness before sitting down in it. "There she is again with that scowl on her face. A grumpy expression is so terribly ageing, don't you think? I always make a point of smiling at myself in the mirror first thing every morning. It lifts the facial muscles. Do you do that, Pembers?"

"I don't have any mirrors at home," replied Pemberley.

"Don't you? Perhaps I should have guessed that. Oh look, here comes Flatface."

Kitty Flatboot approached the table and gave Churchill a sour look as she readied herself with her notepad.

"What you havin'?" she asked.

"I'll have an egg salad sandwich, please, with sliced radishes. The same for you, Miss Pemberley?"

"Just cucumber for me, please."

"With egg salad?"

"No, just cucumber on its own, please."

"And a pot of tea for two as well, please, waitress. No smile today?"

"Why you always talkin' about smilin'?"

"Because there isn't a great deal of it going on around here. I think, as a nation, we need to do more smiling. Don't you agree, Pembers?" asked Churchill with a forced grin.

"I don't think smiling comes naturally to the British," replied Pemberley. "I think we're all worried that it makes us look suspicious."

"What nonsense."

"I know that I feel suspicious of people who smile a lot. I always assume they're trying to make up for something."

"Please bring our order quickly, won't you, waitress? My secretary is rather hungry and it's making her terribly grumpy."

Kitty Flatboot gave a sulky nod and departed.

"You can be glum company sometimes, Pemberley. I was only trying to sprinkle a little cheery dust about the place."

"Oh look, Mr Harding is sitting just over there," said Pemberley.

Churchill felt a rush of heat to her face. "Is he now?"

"Yes, just there. Look!"

"It would be rude to turn round and stare at him, Pembers."

Churchill's face felt warmer still as she watched Pemberley wave at the shop owner. She felt certain he would have heard about the incident at Ashleigh Grange by this stage.

"He's coming over," said Pemberley.

"Well, I'm sure there's no need for that. Oh hello, Mr

Harding. How are you?"

Churchill picked up the menu card and fanned herself with it in a desperate bid to cool her face down.

Mr Harding's eyes twinkled. "I'm very well thank you, Mrs Churchill. And you?"

"I can't complain, Mr Harding. Thank you for asking."

"Oh good. We certainly don't want any complaining, do we?"

"I can't abide people who complain. It's such a wearisome trait."

"It certainly is."

A pause ensued, and Churchill waited for Mr Harding to mention the rumours he had heard from the previous night.

"Have you ladies ordered lunch?" he asked.

"We have," replied Churchill with relief. "An egg salad sandwich with sliced radishes for me and a cucumber sandwich for my trusty assistant."

"Both excellent choices, if I may say so."

"Thank you, Mr Harding."

"I've just enjoyed some spotted dick with custard myself."

"Another excellent choice." Churchill began to feel increasingly hopeful that news of the incident on the colonel's estate hadn't reached his ears.

Kitty Flatboot placed a tea tray on the table.

"Is your chair a'right today?" she asked Churchill.

"Perfectly fine thank you."

"Mrs Churchill's chair broke last time she was 'ere," Kitty explained to Mr Harding. "Fell flat on the floor she did."

An intense hatred for the waitress burned in Churchill's chest as she watched her walk away.

"It was a defective chair," Churchill added bitterly.

"A defective chair? Poor you Mrs Churchill," said Mr Harding. "It must have quite ruined your day."

"It was nothing, my day was absolutely fine."

"Were you harmed?"

"No not at all. You recommend the spotted dick do you Mr Harding?"

"Oh yes, with the custard too. Well I won't keep you ladies a moment longer, I must go and pay my bill. Do enjoy your lunch."

"Oh, thank you, Mr Harding. Do have a wonderful afternoon, won't you?"

"I shall certainly endeavour to."

He left them and strolled over to where Kitty Flatboot was waiting beside the till.

"How mortifying Pembers," hissed Churchill. "Now Mr Harding knows about the chair incident and if he also knows about the breeches incident... oh, the thought is unbearable!"

"There's no point in worrying about it," replied Pemberley. "What's done is done. Consider it as water off a duck's back."

"Easier to do if you're a duck. Oh look, Flatface has muddled up Mr Harding's change again, she really doesn't deserve to keep her job here."

The two ladies watched as coins were passed back and forth between Mr Harding and Kitty Flatboot. Mr Harding eventually seemed satisfied and left the tea rooms.

"Let's keep an eye on her now, Pembers, and see just how many of those coins find their way inside the till."

Both women watched intently as Kitty counted each coin back into the till and slammed it shut.

"Pah!" scorned Churchill. "She must have known we were watching her."

Kitty looked up and gave them an icy stare.

Chapter 31

"THERE'S another option that springs to mind when considering the terrible murder of Mr Rumbold," said Churchill to Pemberley as they walked back down the high street to their office.

"Which is what?"

"The possibility that either Mr Harris or Mr Downs used a frying pan from their own homes."

"In which case, wouldn't their wives have noticed a missing frying pan?"

"You'd have thought so, wouldn't you?"

"Unless the murdering cad came up with an excuse for taking a frying pan out with him of an evening."

"I can't begin to think what sort of excuse he would have come up with, but it's a possibility isn't it, Pembs?"

"Pembs?"

"Doesn't sound right, does it? I'll stick to Pembers."

"Or even Miss Pemberley, perhaps."

"It's just a little cumbersome when I want to get a point across quickly. Oh, here comes the chief inspector heading our way. Doesn't he have an odd walk? I've not noticed that about him before. He's walking like he has something stuck up his... Good afternoon, Chief Inspector Ll... Llooly... Lendy..."

"Llewellyn-Dalrymple," he replied gruffly.

"Of course, I hadn't forgotten. I knew it was that all along. It's just that sometimes my tongue doesn't roll itself properly. Do you ever experience that phenomenon?"

"No, I can't say that I do. How are the injuries?"

"What injuries?"

"From the chafing."

Churchill gave a start. "*Chafing?*"

"That's why you removed your breeches in the colonel's garden, wasn't it?"

"Oh, you make me blush with the directness of your questions, Chief Inspector. The chafing injuries are recovering quite well, thank you." Churchill felt her toes curl with embarrassment.

"Terrible business, chafing," he continued. "I once owned a pair of canvas breeches, and what a fabulous, hard-wearing pair they were. Then I made the mistake of hoofing it up and down the three highest peaks in the Lake District while wearing them. It felt as though my loins were on fire after that, and it took about three months for the skin on my inner thighs to grow back."

Churchill winced. "I'm so pleased that you understand my predicament, sir."

"Oh yes, I thoroughly understand it. Much as I had once loved those breeches, I filled the pockets with heavy stones after that experience and drowned them in Lake Windermere."

"Goodness me!"

"Poor breeches!" protested Pemberley.

"You obviously haven't experienced the woes of severe chafing, my dear lady," he said, directing his remark to the waif-like secretary.

"She doesn't understand it at all, Chief Inspector," said Churchill. "It's an affliction that only chafing sufferers such as you and I could comprehend. Terrible news about Mr Rumbold."

"Dreadful indeed."

"Any news on the owner of the frying pan?"

"Maybe yes and maybe no." The chief inspector stroked his red moustache, then gave a cough. "Which imaginary frying pan might you be referring to, anyway?"

"Oh, we know all about it. We saw the constables fish it out of the duck pond."

"It doesn't exist. And I'd like to make it clear that I have no wish to hear either of you gossiping about it either."

"Well, how can we if it doesn't exist?"

"Exactly. Let's leave it at that then, shall we?"

"We understand each other perfectly, Chief Inspector," said Churchill with a wink. "Any suspects?"

"Funny you should mention that, actually, because one individual has suddenly become of particular interest to us."

"Who might that be?"

"I couldn't possibly say."

"Is it the mysterious man we haven't yet identified? That one with the square chin and spectacles who likes egg sandwiches?"

"Who's he?"

"I wish I knew."

"Whoever he is, it's not him. Anyway, I must get on with business, as I think we may be making an arrest imminently." He rubbed his hands together and grinned. "Cheerio, ladies!"

Churchill stomped her foot as she watched the chief inspector's form disappear down the high street. "Oh, darn it, Pembers, they're a step ahead of us. And I so wanted to beat them to it!"

Chapter 32

CHURCHILL SPENT the rest of her day studying the incident board. She rearranged photographs, notes, pins and lengths of string, then paced the office floor deep in thought. She slept badly that night and returned to the office early the following morning to rearrange everything on the incident board once again.

Was the culprit Mr Downs? Or could it be Mr Harris? Although they seemed to be the two most likely suspects, Churchill couldn't ignore the picture of Mr Woolwell, whom she hadn't really considered yet. And then there was the colonel. Could it be the colonel? There were still unanswered questions in her mind from the cocktail party, could there be answers to them? Or were they unnecessary distractions?

Churchill paced the floor again and had already worked her way through a plate of cherry and almond tarts before Pemberley arrived.

"Goodness, Mrs Churchill, you're here early."

"I never sleep well when I have a case to crack, Pembers."

"Oh dear. I fear you're expecting too much of yourself. It's not essential that you beat the police at their own game, you know."

"Ah, but I'm the competitive sort, Pemberley! There's nothing that gives me fire in my belly as much as a bit of competition."

"I get that from garlic. It doesn't agree with me at all."

"You *need* fire in your belly, Pembers! It's what motivates one to get up each morning and do battle with the day!"

"Should I eat more garlic, then?"

"Oh, I don't know." Churchill glanced disconsolately at the plate which was now devoid of cherry and almond tarts.

"I don't think this battling-with-the-day-business is my sort of thing," continued Pemberley. "I like a to-do list, but I can't say that I enjoy a battle with anything. It's rather a confrontational way of doing things. Anyway, I almost forgot to tell you that there's quite a commotion going on at the cookshop."

"The cookshop?" Churchill felt her heart stop. "Surely not?"

"I saw it with my own eyes."

"Well, I think I need to view it with mine in that case." Churchill put her hat on and picked up her handbag.

The two ladies left their office and walked along the cobbles to where a small crowd was standing outside the cookshop. The sun was warm but Churchill felt a chill as she noticed Chief Inspector Llewellyn-Dalrymple's shiny police car parked beside the crowd.

"What's happening?" Churchill shouted to PC Gussage, who was guarding the door of the cookshop.

"I'm not allowed to say," he called back.

"Oh, go on!" shouted Churchill. "It'll just be between you and me, Constable!"

"And the fifty other people hanging about here!" he retorted.

"Oh, they don't matter a jot! Has there been a burglary?"

PC Gussage turned away without giving a response.

"Now he's ignoring me, isn't he, Pemberley? Typical."

Churchill tried to peer in through the cookshop windows but her view was obscured by the tall display of jelly moulds.

"Oh dear, I do hope the thieves haven't taken too much. Poor Mr Harding. Why burgle such a charming man? Whatever did he do to anyone? It always narks me that the most awful of things happen to the most pleasant of people. Life is so terribly unfair, isn't it, Pembers? Oh my goodness!" Churchill gave a shriek and was only just saved from falling to the ground by the swift action of her secretary.

The cause of her distress was the appearance at the cookshop door of Mr Harding wearing handcuffs, accompanied by Chief Inspector Llewellyn-Dalrymple and Inspector Mappin.

"No!" cried Churchill as Pemberley propped her up. "Tell me it's not true!"

"We don't know what's happened yet," replied Pemberley.

"But they've handcuffed him! This must be some sort of mistake. Mr Harding wouldn't hurt a fly!"

"How do you know that? You only met him a few days ago."

"I'm an expert judge of character, Pembers! I feel these things in my waters."

Mr Harding glanced over at them with a sorrowful

look before bowing his head and stepping into the police car.

The crowd parted, allowing the car to trundle the hundred or so yards to the police station.

"He's innocent!" Churchill called out as the car rumbled past them over the cobbles.

"He might not be," said Pemberley. "You just never know with these things. We don't even know what he's been arrested for."

"Murder," said a voice next to them.

"*What?*" exclaimed Churchill. "How do you know that?" She turned to the woman who had spoken. She wore a hat with a large feather in it and her face seemed strangely familiar.

"I just do," replied the woman curtly. "You're Mrs Churchill, aren't you? I once caught you trampling on my geraniums."

"In the course of an investigation, I must add. Hello again, Mrs Mappin. Why on earth has your husband got our dear Mr Harding in handcuffs?"

"I've already told you. Murder."

"Not *the* murders, though?"

"What other murder has there been?"

"Oh!" wailed Churchill. "Pembers, what a terrible day this is turning out to be. Mr Harding will never recover from this!"

"He should have thought about that before he went around murdering people," Mrs Mappin said calmly.

"What evidence do they have?" retorted Churchill.

"The frying pan," replied Mrs Mappin.

"How do you know about the frying pan? It's meant to be a secret."

"How do *you* know about it?"

"We saw it being pulled out of the duck pond, didn't

we, Pembers? I don't see how the frying pan can be connected with Mr Harding, anyhow."

"It came from his cookshop," said Mrs Mappin.

"Surely most of the frying pans in the village are from his cookshop."

"Not at the prices he charges. I go to Heythrop Itching for mine. I refuse to go anywhere near his shop because he always charms me into purchasing something."

"Mr Harding sells premium-quality cookware," said Churchill. "I'm quite sure you can get cheaper wares at that Itching place, but it most likely wouldn't last five minutes. And anyway, Inspector Mappin has it all wrong. He can't just go and arrest poor Mr Harding because he happens to be selling frying pans that resemble the one found in the duck pond."

"The frying pan merely sealed his fate," said Mrs Mappin.

"What do you mean by that?"

"I'm not at liberty to say." Mrs Mappin tightened her lips.

"Oh, go on," whispered Churchill. "I'm a private detective, Mrs Mappin. You can tell me."

"We *both* are," chipped in Pemberley.

"That's right. We *both* are," said Churchill. "And we can't claim to possess even half the investigating skills of your fine husband. But we try our best, don't we, Miss Pemberley?"

"We do indeed," added Pemberley. "And cases like this aren't easy to crack. Inspector Mappin must have worked inordinately hard to come up with the idea that Mr Harding is the culprit."

"Oh, he does work hard," agreed the inspector's wife with a nod.

"And with sterling results," continued Pemberley. "He

clearly combines his intricate sleuthing mind with a relentless work ethic. He leaves no stone unturned."

"I agree," said Churchill. "No stone remains in situ when Inspector Mappin is on the case. Now, many of us can turn stones, of course, but could we all identify the culprit?"

"No, that takes a unique skill," said Pemberley. "He must have done some truly thorough investigation into the affairs of Mr Harding."

"So he did," said Mrs Mappin. Then she lowered her voice to a whisper and continued, "He discovered that Mr Harding owed money to both deceased men."

"Is that so?" whispered Churchill in reply.

"Yes. He had racked up a number of debts from card games."

"Goodness me! Who'd have thought it?" Churchill replied.

"And there were other rumours, though I've never been one for rumour, and Mr Harding has always struck me as a respectable gentleman. In fact – and don't tell Inspector Mappin this – I've always considered him to be a bit of a dish."

Churchill gripped her handbag tightly, feeling a pang of jealousy. "I see. A dish, eh? Who'd have thought that?" She refused to believe that Mr Harding had gambling debts and strongly objected to the thought of him being ogled by other ladies in the village. She preferred to think that she was the only one who had noticed his many charms.

"So your husband's theory is that Mr Harding murdered Mr Williams and Mr Rumbold because he owed them money," Pemberley probed quietly.

"That's it, in a nutshell," replied the inspector's wife. "But you didn't hear it from me."

"Of course not," said Pemberley. "This information is safe with us, isn't it, Mrs Churchill?"

"I suppose so," she replied, "but if you were to ask me what I think, I'd have to tell you that your husband's way off the mark, Mrs Mappin. I suppose he needs to demonstrate to the populace of Compton Poppleford that he's prepared to arrest people, but it's a shame that he decided to pick on poor, innocent Mr Harding."

"Just a moment ago you were singing my husband's praises!" said Mrs Mappin.

"We were, yes. But on this occasion he is sadly mistaken. And what's more, I intend to prove it."

"Really?" said Pemberley. "Inspector Mappin may be right, you know."

"Of course he's right!" snapped Mrs Mappin.

"We shall have to wait and see," retorted Churchill, setting her jaw. She had no idea how to prove Mr Harding's innocence, but felt resolved to do it somehow or other.

Chapter 33

"IT'S AWFULLY unprofessional for Inspector Mappin to share the details of a case with his wife," commented Churchill as she slammed her handbag down on her desk.

"Ah, but it's just as well he did, otherwise we wouldn't have found out why he'd arrested Mr Harding," said Pemberley.

"He's arrested him because he's an easy target. Poor Mr Harding."

"The inspector must have had some evidence. He must have discovered that Mr Harding had accumulated these gambling debts. And, more importantly, that the debts were owed to the two men who have been murdered."

"He's not a *gambler*, Pembers, he's a *card player*! I like a game of bridge myself, as you know. He should have come and played a few hands with me rather than getting involved with that dirty-fingernailed brigade. And that's by the by. My original point – that Inspector Mappin is unprofessional – still stands."

"Surely Detective Chief Inspector Churchill told you details about the cases he worked on?"

"He didn't, actually. He was a man of great tact and remained quite determined that police business should be left on the doorstep of our home each and every evening."

"Didn't anyone ever take it?"

"Take what?"

"The police business left on your doorstep every evening. They might have seen it as they were passing and decided to swipe it."

"No, I mean... Oh, I see, Pembers. You were having a little joke with me. I'm not really in the mood for jokes at the present time."

"You were speaking metaphorically."

"Well, perhaps I was and perhaps I wasn't. I'm not really sure."

"But I thought you learned all your detective skills from your husband's many years at Scotland Yard?"

"I did."

"But how could you do so if he left it all on the doorstep every day?"

"By reading his mind, of course."

"Is that so?"

"There's no need to look so impressed, Pembers." Churchill sat down behind her desk. "Oh, I suppose it's because you've never been married. Being a spinster, you won't have realised that it's terribly easy to read a husband's mind. Especially a husband you've been married to for many years. They give everything away through their mannerisms. In fact, during our latter years together there was little need for us to speak at all as I knew every little thing he was thinking."

"That doesn't sound like much fun."

"Who ever said marriage was fun, Pembers?"

"Did he know everything you were thinking?"

"No, not at all! It would be most ungentlemanly to

even hazard a guess at what might be occurring in a lady's mind. Would you like someone to read your mind, Pembers?"

"I wouldn't be averse to the idea."

"I can't see why anyone would wish to. A lady's thoughts are her own, I say. Please would you make us some tea, Pembers? I feel terribly drained."

Churchill was able to muster just enough strength to purchase some Eccles cakes from Simpkins the baker. It was only after they had been washed down with a hot cup of tea that she began to feel marginally refreshed.

"Whatever happened between Mr Harding and those gardening types, I think it's as plain as a pitchfork that he simply fell in with a bad crowd."

"Is it a bad crowd?"

"Well, two of them have been murdered Pembers. One doesn't get murdered when one goes about life in an orderly and respectable manner."

"You might if you were in the wrong place at the wrong time."

"In which case one needs to ensure one goes elsewhere. What I mean, Pembers, is that those grubby gardeners were all up to no good. All this bribing-the-colonel business is only the tip of the iceberg."

"The colonel must be up to no good as well."

"He's completely blameless, Pemberley. He told us quite openly that they all keep bribing him. He can't help it if they insist on throwing money at him, can he?"

"And keep hiding it in marrows."

"Exactly. What can he do if they're determined to hide money inside marrows in the grounds of his estate?"

"Fire his shotgun at them, like he did at us?"

"That was a mistake, for which he profusely apologised."

"Did he?"

"I believed he did. And he fired it into the air, not directly at us. Anyway, you're missing my point, Pembers. My point is that the colonel is innocent."

"As innocent as Mr Harding?"

"Exactly. Why do you have that odd smile on your face, Pembers? It's most unbecoming. Oh, I see. You don't believe Colonel Slingsby and Mr Harding are innocent after all. Is that it?"

"It's not that I don't believe they're innocent. I just think they're both suspicious. We don't know whether they're guilty or innocent; they're probably somewhere in-between."

"And this is where being a good judge of character comes in useful, Pemberley. It's quite obvious to me that Mr Harding and the colonel are innocent of murder, and are merely suffering a tarnish to their reputations as a result of their vague association with those soiled gardeners."

"There are only three of them left now."

"There are indeed, and what does that tell you, Pembers?"

"I don't know."

"All we need is for one of them to murder the other two and then we'll have our murderer. He's the guilty one. *And then there was one.*"

"But what if it's *none*?"

"How could that happen?"

"It happened before in one of Atkins's cases. Do you remember reading about it? When they were all stuck on a remote island?"

"Oh yes, I recall."

"If Mr Harris, Mr Downs and Mr Woolwell are murdered we will have no idea who the murderer is. And anyway, I don't want them to be murdered. Or anyone else, for that matter. I think it terribly sad that we've already lost Mr Williams and Mr Rumbold, and we need to ensure that this dreadful killer doesn't strike again. Maybe he won't now that Mr Harding has been arrested, but perhaps he will? It's quite scary, Mrs Churchill. I don't like it at all."

"We must get back to it. We need to find the murderer before poor Mr Harding is charged with an offence. Let's go and ask Mrs Harris and Mrs Downs if they've had a frying pan mysteriously go missing."

Chapter 34

"OH HELLO, Mrs Harris. We were just admiring this fine crop of jersey royals," said Churchill down at the green-grocer's.

"Half a pound for a penny," she replied, her blonde curls bouncing cheerily.

"I'm sure my secretary would love to buy half a pound, wouldn't you, Miss Pemberley?"

"I don't really eat potatoes."

Churchill gave a shrill laugh. "But they're a staple item, Miss Pemberley! What on earth could you possibly be eating instead?"

"I prefer bread."

"Bread with your roast beef? Whoever heard of such a thing?" With a fixed smile on her face, Churchill whispered out of the side of her mouth, "Just buy the spuds, Pembers. We're using them as a conversation starter."

"But I don't like—"

"*I'll* eat them."

"Half a pound of potatoes is it, then?" asked Mrs Harris, placing them in a paper bag.

"Yes please," replied Churchill. "I always find that I boil too many. Do you boil too many, Mrs Harris? If so, I can recommend frying the leftovers with a bit of dripping. It's one of the most delightful morsels I have ever eaten. Forget the fad for French cookery; potatoes and dripping are all Britain needs. Of course, one does require a decent frying pan. Do you have a decent frying pan, Mrs Harris?"

"I used to."

"*Really?*" Churchill's heart began to pound with excitement. "I see. It went missing, eh?"

"No, the dog broke it. He ran off with it down the garden path. He had the handle in his mouth and knocked the round bit off against the gatepost."

"Oh, I see."

"He lost some of his teeth at the same time. I've been meaning to replace the frying pan, but the cookshop here is extremely overpriced. I hear there's a good one in Heythrop Itching."

"Indeed. Well, thank you for the potatoes, Mrs Harris. Good morning to you."

"Oh hello, Mrs Downs, what a fine piece of rump," said Churchill down at the butcher's.

Mrs Downs' bulldog face smiled.

"I do like to fry a bit of rump steak," continued Churchill. "Do you fry your steak, Miss Pemberley?"

"I don't really like steak."

"Just pretend you do," hissed Churchill from the side of her mouth. Then she smiled and addressed Mrs Downs again. "Do you like to fry your steak, Mrs Downs?"

Mrs Downs nodded and rolled her eyes.

"But it's very important to have the right sort of frying

pan, don't you find, Mrs Downs? Do you have the right sort of frying pan at home?"

Mrs Downs's face fell.

"Oh, I see. What does that face mean, Mrs Downs?"

"Don't go askin' me about fryin' pans," the woman growled as she wrapped up a piece of steak.

"Oh, I'm sorry. I didn't realise it was such a sensitive topic."

"I know what you're playin' at," she scorned, jabbing a beefy finger in Churchill's direction.

"Playing? I'm not *playing* at anything. I'm simply buying some—"

"I 'eard about you up at the colonel's place without yer skirts on. And if you dare suggest my Colin murdered Rumbold with that fryin' pan what they found in the duck pond I'll throttle yer with a string o' sausages!"

"Oh goodness!" said Churchill, taking a step back. "Mrs Downs, I would never, ever consider such a thing. I—"

"That'll be a shillin' fer the steak."

"Oh yes, of course," replied Churchill, rummaging around in her handbag for her purse. "I hope you didn't think I was accusing—"

"I know exac'ly what you was doin'," replied Mrs Downs, hurling the wrapped-up steak at Churchill, who just managed to save it with a high catch.

"Thank you, Mrs Downs," said Churchill, warily sliding a shilling across the counter. "And good day to you."

"What a terrifying woman," said Pemberley once they were a safe distance from the butcher's shop. "She looks like a bulldog, but I didn't expect her to behave like one."

"I wasn't even expecting her to speak," replied Churchill. "That was a surprise indeed."

"You can't blame her for being annoyed," said Pemberley. "You were implying that her husband had murdered Rumbold."

"Oh no, not at all. I merely inquired about the whereabouts of her frying pan. I had hoped she would accept the question on the face of it, just as Mrs Harris had done. I didn't expect her to use any guile."

"Some people are cleverer than we give them credit for."

"I wouldn't exactly call her clever, Pembers. It's because she knows that her husband clonked Rumbold on the head with their frying pan that she reacted so defensively. That unpleasant encounter in the butcher's shop was the reaction of a guilty woman! What we must do right away is ascertain the location of Mr and Mrs Downs's frying pan. If it's missing from their home we can safely assume it was used as the murder weapon."

"But what if they didn't have one in the first place?"

"She didn't deny that they'd ever owned one, did she?"

"No, she didn't give an indication either way."

"Surely every household has a frying pan, Pembers?"

"We can't make that kind of assumption. Atkins always used to say that only foolish detectives make assumptions."

"Well, that really does go without saying. He was hardly offering much insight there, was he?"

"So we cannot assume that the Downs household owns, or ever owned, a frying pan."

"Oh darn it, Pembers. How do we find out? Poor Mr Harding is festering in Compton Poppleford police station all the while."

"It won't be so bad for him just yet. They'll only be at

the cup-of-tea-and-interview stage. There may even be biscuits."

"I do hope so. Our work needs to be two-pronged henceforth, Pembers. The first prong is to identify the murderer and the second is to build the case for Mr Harding's innocence. I've just the idea for the second prong, but I'll need to buy some new buttons for my cerise cardigan."

Chapter 35

"WE'LL NEED to go to the haberdashery shop if you want buttons," said Pemberley.

"Won't we just," replied Churchill.

"But it'll mean having to speak to Mrs Thonnings."

"It will indeed."

"But you don't like her."

Churchill gave a laugh. "My dear second-in-command, how could I possibly have a strong opinion about the woman? I barely know her."

"But you've been terribly uncomplimentary about her recently. Ever since you heard of her past liaison with Mr Harding."

"*Uncomplimentary* is rather a strong word, Pembers. I merely commented on the artificial colouring of her hair."

"And the cheapness of her blouses."

"Simply stating a fact."

"And a few other snide remarks."

"Perhaps I was having a bad day. Anyway, come along. I need buttons."

. . .

Mrs Thonnings' haberdashery shop was a warm, cosy little place stacked high with ribbons, zips, buttons and bows of every colour imaginable. A tabby lazily groomed itself on the countertop, while Mrs Thonnings sat on a stool behind the counter reading a romance novel. She pushed her horn-rimmed glasses up onto her shiny orange-hued hair and greeted Churchill and Pemberley with a warm grin.

"How lovely to see you in here again, ladies!"

"Good morning, Mrs Thonnings," said Churchill, trying not to think about her locked in a fond embrace with Mr Harding. "I'm on the hunt for some buttons for my cerise cardigan."

"Of course." Mrs Thonnings slid off her stool and spent the next five minutes showing Churchill the many types of buttons she felt might be suitable. Churchill eventually chose an attractive pearl-effect set and Mrs Thonnings popped the buttons into a small, striped paper bag for her.

"I suppose you've heard the news about our poor cook-shop friend," ventured Churchill.

Mrs Thonnings tutted and shook her head. "Dreadful news. I never would have thought it of Jeffrey."

"Jeffrey?"

"Mr Harding."

"Oh, he's a Jeffrey, is he?' Churchill was surprised to realise she had never found out his forename. "It's certainly an awful shock," she continued. "It must surely be a mistake on Inspector Mappin's part."

"Perhaps it is," said Mrs Thonnings with a sigh. "After all, he only mentioned the fact that murdering his creditors would be a solution to his debt problems on one occasion."

"What?!" replied an astounded Churchill. "He actually admitted that he would consider murdering the people he owed money?"

"He only said it once as a joke," said Mrs Thonnings, "and I don't think he would ever have gone through with it."

"No, I'm sure he wouldn't have. It's quite common to joke about murdering people these days," said Churchill.

"Is it?" said Pemberley.

"Oh yes," replied Churchill. "If I'd actually murdered all the people I'd said I was going to I'd have been hanged for it by now."

"I don't recall you ever joking about murdering anyone, Mrs Churchill," said Pemberley. "And it's not terribly funny, either."

"You do take life rather seriously, Miss Pemberley," said Churchill with a chuckle.

"I must admit that I felt slightly concerned when Jeffrey joked about murdering them," said Mrs Thonnings, "but I put it down to a bad evening at the card table and he didn't mention it again, so I thought it had all been forgotten about. In fact, I was under the impression that he was beginning to repay some of his debts."

"So his debts were no secret to you?" asked Churchill.

"His debts were the worst-kept secret in Compton Poppleford!" replied Mrs Thonnings with a laugh. "We all knew about them, didn't we?"

"Well, *we* did!" Churchill chimed in, adding a false laugh. "Goodness, we've often talked about poor Mr Harding's debts, haven't we, Pembers?"

"Have we?"

"Yes!" retorted Churchill, itching to give her secretary a sharp jab with her elbow so she would play along. Churchill felt rather irritated that, as the village's private detective, she hadn't been privy to its worst-kept secret.

Mrs Thonnings's face had assumed a distant expression.

She picked up a length of red ribbon that had been lying on the counter and began threading it absent-mindedly through her fingers. "Yes, it was the reason Jeffrey and I separated," she said. "His gambling habit was completely out of control."

"Was it really?" asked Churchill incredulously. She hadn't felt so disappointed in a man in a long time.

"Yes, it's such a shame, isn't it?" said Mrs Thonnings. "He's such a well-educated, sophisticated, charming chap, yet he fritters all his money away on card games. I kept telling him he needed to get better at cards and then he might earn something back, but he never was a naturally gifted card player."

"Well, that is a big shame," said Churchill, feeling genuinely sad about Mr Harding's situation. "But being a gambler and owing money isn't the same thing as being a murderer, is it?"

"Oh, absolutely not," said Mrs Thonnings, "and I don't think Jeffrey would have murdered those gardeners. He never did like getting his hands dirty; he has quite pristine habits. If he was going to murder someone he would probably choose poison so he could remain a safe distance from the victim at the time of death."

"Goodness, you appear to have given the matter some thought, Mrs Thonnings."

"I must admit that I have! I've been thinking about it ever since Jeffrey was arrested this morning, and I've come to the conclusion that he couldn't have murdered those men. And even if he had, he would have done it with poison."

"Have you told Inspector Mappin all this?"

"Not yet. He hasn't asked me."

"Well, I think you should go and tell him right away! It might result in poor Mr Harding being released."

"The police are hardly going to listen to me. I'm just the silly little lady who runs the haberdashery shop."

"You need to make them listen to you, Mrs Thonnings! They need to know that they've got the wrong man."

"But have they? What if he's the murderer after all? I'd look quite foolish then, wouldn't I?"

"You must go down there and say your bit, Mrs Thonnings. By all accounts, nobody knows Jeffrey the way you do. Do you think he's capable of being a murderer?"

"No."

"You must go down and tell them, then. Miss Pemberley and I will mind your shop."

"I don't want to put you to any trouble. I can pop down there later."

"There's no time like the present, Mrs Thonnings!" continued Churchill. "You need to speak to that wretched Inspector Mappin while all this is fresh in his mind. It won't do to delay. You might even meet the chief inspector down there, but don't be cowed by him. He's a waste of space; in fact, they all are. But you must go and do your bit."

"Right, well I'll just fetch my hat. Is it chilly out? Do I need my coat?"

"You'll be fine in just your cardigan, Mrs Thonnings. We'll look after puss here. What's his name?"

"Mr Tiddly," she replied as she put on her hat.

"Good morning, Mr Tiddly," said Churchill. The tabby hissed at her and jumped down from the counter.

"Go on, Mrs Thonnings, toddle off. Miss Pemberley and I will steer the ship while you're gone."

. . .

"I'm not sure about this, Mrs Churchill," said Pemberley after Mrs Thonnings had departed. "I don't like working in shops."

"It'll only be for five minutes, Pembers, and with a bit of luck no customers will come in."

"Was it wise to send Mrs Thonnings off to the police station like that?"

"We need to get poor Mr Harding off the hook, Pembers. If we leave matters as they are it'll take the sloth-like Inspector Mappin about a week to get round to talking to Mrs Thonnings, if at all, and all that time Mr Harding will be rotting in the cells of Compton Poppleford police station."

"Ugh. Actually rotting?"

"It's not a nice thought, is it? That's why we're doing everything we can to help him. I just know that man's innocent."

The bell over the door gave a tinkle, and a tall, large-nosed lady dressed in black walked in.

"Oh, darn it, Pembers," whispered Churchill. "It's the grieving Mrs Rumbold."

"Oo!" exclaimed Mrs Rumbold, stopping and staring at the two ladies behind the counter. "What are you doing in here? They haven't arrested Nora as well, have they?"

"Nora?"

"Mrs Thonnings."

"Oh, her. No, they haven't. She's gone down to the police station to plead Mr Harding's innocence."

"I don't know why she's done that. He clearly did it. He owed my husband and Mr Williams two hundred pounds each. And I hear he doesn't have an alibi for either murder."

Churchill sighed and wondered why everyone seemed to know more about the case than she did.

"Please accept our condolences, Mrs Rumbold, for the tragic demise of your husband."

Mrs Rumbold gave a sniff. "Thank you."

"Did your late husband ever pursue Mr Harding for the money he owed him?"

"Oh yes, but it didn't make any difference."

"Did he threaten him?"

"Several times, apparently. With a hoe."

"And what did he do with the hoe?" asked Churchill.

"Just waved it around menacingly, I believe. That's what he told me, anyway. If men get up to violence they don't usually admit it to their wives, do they?"

"So you think your late husband may have been violent toward Mr Harding?"

"I don't like to think he was, but what do I know? There's usually a lot of whiskey involved when these card games are underway, and we all know what men are like after a drop too much, don't we?"

"But did your husband take his hoe to the card games?" asked Pemberley.

"Goodness me, no," laughed Mrs Rumbold. "But he often took his dibber because that fitted into his pocket easily."

"Dibber?"

"A short, pointed stick used to make holes in the ground for seeds."

"Or to make holes in someone's face," added Pemberley.

Churchill startled. "Really, Pembers? You know of that happening, do you?"

"It was just a guess," she replied.

"Did your late husband ever make holes in anyone's face with his dibber, Mrs Rumbold?"

"I honestly couldn't tell you."

"But you wouldn't rule it out?"

"Men will be men, Mrs Churchill. When there are cards, money, whiskey and sharp gardening implements at play, who knows what can happen?"

"Well, quite!"

"I'd like three yards of rickrack, please. Black."

Chapter 36

MRS THONNINGS RETURNED to the haberdashery shop a short while later.

"I've told them everything I can," she said.

"Which was what?" asked Churchill.

"That Jeffrey used to joke about murdering his creditors."

"But you emphasised that it was only a joke, didn't you?"

"Oh yes."

"And you told them that he couldn't possibly be a murderer?"

"Yes, I did. They didn't write that bit down, though."

"What did they write down?"

"Only the bit about him joking about murdering people."

Churchill clenched her teeth. "Thank you, Mrs Thonnings. I'm not sure it will have done the trick, but at least you tried."

"I did try," said Mrs Thonnings. "And that's the most important thing, isn't it?"

"Indeed it is," replied Churchill through her teeth.

"I fear that we have only made matters worse for Mr Harding in getting that orange-haired, cheap-bloused woman involved," said Churchill after they had left the haberdashery shop.

"She did try," said Pemberley.

"Not hard enough, if you ask me."

Pemberley sighed. "It's not looking good for Mr Harding, is it?"

"What on earth are you talking about, Pembers? Of course it is."

"But what with Mrs Rumbold telling us about all the unpleasant business with hoes and dibbers and cards and whiskey, and all that malarkey, it sounds like a rather cutthroat world to me."

"It doesn't sound very pleasant, does it? But neither does it make our delightful Mr Harding a murderer."

"But if Rumbold was threatening him with his hoe or dibber, and possibly using those tools as weapons against him, surely it could have caused Mr Harding to snap."

"Mr Harding doesn't strike me as the sort of man who snaps, Pemberley."

"You barely know him! You didn't even know his name was Jeffrey and you had no idea he had gambling debts, though the rest of the village supposedly did."

"There's no need to rub it in, Pembers."

"I'm not. I'm merely stating that it's difficult to defend a man when you really know very little about him."

"I was hoping to learn more, but then that interfering Mappin arrested him."

"I think Mr Harding may well have snapped. He owed

Rumbold and Williams money, and what's more they were harassing him for repayment."

"How do you know that?"

"Because Mrs Rumbold told us! She said they pursued him, remember? That's enough to make any sane man lose his rag."

"Let's just consider for a moment that it's possible he did commit murder. I think you've hit the nail on the head, Pembers, when you talk of a sane man losing his rag. That's the only reason he could ever have done such a thing. He lost all his hard-earned money in the card games, and those grimy, gardening types no doubt harangued him about it all. Then he most probably got poked in the face by a dibber, and that was the very last straw. Oh, and Mrs Thonnings had left him into the bargain. It's no wonder the poor man decided to commit murder. He just needed a little peace and quiet."

"So you do think he could have done it after all?"

"No, Pembers. No, I don't. He just has to be innocent. I was simply coming up with a possible motive, and I realise now that he did have one. Then again, I think we all have a possible motive, don't we?"

"Even me?"

"Yes. Even you, Pembers."

"But why would I murder two gardeners?"

"Because one of them traipsed mud into our offices the other day."

"That's not a good enough reason."

"In some people's minds it is, Pembers. Now, let's return to the most obvious fact of this case, and that is Mr Downs's guilt. I've no doubt that he's our man."

"Mrs Downs was very snappy about him, wasn't she?"

"Exactly. A previously mild-mannered woman who simply nodded and smiled in the right places hurled a piece of rump steak at me and was terribly defensive about her frying pan and her husband."

"She's covering something up."

"That's exactly what I think, Pembers. But the question is, what?"

"Her murdering husband?"

"I think it could well be that. So you see, that's why I know Mr Harding is innocent. It's because Mr Downs is so guilty."

"Perhaps they both did it."

"Impossible. I can't imagine Mr Harding ever colluding with that man. Let's just work on the premise that Mr Downs is responsible. Now, what we need, Pembers, is evidence."

"Such as what?"

"That's the question, isn't it, Pembers? And I don't like to try to answer it now, because if I make an attempt to predict what form that evidence may take my mind will become closed off to other possible forms of evidence."

"That makes sense."

"Oh, good. A detective always needs to keep an open mind, you see. You don't need me to tell you that, Pembers. You probably heard it all the time from Atkins."

"No, I don't think I ever heard him say that."

"Well, he should have. So you ask me about evidence, Pemberley, and I simply reply that *anything could be evidence*. What we possess is the skill to find it."

"Do we?"

"I hope so, don't you? Otherwise we couldn't very well call ourselves detectives."

"Some days I feel like a detective but others I don't. I don't feel particularly detective-like today."

"Well I do, Pembers, so indulge me. Where shall we go looking first?"

"How about straight to Mr Downs himself?"

"Inspector Mappin forbade us from speaking to him, remember?"

"That's when he was a suspect. But Mr Harding is the only suspect now. Mappin's probably forgotten that Mr Downs even exists."

"Perfect logic, Pembers. Yes, let's go and see him. Do you know where he lives?"

"Down Cackrudge Lane. But it's daytime, Mrs Churchill, so he'll be down at his allotment."

Chapter 37

BIRDSONG CARRIED on the honeysuckle-scented breeze as Churchill and Pemberley walked across the allotments. Churchill felt a lump in her throat as they passed the heavily barricaded allotment that had belonged to Mr Rumbold. Mr Williams's allotment lay just beyond it, and a few weeds were already beginning to sprout between the carrot-tops.

"Oh dear," said Pemberley as she wiped a tear from her eye. "It's so awfully sad to see the allotments falling to rack and ruin."

"They're not quite that bad yet, Pembers," said Churchill. "Someone else will rent them soon, I'm sure."

"But one of them's a murder scene! I don't think anyone would like to cultivate anything on a murder scene. What sort of plant would want to grow there?"

"I shouldn't think the plants are too fussy."

"Oh, but they're very fussy indeed," said Pemberley. "I can't get anything to grow in my garden."

"But your garden isn't a murder scene, Pembers."

"Yes it is."

"What? When?!"

"About 1832, I think."

"Good grief! Do you know what happened?"

"I think it was a drunken fight. And that's why nothing will grow there now."

"Isn't that more likely down to your gardening skills rather than the grisly history of the plot?"

"What gardening skills?"

"Do you possess any?"

"No."

Churchill sighed. "I sometimes wonder how many wasted minutes and hours are spent in conversations that end up in a dead end. We're on the lookout for Mr Downs, aren't we, Pembers? You'll have to remind me what he looks like as I've only seen the chap once, and that was when he was busy escorting Barry Woolwell out of the pub."

"He's just over there," replied Pemberley, pointing at a lean, hook-nosed man who was leaning on a spade and watching them from a well-tended allotment close by.

"Oh yes, so he is. Lovely! Let's go and have a natter with him, shall we?"

A scruffy Jack Russell left the gardener's side and cantered over to them, barking furiously. They tried to ignore it and walked over to where Mr Downs stood.

"Quiet, Sparky!" he shouted at his dog. "Afternoon, ladies," he said, fixing them with a steely stare. He had smears of dirt on his face and the hand resting on the handle of the spade was covered in mud. "I've been expectin' you."

"Golly! Have you really Mr Downs? Why's that, then?" asked Churchill.

"'Cause you're always askin' folk questions. I've seen yer, I 'ave, with these very eyes."

"How extremely observant of you, Mr Downs."

"Oh, I is. I don't miss nothin', me. Quiet, Sparky!"

"Jolly good."

"I knowed it wouldn't be long afore you came a-speakin' ter me."

"Not only are you observant, Mr Downs, but you are also adept at predicting other people's behaviour."

"Oh, I does that an' all. I knows what people's up ter, and I knows what they be plannin'. Sometimes I knows it afore they even knows it 'emselves."

"What wonderful powers of deduction, Mr Downs. You should become a detective."

"Quiet, Sparky! That I should. I got a nose for it."

Churchill glanced at his enormous hooked beak.

"You certainly have a nose, Mr Downs."

"For it."

"A nose for it. Yes indeed. Very much so. For what, exactly?"

"Detectivin'!"

"Oh, of course. Is that a word, is it? Anyway, we must press on. You're no doubt aware that I'm—"

"Mrs Churchills. Private detective. You bought Atkins's place."

"Churchill without an 's'. But other than that, you are exactly right."

"And yer wants ter know who's been a-murderin' folk?"

"Don't we all, Mr Downs?"

"You thinks I might 'ave 'ad sumthin ter do with it. Quiet, Sparky!"

"No, that's not quite true. We were wondering whether you might have any idea who the culprit could be."

"I gots me some ideas."

"Would you care to share them with us?"

He leaned on his spade again and squinted up at the sun.

"'E's got a grudge."

"Who has?"

"The culprit."

"Oh, him. Yes, I'd say that he has a grudge all right."

"An' 'e's likely ter be left-'anded."

"Really? What makes you so sure of that?"

"'Cause of the way the gun was fired and Rumbold was tied up. Quiet, Sparky!"

"Couldn't we put the noisy dog in the toolshed for a bit?"

"Nope. 'E don't like it in there."

"I don't suppose he does. But the wooden walls would muffle the noise a little, wouldn't they?"

"I ain't puttin' no dog o' mine in no tool shed, Mrs Churchills."

"Churchill. Fine, then. You state that you know that the culprit is left-handed because of the manner in which he fired the gun and tied Mr Rumbold up. How do you possess such a detailed knowledge of the case?"

"I just do is all."

"But how?"

"I ain't got all day ter explain it, Mrs Churchills. Just take it from me."

"Churchill. May I ask you a question?"

"An' 'e's got money woes."

"Who has?"

"The culprit."

"The left-handed chap with a grudge?"

"Quiet, Sparky! That's the one. Money woes an' all."

"Money does appear to be a common theme throughout this investigation. Do you know anything about the marrows in Colonel Slingsby's garden, Mr Downs?"

"I've 'eard of 'em."

"Have you seen them?"

"Yeah, I seen 'em an' all."

"Did they belong to Mr Rumbold?"

He scratched the side of his large nose. "Of sorts."

"What does that mean?"

"As I understands it, them marrows performs what I calls a transactional role."

"Do you mean that people hide money in them?"

His eyebrows raised. "Couldn't say."

"You know they do, don't you, Mr Downs?"

"Yer've seen 'em 'ave yer? Quiet, Sparky!"

"Couldn't we put him in the tool shed for just two minutes? I realise he doesn't like it in there, but it would only be for two minutes and then he could come out again and bark away to his heart's content."

"Nope. Whaddya know about them marrows?"

"We counted the money. There were two hundred gold sovereigns in one marrow alone. But how is this connected with the murders of Mr Williams and Mr Rumbold?"

He scratched his nose again. "Dunno."

"Mr Downs, you seem quite certain that the murderer is a left-handed chap with a grudge and money woes, yet you refuse to speculate on how a marrow stuffed with coins might be involved."

"It ain't the marrow what dunnit."

"Clearly not. But the money stashed within it was clearly intended for someone. Who might that someone be?"

"The colonel, I s'pose. Quiet, Sparky!"

"Why?"

"I dunno why yer askin' me all this, Mrs Churchills. Yer already know about the bribes an' all that."

"Chur*chill*. Did you ever bribe the colonel, Mr Downs?"

"Yeah, course. We all does it. That's 'ow we wins the prizes."

"But if everyone bribes the colonel, how does he decide who to award the prizes to?" asked Pemberley.

"'E judges it on merit."

"In which case there would seem to be no point in bribing him at all," ventured Churchill. "If everyone agreed not to bribe him he would judge the vegetables on merit, which is what he has to do anyway given that everyone bribes him. You could all save yourselves a bit of money."

"Yer could look at it like that."

"And it's not as if the colonel needs the money, is it?"

"But 'e do, yer see. 'E's got money woes 'imself."

"Really?"

"Yeah. 'E's got that 'uge 'ouse an' 'e's got all them servants and whatnot, and 'e ain't got enough money to pay fer it all."

"What about his inheritance?"

"'Is brother spent most of it."

"Oh dear, really? Siblings can be dreadfully inconvenient at times. I'm quite pleased that I don't have any."

"Poor you, Mrs Churchill," said Pemberley. "Does that mean you grew up alone?"

"Of course not. I had my mother and father to look after me, and Strudel the cat. And when I was sent off to school there were lots of girls there. I can't say I made friends with many of them, but there were lots there. Anyway, I don't want to waste time talking about my childhood. We have a killer to catch!"

"They've got ol' Jeffrey 'Ardin', anyways," Mr Downs chipped in. "They won't go lookin' for no one else now."

"I sincerely hope they do. The poor man's innocent! Don't you believe he's innocent, Mr Downs?"

"'E might of 'ad an 'and in it. Quiet, Sparky!"

"He had no hand in it whatsoever, did he, Pembers?"

"My mind isn't made up quite yet."

"It's extremely unlikely to have been him though, isn't it?"

"Possibly, but I—" Pemberley began.

"It's *not* him," interrupted Churchill. "When you say *had a hand in it*, Mr Downs, are you suggesting that Mr Harding may have been the murderer's accomplice?"

"Yeah, 'e could of been."

"Nonsense! Have you ever owned a frying pan, Mr Downs?"

"Yeah." Then his face changed. "Now 'ang on a minute. You ain't suggestin'—?"

"I'm not suggesting anything, Mr Downs! We'll be off now. Goodbye to you and your lovely dog!"

The two ladies marched away as quickly as possible with Mr Downs calling after them. "It weren't me wot dunnit! I ain't never 'it no one over the 'ead wiv a frying pan!"

Chapter 38

CACKRUDGE LANE WAS a puddle-filled track with small, ancient-looking cottages slumped either side of it.

"With Mr Downs at his allotment and Mrs Downs at the butcher's, we should be able to peer through their windows without too much trouble," said Churchill. "Which cottage is it? If you can call these cottages. They're more like huts, really, aren't they?"

"The one with the roof covered in moss," replied Pemberley.

"I see the one you mean."

"It needs to be re-thatched."

"It needs to be knocked down; it doesn't look fit for human habitation." Churchill peered in through the little casement window. "I can't see a thing in there. It's too dingy and I don't think these windows have been cleaned since the eighteenth century. Presumably there is some form of access at the rear?"

"I should think so," replied Pemberley, walking on past the row of cottages.

Churchill followed her until they reached a narrow path between the end cottage and a tall hedge.

"Let's go down this little snicket," said Pemberley.

"A what-did-you-call-it?" asked Churchill, following her into the narrow lane.

"It's what they say up north."

"Do you have northern connections, Pembers?"

"My father once met a man from Darlington."

"Good for him. Oh look, the privies."

The snicket opened out into a cobbled back yard behind the cottages, where a row of tumbledown brick lavatories stood. Washing lines criss-crossed the yard, and shirts, vests, aprons and knickerbockers billowed in the breeze.

Ducking between the pieces of laundry, the two women finally located the back entrance of the Downs's moss-covered home.

"Ah yes, there's a better view through here, Pembers," said Churchill, peering in through another little window. "I can see a stove with all manner of cookware stacked around it. There's a saucepan, and I think I spy a colander. There's a large earthenware dish of some sort... Oh and it looks like there's another little Jack Russell terrier in here too. Hello little fellow!"

The dog responded with a bark.

"Can you see a frying pan?"

"Not yet, Pemberley, which I must say is quite promising. There's a kettle..."

"And a frying pan?"

"I'm still looking! It's not easy squinting through this tiny little window, you know. It would be a darned sight easier if we could actually get inside the place."

"Why don't we just do that, then?" replied Pemberley, opening the little door next to the window.

"What? Just walk in? You mean to say that it's unlocked?"

"Of course it is. No one ever locks their doors in what you like to call the provinces."

"But what about burglars?"

"They're just something you get in big cities. No one's got anything worth stealing around here."

"I imagine that to be true," said Churchill, glancing up at a pair of patched long-johns swinging on the washing line. "Come on, then. If we're going in let's make it quick. It won't take a moment to identify whether there is a frying pan on the premises or not. Let me go first, though. My eyesight is keener than yours."

Churchill bustled in through the little doorway into a low-ceilinged room and was immediately met by the sound of furious barking. Within half a second the terrier had flung itself at her and locked its jaws onto her tweed skirt.

"Oh darn it!" she cried. "I wasn't expecting it to do that!"

The little dog growled as its razor-sharp teeth gripped tightly around the bottom of her skirt.

"Can't you get it off, Pembers?"

"How would I do that?"

"Just pull it or something."

"It might bite me!"

"It's biting my skirt! This is Harris tweed!"

"I'd rather its jaws were locked on to something inanimate rather than a body part. It's certainly the lesser of two evils."

"Oh, is it indeed? That's fine for you to say when you haven't got a demonic Jack Russell chewing up an item of clothing that was made-to-measure at great cost."

Pemberley walked over to the stove. "I can't see a frying pan."

"I refuse to even commence the search for a frying pan until this animal has been removed from my clothing. Pembers, how about that steak we bought? Get it out of your shopping bag and wave it under the dog's nose."

"But it cost——"

"I know how much it cost, but I paid twenty times more for this fine skirt. Just get it out and wave it at him."

Pemberley retrieved the steak from the shopping bag, unwrapped it and tentatively held it by one end.

"Here, little doggy," she said. "Look what Auntie Doris has for you!"

The dog ignored her and continued to growl at Churchill.

"He didn't hear you, Pembers. Waggle it about a bit and get the scent wafting over to him. In fact, bring it closer. He needs it waved right under his nose."

"He might go for it!"

"That's exactly what we want him to do!"

"But what if he takes a chunk out of my hand as well?"

"Just waggle the steak, Pembers. Jiggle it!"

"He doesn't want it."

"Oh, give it to me, will you?"

Pemberley did as she was asked and Churchill waved the steak above the dog's head.

"Here, doggy, doggy, doggy! Look at this lovely steak! Much nicer than Churchy's skirt, you little blighter! Now get off!"

The steak had no effect on the dog, which remained where it was, jaws locked and snarling.

"We could cut it off," suggested Pemberley.

"What do you mean?"

"We could just cut off the piece of skirt it's hanging on to."

"I'm not allowing a pair of scissors anywhere near my skirt, Pembers!"

"Then it appears we are quite stuck."

"Not a bit of it. Just look for the frying pan, then we can get out of here. This beast is merely guarding his territory. Once we're out of this place he's bound to let go."

"I can't see a frying pan anywhere," said Pemberley, searching around the small iron stove.

"Me neither, Pembers," said Churchill, cautiously removing her eyes from the dog for a short while to survey the simple room. "There we have it, then," she said. "No frying pan, ergo Mr Downs used it to incapacitate his poor friend Mr Rumbold before leaving him to drown in the duck pond. Dreadful! Despicable! He must be detained at once, Pembers. And after that he shall face trial."

"Oh look, here's a frying pan." Pemberley retrieved a pan from a hook on the wall beside the pantry.

"Oh, darn it. Really?" Churchill's heart sank.

"But perhaps Mr and Mrs Downs owned two frying pans?"

"I don't see why they should have, but it's possible. In which case Mr Downs may still be the murderer."

"Uh oh," said Pemberley, glancing over at the little window.

Churchill noticed a shadow passing it, like a cloud moving across the sun. "Oh dear indeed."

The door swung open. "Everything all right in here? I heard barking."

The voice came from a large lady with a square face and long grey hair. Churchill stifled a groan. It was Mrs Higginbath.

In one swift move Churchill tossed the steak into the frying pan Pemberley was still holding and hastily armed herself with an excuse.

"Mrs Churchill? Miss Pemberley?"

"Mrs Higginbath! How lovely to see you again! Miss Pemberley and I were just about to fry some steak as a surprise for Mr and Mrs Downs. Do you live next door?"

"It would be a surprise for them indeed," replied Mrs Higginbath, staring at the frying pan. "Yes, I do. What's Spark doing attached to your skirt?"

"Spark? Not Sparky?"

"No, Sparky's the quiet one. Spark's the one who's got your skirt in his mouth. He must have felt quite threatened."

"Entirely our fault, Mrs Higginbath. We weren't sure how to warn the dog that we were cooking up a surprise for Mr and Mrs Downs. He's taken it quite badly."

"It's because he knows something's afoot, that's why. He's not stupid, and neither am I. If you think I believe your cock and bull story about cooking a surprise steak you really are more foolish than you look."

Chapter 39

"THE WHOLE THING can be explained in quite simple terms, Inspector Mappin," said Churchill, seated in the police station with Pemberley beside her. "But I would really appreciate it if you could remove your dog from my skirt, Mrs Downs."

The bulldog-faced lady stood over them, her handbag clutched firmly in her hands. "I already told yer. Only Colin can get the dog off."

Inspector Mappin sighed. "Mrs Churchill, you do realise that policing in Compton Poppleford is stretched to its utmost limits with all this murder business going on, don't you? Do you think I have any time at all for your nonsense?"

"Of course not, Inspector. I repeatedly told Mrs Higginbath that it was completely unnecessary to involve the strong arm of the law, yet she insisted on telephoning you. The woman bears a grudge against me, Inspector, and all because I once let slip something that wasn't entirely complimentary about her nephew. She still won't even let me join the library!"

"You broke into me 'ouse!" scorned Mrs Downs.

"We were merely making routine enquiries, Mrs Downs. Miss Pemberley and I had simply popped our heads in through the door. We had no idea we would be set upon by a crazed hound!"

"'E's a guard dog!"

"And a very effective one, Mrs Downs. But we didn't break into your house. The door was unlocked, and we didn't take anything either."

"You took me fryin' pan!"

"Miss Pemberley, please will you return the frying pan to Mrs Downs? We were herded out of there by Mrs Higginbath so swiftly that we forgot to put it back on its hook. Look, you can have the steak too. We paid good money for that, as you well know."

Inspector Mappin cradled his head in his hands. "How long will it be before your husband gets here, Mrs Downs?"

"Dunno. One o' the Flatboot boys was sent to fetch 'im."

"And you're quite sure that only your husband can remove the dog from Mrs Churchill's skirt?"

"Yeah, and she's lucky it's only 'er skirt. Colin's trained 'im to bite people's legs."

Churchill winced and glared at the fearsome terrier locked on to her skirt.

"How many frying pans do you own, Mrs Downs?" asked Pemberley.

"Just this one." She scowled. "What else 'as to 'appen for you two to get it into yer thick skulls that my Colin ain't the murderer?"

Inspector Mappin sighed again. "Is that what this is all about, Mrs Churchill? Do you suspect that Mr Downs is the murderer?"

"No, Inspector! Absolutely not! Now, I can't deny that

Miss Pemberley and I have been conducting some enquiries regarding the ownership of frying pans around the village, but there was no intention to accuse anyone of anything. In fact, all our work thus far has merely been an attempt to prove Mr Harding's innocence."

The inspector snorted.

"He didn't do it! Someone else hit Mr Rumbold with the frying pan, not Mr Harding. And whoever it was must be missing a frying pan. As soon as we noticed the frying pan hanging on the wall in Mr and Mrs Downs' cottage we immediately said, *Ah so it's clearly not Mr Downs, then, because there's the frying pan.* Didn't we, Miss Pemberley?"

"Something similar to that."

"Yes, well I can't recall my exact words, but they were broadly similar, weren't they? And as soon as we said that, we were just about to leave when this savage creature latched on to my skirt. Which is Harris tweed, by the way, so you must understand that I'm particularly upset about it. So you see, I have already lost out, Inspector, and I don't think this incident should take up any more of your precious time. Or ours, for that matter."

"Mrs Churchill," said the inspector wearily, "I don't believe you had any malicious intent when you entered the property of Mr and Mrs Downs this afternoon."

"Thank you, Inspector."

"However, you are guilty of being nosey to the point of disruption and great inconvenience to many law-abiding citizens. This is the second time you've been caught trespassing in the last week, Mrs Churchill."

"And Miss Pemberley, too."

"You place an unreasonable expectation on your assistant to tag along with you. You drag her into it."

"I don't *drag* you, do I, Miss Pemberley?"

"Mrs Churchill, if I hear any more reports of trespass I

shall have to take these matters very seriously indeed. You buzz about this village like a bee in search of honey, and it's becoming extremely annoying. One of these days you're likely to get swatted."

Churchill gritted her teeth, wishing she could swat the inspector with her handbag.

"I wish ter press charges!" announced Mrs Downs.

"We're too busy for that," retorted Inspector Mappin. "We've got a murderer to prosecute."

"I wish to plead Mr Harding's innocence!" said Churchill.

"Just stay out of it, you!" snapped the inspector. "Just *please*, for once, Mrs Churchill, allow the law of the land to roll on without poking a stick into its spokes."

Chapter 40

"BEES DON'T SEARCH FOR HONEY," grumbled Pemberley as they walked up the high street after leaving the police station. "They make honey. I wanted to tell Inspector Mappin that, but he would only have become even crosser."

"And it wouldn't have made any difference, my dear, Pembers. The chap is completely hapless. He doesn't know his elbow from a bar of soap."

"That must cause serious problems during his morning ablutions."

"Absolutely, it must. And to think that poor Mr Harding is withering, positively perishing, in the cells of that dismal police station while Mappin and the chief inspector discuss the cricket over tea and biscuits. It's just..." Churchill paused to wipe a tear from her eye. "Oh, the injustice of it all, Pembers!"

"At least Mr Downs managed to remove Spark from your skirt."

"I suppose I should be grateful that his teeth didn't leave

even the slightest hole. That's Harris tweed for you. One can expect nothing less from the Outer Hebrides; everything has to be hard-wearing up there. Inspector Mappin wouldn't last five minutes. He'd be swept away the instant it blew a hoolie."

"Is that the colonel's Daimler parked outside the cook-shop?" said Pemberley.

"It jolly well appears to be, doesn't it?"

"But the cookshop's closed, so what's the colonel doing there?"

"I don't know."

The two ladies halted in their steps and watched from a distance as the cookshop door opened and the lean form of Colonel Slingsby stepped out. Churchill's eyes were drawn to a large bag, which he carried in one hand. He looked around as Pattison opened the car door for him. Then he climbed inside.

"Did you see the valise in his hand, Pembers? What could he have stashed in there?"

"He's removing evidence!"

"What evidence?"

"I wish I knew."

The Daimler turned around in the road, then drove away from them.

"He can't be removing evidence," said Churchill. "Mr Harding hasn't done anything wrong."

"But can we actually be certain of that?"

Churchill felt her heart sink as she questioned, for the first time, whether her continual defence of Mr Harding was misplaced.

"Well, I don't suppose we can be completely certain, can we? If the man was provoked by a dibber to the face, or whatever it was, and there were whiskey and cards and money involved, then maybe... just maybe... there's a slight, teeny-weeny possibility that he may not be completely above board."

Pemberley allowed a respectful pause to pass before replying. "It's usually sensible to keep an open mind."

"Yes indeed. Common sense must prevail at all times. But at this moment I'd like to know what the colonel has just removed from Mr Harding's business premises."

"A frying pan, perhaps?"

"Can we, just for one moment, stop considering frying pans? I'm rather tired of them, if truth be told."

"His missing gun?"

A chill ran down Churchill's spine. "Oo, Pembers! That might be it! But how does the colonel intend to explain its reappearance?"

"Perhaps he'll keep it hidden."

"Oo, yes! Plenty of hiding places in that ancestral seat of his. There will be trapdoors, hidden compartments, lofty attics and all sorts. There may even be a priest hole. No one would find it for generations. Just a moment, though, Pemberley. If we're saying that the colonel was removing his gun from Mr Harding's shop, that suggests Mr Harding is the murderer."

"It suggests it, but we can't be certain. And we did just decide that it's best to keep an open mind."

Churchill nodded bravely. "We did indeed. We must consider all possibilities, no matter how unpalatable they are."

"That's just what Atkins used to say."

"Did he? Oh good. We've finally found something he and I agree on. Now then, Pembers, I would like to speak to the colonel again but I'm not sure how to go about it. It wouldn't do for us to simply invite ourselves back to Ashleigh Grange, especially after the incident with the marrows and my breeches. How else can we gain an audience with him? The old crumb doesn't seem to venture away from his home too often."

"I think I have an idea."

"Really, Pembers?"

"But it may involve riding a bicycle."

Chapter 41

"NEVER UNDERESTIMATE the power of food, Pembers," said Churchill the following morning. "I've realised that if I pedal toward the picnic in the basket on the front of my bicycle I'm able to stay in the saddle."

"Hurrah, Mrs Churchill. You've learned how to bicycle in a straight line!"

"I've always known how to do that, Pemberley, but for some reason reminding myself of the sandwiches, pork pie and pickled onions improves my balance. You didn't forget the cherries and Madeira cake, did you?"

"No, they're in my basket."

"Wonderful. And the lemonade?"

"That's in my basket, too. I didn't want to take the risk of putting any glassware in yours."

"And I wouldn't have wanted you to, Pembers. I'll leave the glassware transportation to you. Oh, how I do love a picnic. When shall we stop and eat it?"

"Don't forget that the picnic is part of our ruse, Mrs Churchill."

"But we still get to eat it, don't we?"

"Yes, but we need to carry out the ruse first."

"Must we?"

"Don't you want to find out what the colonel has removed from Mr Harding's cookshop?"

"Of course I do, and I shall be even more determined after a slice of pork pie."

"We haven't even bicycled a quarter of a mile yet, Mrs Churchill."

"Nonsense, we must have travelled three miles by now."

"We can't have. We've only just passed the old water pump."

"Trust you to notice something as dull as an old water pump, Pembers."

"I like to keep an eye out for landmarks."

"I can feel my balance going now I've learnt that we're not even at the half-mile mark."

"Keep bicycling toward the picnic, Mrs Churchill."

"I am! But at this rate I'll never catch up with it. Is this really worth our while, Pembers?"

"Of course it is. This level of effort and determination is what's required to crack the case."

"I like that sort of talk, Pemberley. You almost sound like me. I must add that this new pair of breeches is quite comfortable. I hadn't realised that funny little ladies' outfitters by the bric-a-brac shop was any good."

The two ladies continued their journey along the hedge-lined lanes that led to Ashleigh Grange. Pink and white dog roses, powder blue cornflowers and flashes of scarlet pimpernel brightened the hedgerows. The sun shone and Churchill perspired.

The tall gateposts of Ashleigh Grange eventually

loomed into view. As soon as she saw them, Churchill paused beneath the shade of an oak tree.

"Thank goodness we're there," she puffed. "And now we wait."

"We can't wait," replied Pemberley. "That will look suspicious. We need to arrive spontaneously whenever he appears."

"How can we arrive spontaneously when we've planned this in advance?"

"We'll have to bicycle to and fro along this stretch of road."

"Pedal continuously? Are you trying to drive me to a fit of exhaustion, Pemberley?"

"No, I wouldn't wish to do that at all. But don't you see that if the colonel finds us standing under this tree he'll know we're here to seek him out."

"Indeed I do see that, Pembers. A nice slice of pork pie and a swig of lemonade will see us on our way. Don't you agree?"

The two ladies paused for a spot of refreshment, then remounted their bicycles.

"To and fro then, Pembers?"

"Yes, while keeping the gateposts within our sights at all times. Doing so will ensure that we're close by when the colonel's car appears. Then we can have our 'spontaneous' chat with him."

"And ask him what's in his valise?"

"We'll have to think of something a little less direct than that."

"Such as: what were you doing sniffing about in the cookshop, colonel?"

"A bit too direct, I feel."

"I know what you mean, Pembers. What we really need is something along the lines of: *Oh hello, Colonel. Lovely day, isn't it? We're just bicycling out to have a picnic on the bank of a babbling brook. How marvellous to happen upon you like this.* I'll throw in a question after that, but I will think of the exact phrasing on the spot. I pride myself on being able to improvise well in conversation. Now, what happens if the colonel's car doesn't appear?"

"There is a chance he won't be making any excursions today."

"Then what?"

"Then we'll just eat our picnic."

"When exactly?"

"Shall we improvise?'

"Oh yes, I'm good at improvising. Let's go."

The two ladies pedalled past the gates of Ashleigh Grange before turning around and pedalling past again. They did this three times before Churchill's legs began to complain.

"I'm sorry, Pembers. The spirit is willing, but the flesh is weak. It must be the heat."

"Your flesh doesn't like heat?"

"It does, but it doesn't enjoy having to do a lot of moving about in it. And I'm worried the Madeira cake will spoil if it spends any longer in your basket."

"Do you want to sit down and eat some cake, Mrs Churchill?"

"Oh, I do, Pembers! I very much want to!"

"Let's do four more passes past the gates first."

"It'll be the end of me, Pemberley, it really will. I can picture the wording on my tombstone now. *Here lieth Annabel Churchill, who pedalled herself to death.*"

"That sounds rather dramatic, Mrs Churchill."

"That's how serious the matter has become. I'm dramatically close to complete collapse."

"Oh, look! Here comes the colonel's Daimler."

Churchill had never seen a more pleasing sight than that of the shiny red and cream car bumping down the long driveway toward the gates.

"Get pedalling!" said Pemberley. "We've just bicycled out from the village, remember? And we're on our way to the babbling brook."

"Surely it'll be just as convincing if we're walking alongside our bicycles."

"We won't get there quickly enough. The car's nearly at the gates."

"Oh, darn it, Pembers," said Churchill as she clambered onto her bicycle again. "This really is the last time I'm getting on one of these contraptions. They don't agree with me at all."

"One final push, Mrs Churchill. We can do this."

The car stopped and the chauffeur climbed out to open the gates. The two ladies pedalled toward him as he got back into the car and drove on through. Then he got out again and closed the gates behind him.

"What a palaver it must be to be upper class," said Churchill as they neared the gateposts. "All that gate opening and closing, and the endless fussing over the family silver. Hobnobbing with the right set and all that business. How wearisome it must be."

"They have staff to do most of it."

"But the staff must be managed, Pembers. Remember the Colonel saying what a bind they were? One almost feels sorry for the old bean."

"I don't."

They reached the first gatepost.

"Here we are, Pembers. We timed it perfectly to intersect with the path of the colonel's car."

No sooner had Churchill spoken than an almighty honk catapulted her out of her saddle and into the road.

For a brief moment the earth seemed to stand still as she lay prostrate on the ground.

Then an angry voice broke the silence. "Where'd you two spring from, eh? Was yer purposefully tryin' to get 'it by me car?"

"I can explain," said Churchill through a mouthful of grit. As she pushed herself up into a sitting position she felt a sharp pain in her shoulder. Her bicycle lay next to her, its wheels still spinning. Pemberley's bicycle also lay on the ground. The slender assistant was on her feet, brushing the dirt from her skirt.

"Oh, it's Mrs Churchill, ain't it?"

Churchill squinted up into the sunshine and saw the silhouette of the chauffeur standing over her.

"I'm right sorry, Mrs Churchill! You didn't 'alf gimme a fright!" The chauffeur held out a gloved hand and helped her to her feet. "Yer don't often see folks bicyclin' down this lane. I didn't expect yer to be 'ere."

"I understand, Pattison, please don't worry. I suppose I should have made use of my brakes, but in all truth I don't know how to use them."

"Not ter worry, Mrs Churchill. Not ter worry." Pattison took her arm and guided her toward the car. "I'll take yer both up to the 'ouse to get patched up."

"I'm sure there's no need—"

"I insist, Mrs Churchill, I insist. Leave the bicycles 'ere and I'll collect 'em shortly."

"Thank you, Pattison. We'll bring the baskets with us, though."

Although her knees were scuffed and her shoulder hurt, Churchill felt pleased that Pemberley's plan to speak to the colonel had worked so well. She smiled and thanked Pattison as he opened the door of the Daimler for her to climb in.

She opened her mouth to greet the colonel, but her jaw remained slack when she saw that it wasn't the colonel sitting in the car at all.

It was Kitty Flatboot.

Chapter 42

"THERE'S no need for refreshments, Miss Flint," said Churchill. "Miss Pemberley and I have brought a picnic with us. It's a little mangled but still perfectly edible."

"This egg sandwich has a stone embedded in it," said Pemberley.

"Remove it then, Miss Pemberley; the sandwich will taste just the same. We don't want to put Miss Flint to any trouble providing refreshments when we've brought our own." Churchill combined an embarrassed smile at the colonel's housekeeper with a withering stare, mindful of Miss Flint's indiscretion about the breeches.

The two ladies sat in the drawing room of Ashleigh Grange with Kitty Flatboot, while Miss Flint hovered about like an irritating fruit fly. The girl avoided making eye contact with them and picked at her fingernails. Churchill's gaze was continually drawn to the item lying on the floor beside Kitty's chair: the battered leather valise she and Pemberley had seen the Colonel remove from the cookshop the previous day.

"So, what needs patching up, Mrs Churchill?" asked

Miss Flint. "Do you require sticking plasters for your knees?"

Initially determined to decline any offer of help, Churchill had to reluctantly acknowledge that her knees were quite sore beneath her new breeches.

"I suppose I do, Miss Flint, thank you. But we won't detain you any longer than is necessary. The colonel is to be out all day, you say?"

"Yes, he's just gone out on a shoot with the Earl of Strangford."

"I see. Thank you."

"I shall inform him of the unfortunate accident with the chauffeur as soon as he returns."

"Oh, there's no need."

"But I must! He will be most concerned to hear about it."

"It wasn't an accident, as such; merely just a little inter-section of bicycles and car. Nobody actually bumped into anyone."

"I shall inform him all the same," said Miss Flint as she left the room.

Churchill sighed and glanced at the valise again. *Could it really contain the gun used to murder Mr Williams? If so, why was Kitty Flatboot in possession of it? And what was she even doing at Ashleigh Grange?*

Churchill turned to look at Pemberley. As their eyes met, she immediately knew that they were wondering the same thing.

Churchill washed down a piece of gritty sandwich with the lemonade, which had remained surprisingly intact in its bottle. Then she cleared her throat. "Are you a regular visitor to Ashleigh Grange, Miss Flatboot?"

The girl looked up from her fingernails. "Yeah, sometimes."

"A sometimes regular visitor?"

"Yeah."

Churchill and Pemberley exchanged a glance and Churchill rolled her eyes.

"Do you do work for the colonel, Miss Flatboot?"

"Nope."

"I see. I suppose you're ordinarily quite busy working for Mrs Bramley, aren't you?"

"Yeah."

"I hope you don't consider this question intrusive, Miss Flatboot, but what is the nature of your acquaintance with Colonel Slingsby?"

The girl shrugged. "Friend of the family."

Churchill glanced at Pemberley again, desperate to ask her why on earth the colonel would fraternise with this notoriously rustic family. "Has he known your family for long?"

"I reckon so. He's old, ain't 'e?"

"He's given you his valise, I see."

The girl looked down at the bag as if she'd only just noticed it sitting there. "Yeah, that's for me ma."

"Is it indeed? I do hope she can make good use of it."

"Yeah, ev'ryone will."

Churchill turned to Pemberley and raised an incredulous eyebrow.

Miss Flint returned with some sticking plaster, interrupting the subtle interrogation. "You may find it more comfortable to apply this in the colonel's mother's dressing room, Mrs Churchill," she said. "You know where it is, don't you? I believe you used it during your last visit."

"I believe I did. Thank you, Miss Flint," said Churchill through gritted teeth.

· · ·

Pattison drove Churchill and Pemberley back to their office, dropping Kitty Flatboot at Cherrybrick Farm on the way.

"Day off today, Miss Flatboot?" asked Churchill.

"Yeah, I gets Thursdees off 'cause I does Saturdees."

"Jolly good. Well, do enjoy the rest of your day."

As Kitty dragged the valise out of the Daimler, Churchill peered at the sprawling, ramshackle farm buildings through the polished window. A goat returned her stare. There was something which didn't seem right about the Flatboot family.

"They all live here, do they? The Flatboots?"

"Yes, several generations," replied Pemberley.

"Goodness. There really must be hundreds of them, as Mrs Bramley said."

A group of scruffy, apple-cheeked children ran out to the car and Pattison wound down his window to hold out a bag of sweets for them.

A snotty-nosed boy knocked on Churchill's window.

"Sweets at the front of the car, dear," she shouted through the glass, pointing at the chauffeur. "Shouldn't you be in school?"

The Daimler turned around, slowly navigated its way through a brood of chickens, then continued on its way.

"Goodness me, Pembers," said Churchill. "You and I have a lot to discuss when we get back to the office."

Chapter 43

"WHAT ON EARTH, in the name of St Francis the Brave, can the explanation for all these shenanigans possibly be?" Churchill slammed her handbag down on her desk.

"It gets worse," replied Pemberley.

"*Worse*? How?! What do you mean?"

"I know what's inside the valise."

"How?"

"I looked inside it."

Churchill stumbled over to her chair and slumped into it. She retrieved a handkerchief from her jacket pocket and wiped her brow. "You looked inside the valise, Pembers? When? Did you seek Kitty's permission?"

"No. I engineered a peek while you were in the colonel's mother's dressing room applying your sticking plaster."

"Please elaborate."

"You may have noticed there was a framed photograph on the wall behind the chair Kitty was sitting in."

"I didn't, but pray continue."

"While you were gone the room fell quiet, so I

decided to declare an interest in said photograph, loudly stating that its setting looked familiar to me. It didn't, of course, but I knew that Kitty would be none the wiser, whereupon I got up from my chair and excused myself to Kitty, asking if she minded me taking a closer look at the photograph. Not wishing to be in my way, the sullen girl got up and went to stare out of the window. Don't forget that the valise was lying by the side of her chair."

"I hadn't forgotten."

"So I stepped forward to peer at the photograph, which I had no interest in at all, and while doing so dropped my slice of Madeira cake all over the valise."

"You had a slice of the cake?"

"Yes, didn't you?"

"No. Is there any left?"

"A little."

"I could have done with a slice of that. You should have offered me some, Pembers."

"Anyway, back to the valise. After dropping my cake on it I emitted an oopsy-daisy sort of sound, then proceeded to make a great fuss of picking up the pieces and wiping the crumbs from it. I told Kitty not to worry and to stay where she was, and that I would see to it all. The girl obliged and allowed me enough time to furtively undo a strap. I just about managed to pull the case open on one side so I could see into it."

Churchill leaned forward, her eyes wide. "And what was inside?"

"Coins," replied Pemberley. "Sovereigns. Just like the ones we found in that marrow. In fact, they could be the very same ones."

Churchill gasped. "No gun?"

"I couldn't see one, but I didn't have much time. I

knew that if I spent too long clearing up my cake mess Kitty would grow suspicious."

"Good thinking, Pembers. It doesn't take much to raise her suspicions. So these coins, then. The colonel has given her some of the money?"

"It would appear so."

"Perhaps he removed the money from the cookshop."

"By all accounts, Mr Harding doesn't have any."

"So the colonel might have used the valise to remove the gun from the cookshop, then hid the gun in his ancestral seat and filled the valise with coins from the marrow. Then, for some reason none of us shall ever be able to fathom, he gave the money to Kitty Flatboot."

"She said it was for her ma."

"That's right, so she did. So why is the colonel giving Mrs Flatboot all that money?"

"Didn't Kitty say that everyone would be making good use of it?"

"Yes, she did! That makes sense now. She must have known it was money and that the countless Flatboots would presumably be sharing it out among themselves. But the question that begs itself, Pembers, is why?"

"Kitty says the colonel is a friend of the family. Perhaps that's the simple explanation."

"But why should he be a friend of the Flatboots? They're from opposite ends of the social strata. It doesn't make any sense. And how does this all relate to the murderer in our midst?"

"Perhaps it doesn't. Perhaps this is entirely unrelated, and therefore any further investigation into it would be a bootless errand."

"But what if the colonel took the gun from Mr Harding's cookshop?"

"We have no way of knowing whether he did or not."

"Oh dear, Pembers, this is terribly confusing. I think I need a slice of whatever remains of that Madeira cake while I reorganise this incident board. The colonel is looking increasingly suspicious to me. I had taken to him quite warmly, but I realise now that there's something rather cloak-and-dagger about the man."

"He's all smoke-and-mirrors."

"Mirrors, smoke, dagger and cloak."

"And don't forget Mr Woolwell and Mr Harris."

"Oh dear, I confess that I had."

"And perhaps Mr Harding is the culprit after all."

"Oh, don't say that, Pembers."

"I thought you had given up defending him."

"I have, but I don't want those pesky police officers solving this case. It won't do. I'm starting to wonder if our time might be better spent reading the minutes from the Compton Poppleford Horticultural Society meetings." She glanced at the large, unopened box beside the filing cabinets. "There could be a nugget or two in there, as the colonel said."

"I shouldn't think there would be anything of use in there."

"Why not?"

"Mirrors and smoke, remember? Dagger and cloak. He's given us all that to read so he can distract us from the real facts of the case."

"Goodness! Do you really think so, Pembers?"

"Yes, it would take us days, possibly weeks, to read everything in that box. In the meantime, he's free to get on with cloaking and smoking and all that business."

"Now I don't know whether to spend any time on them or not."

"I wouldn't bother."

"But there might be something, mightn't there? A little

something." Churchill went over to the box, untied the string around it and pulled out the first folder. "Meeting minutes of the CPHS, 1923. I think we could start with something a little more recent."

"I'll make some tea and update the incident board," said Pemberley.

Churchill found the folder from the previous year and sat down to read it with the remains of the Madeira cake. It wasn't long before they heard the door slam downstairs, followed by footsteps on the staircase.

"Oh no. Who is it, Pemberley? I'm too busy to be bothered by anyone else today."

"Hullo? Mrs Churchill?"

In strode Chief Inspector Llewellyn-Dalrymple.

"Oh hello, Chief Inspector," said Churchill wearily. "I'd offer you a slice of cake but there isn't much left, and I was hoping to have it all to myself."

"Enjoy it, Mrs Churchill, I won't keep you long. How are you? I heard reports of a traffic accident outside the gates of Ashleigh Grange."

"Oh, it was nothing. I'm fine, thank you. We both are."

"Oh good. Marvellous. That Pattison chap drives a shade too fast in that Daimler of his. I've told Inspector Mappin he should slap him with a fine."

"He wasn't at fault today, Chief Inspector, our paths merely crossed. Fairly swiftly, I should add, as we were on bicycles and he was in a motor vehicle. But it was nothing more serious than a few bumps and bruises."

"That is a relief indeed. We received a telephone call from Miss Flint, the colonel's housekeeper, so I thought we'd better follow up. Inspector Mappin would have come but he's rather embroiled in the case at the moment."

"How's the questioning of your suspect going?"

"It's been rather tiresome, I'm afraid. He's hired a

lawyer and that immediately puts a spanner in the works. I always tell suspects not to do it because it means the interviewing business takes three times as long. Lawyers are slippery creatures and rather skilled at applying a layer of grease to the proceedings. I like a nice clean case where charges are brought against the defendant, he stands trial, he's found guilty and then *whomp*, he hangs for it. All in a matter of weeks."

"Oh, gosh! But you wouldn't do that to Mr Harding, would you?"

"It won't be so simple with him. Not now he's got this slippery lawyer chap from Dumbleton Poggs. And don't ask me if that's the name of a village or a law firm, because I have no idea. I must commend you ladies on your incident board. Isn't that a fine-looking thing?"

He stepped closer to the board and surveyed it, nodding all the while.

"Very good indeed," he continued. "I can tell that a good deal of thought has gone into this. It's amazing what a pair of old biddies can cook up."

"Isn't it indeed? Was there anything else, Chief Inspector?"

"No, I don't think there is, actually. I should probably get back to it."

"Indeed you should."

Chapter 44

"I HAD no idea that your waitress was so *au fait* with Colonel Slingsby, Mrs Bramley," said Churchill as she and Pemberley took elevenses at the tea rooms the following day.

"Yeah, so she is. They all is."

"The Flatboots?"

"Yeah."

"Is there a reason for the unusual acquaintance?"

"Yeah, and I ain't discussin' it, 'cause it's shameful!"

"Really? The relationship between the colonel and Kitty Flatboot is shameful, is it?"

"You'll get nothin' more from me on it, Mrs Churchill. It quivers me waters just thinkin' about it."

"Goodness." Churchill took a thoughtful sip of tea.

"All I'll say is, the sooner you catch 'er with 'er 'and in the till the better. I wish I'd never 'ad anyfing ter do with the Flatboots."

"Crikey, Mrs Bramley, you seem quite aerated this morning."

"I am, Mrs Churchill. I is. I can forget about the shamefulness fer a bit, but whenever it's brung up again I gets the quivers."

"I apologise for mentioning it, Mrs Bramley."

"You wasn't ter know, Mrs Churchill."

"Shameful, eh?" Churchill whispered to Pemberley once Mrs Bramley had departed. "I never would have thought it. What's the age gap between Kitty and the colonel. About sixty years?"

"Seventy, I'd say."

"Cripes. You'd think she'd be more interested in boys her own age. Mind you, she is rather plain. I shouldn't think the colonel would be too fussy about that in his dotage. Are you planning to eat that tea cake?"

"I've lost my appetite."

Churchill helped herself to it. "I think we should follow up on other possibilities, Pembers. You were right when you said this whole business with the colonel could be fruitless or bootless, whatever it was. Scandal can be a terrible distraction, can't it?"

"Mr Woolwell could be behind all of it, and we'd have no idea because we haven't yet spoken to the man."

"We tried once, didn't we? When he was three sheets to the wind. And then there's that Stropper Harris chap. He's a strange one."

"Look at all those people walking past the window," said Pemberley.

"Where?" Churchill turned, taking much of the lace tablecloth with her.

Beyond the frilly curtains of the tea rooms she saw a bustle of people passing.

"Something's happened, Pembers. Finish your tea cake."

"It's on your plate."

"So it is." Churchill crammed it into her mouth as she got up from her chair. "Let's go," she said, spraying crumbs everywhere.

They soon encountered Mrs Thonnings in the crowd.

"I wonder who it is this time!" she said excitedly.

"What do you mean?" asked Churchill.

"It has to be another murder, doesn't it? Nothing gets the village quite so excited as a murder."

"It might not be."

"Trust me, Mrs Churchill, there's nothing else that gets Compton Poppleforders this tickled."

Churchill sighed. "It looks like this crowd is heading for the allotments again, Pembers."

"Oh no," replied Pemberley.

"Let me through!" cried out a voice from behind them.

Churchill moved aside to let a young, dark-haired woman in a green coat push past.

"Isn't that Mrs Woolwell?" she whispered.

Pemberley nodded sombrely. "Perhaps she received a telephone call."

"Oh, Pembers." The two ladies stopped suddenly, and the crowd continued to move on past them. "He's the next victim, isn't he?"

Pemberley lifted her spectacles and dabbed at her eyes.

"I'll tell you what this means," continued Churchill. "It means that Mr Harding can't be the murderer because he's still languishing in the police cells, although I'm fairly indifferent to his plight now, having lost my affection for him a few days ago. Let's leave the police to this sorry scene and continue with our own investigation."

"But don't you want to find out what happened to him?"

"We'll find out in due course, Pembers. In the meantime, we need to track down this murderer. He can't keep getting away with it."

Chapter 45

THE TWO LADIES walked up the track toward the cottage Churchill rented from Farmer Drumhead. The bleats of sheep drifted across the neighbouring field and a skylark was singing high above their heads.

"It's a shame about Barry Woolwell," said Pembers. "He was the least annoying of all the gardeners."

"Well, he clearly annoyed someone," said Churchill. "And I've no doubt we'll soon hear further unpleasant stories about money and debts and whiskey and common garden implements being brandished as weapons. Now where's that wretched boy? He's usually knocking around here somewhere.

They followed a track that led into Farmer Drumhead's farm and walked past the hay barn in the direction of the slurry pit.

"He's often around here," said Churchill. "I wonder where else he could be. Oh, there he is, look." She strolled toward an adolescent boy in a cap who sat on a nearby gate chewing a piece of straw.

"Good morning, young Timmy." She doffed her hat. "I

have a shiny farthing here for a boy who is willing to do a spot of work."

The boy sniffed and looked away.

"How about a spot of work, young man? It beats sitting on a gate all day."

"I ain't gonna sit 'ere all day."

"What else do you intend to do? Catapult snails into the slurry pit?"

"Proberly."

"Don't you want to hear what Auntie Churchy's got to offer?"

The boy turned to face her with a sneer. "Auntie?"

"Yes, in return for a generous payment."

"It's only a farthin'."

Churchill sighed. "Auntie Churchy has two shiny farthings here for a boy who is willing to do a spot of work for her."

"Two?"

The boy jumped down from the gate. "What d'ya want doin', Auntie Churchill?"

"Mrs Churchill will do just fine. I'd like someone to do a bit of scouting around for me. And don't worry, it won't be too far from home. It will be at your home, actually. I'd like you to look for anything that is out of the ordinary; an object you wouldn't normally see there. Someone's probably made an attempt to bury it or hide it. Can you think of any good hiding places at Cherrybrick Farm?"

"Yeah, there's loads of 'em! Beneath them 'ay bales in the cow shed, behind the buckets in the stables, the trapdoor in the chicken 'ouse and underneath Grampa's caravan."

"It sounds like you have a number of places to look."

"Yeah, but ev'ryone 'ides stuff under Grampa's caravan. That's the easiest one."

"Why not take a look there first, then? But as soon as you find something, bring it to me and don't breathe a word about it to anyone else. Do you hear what I'm saying?"

The boy nodded.

"I'll give you one farthing now." Churchill pulled her purse out of her handbag. "And the other when you return from your errand."

"Oh, what? I gotta wait for it?"

"You won't get a better offer today, boy. Now, off you trot. Search high and low, please!'

The boy strolled off.

"How do you know you can trust him?" asked Pemberley.

"I don't. I can only hope that the promise of two farthings is greater than the extent of his family loyalty. I'm taking a bit of a gamble."

~

"Poisoned scrumpy!" announced Mrs Thonnings. "Can you believe it?"

"Nothing surprises me any more, Mrs Thonnings," replied Churchill, wondering what the woman was doing in their office.

"They think he drank it late yesterday evening. He was up at his allotment and Mrs Woolwell wasn't too worried when he didn't come home because he often spent the night at his allotment when the weather was warm. I wouldn't stand for it, would you?"

"My late husband never owned an allotment, so I couldn't say."

"Neither did mine. Anyway, that's where they found him."

"At his allotment?"

"Yes. Mrs Woolwell grew concerned when he didn't come home for his breakfast. He usually stays out all night and then has the cheek to turn up asking for breakfast! I certainly wouldn't put up with it. Anyway, he didn't turn up this time and, at about the same time as he normally returned for breakfast, Mr Harris discovered poor Barry deceased by his toolshed."

"So the murderer poisoned his scrumpy, eh?" asked Churchill.

"Yes. They think some fungicide from his toolshed was tipped into it. He kept his jars of scrumpy in there, too."

"He stored fungicide next to his scrumpy stash? It sounds like the perfect opportunity for someone with murderous intent. I bet the killer couldn't believe his luck."

"It does seem rather foolish, doesn't it? Mrs Woolwell had apparently banned scrumpy from the house, so the toolshed was the only place he could store it."

"The fungicide probably contained cyanide," said Pemberley. "It would have been a swift but exceptionally unpleasant death."

"Nasty indeed," said Churchill. "Jam tart, Mrs Thonnings?"

"Oh, thank you!"

"You seem to have learned rather a lot about Mr Woolwell's death, Mrs Thonnings."

"I must say that I quite fancy being a detective. Oh, Mrs Churchill, I'm so envious of your private detective practice! All I do is sit about all day selling bows and ribbons, but you get involved with the nitty gritty of life. Just look at that map on the wall with all those pictures and string and pins! How I should love to have an incident board like that. I'd pretty it up with some bows, of course."

"It's not as glamorous as it looks, Mrs Thonnings," said Churchill.

"Oh, please don't say that! Surely it must be. How I should love to crack a case."

"I'm afraid the case-cracking only comes after many hours of mind-bending, back-breaking work, Mrs Thonnings."

"But you make it look so easy, Mrs Churchill."

"Do I?"

"I see you both walking past my window, deep in discussion and I wonder what exciting discoveries you must be discussing. I'm really quite envious of you, Mrs Churchill."

"Are you?"

"Oh yes, terribly so. If you ever need any assistance on one of your cases you'll ask me, won't you? I would so love to be involved."

"We'll let you know if anything arises, Mrs Thonnings," said Churchill, wary of anyone else trying to shoulder their way into her work.

"Oh, thank you. In the meantime I'm going to prepare a nice meal for Jeffrey. Surely they must have realised he's not the murderer by now. He'll be quite hungry after his long spell in the police cells. The food they serve there isn't fit for a worm."

"You must feel guilty for being so mean about Mrs Thonnings after all those nice things she just said about you," said Pemberley once Mrs Thonnings had left.

"I wasn't mean about her, Pembers, and I'm not sure she said many nice things about me just then; she said she was *envious*. One must always be wary of people who say they're envious."

"Oh, but I thought she was being quite nice."

"You make us some tea, Pemberley, and I'll get on with reading the minutes from the horticultural society." She opened out the file on her desk. "It's a dry old read, you know."

"I suspected it would be."

"'Mr T Williams has proposed that new guidelines be issued for the trimming of the roots of onions to the basal plate.'"

"There could be a clue in that."

"An obscure one, perhaps. 'Mr J Rumbold reported that the incidence of splits in leeks was on the increase.'"

"That's a shame. Poor leeks."

"When Mrs Thonnings talks about our exciting discoveries she has no idea how many hours we spend doing this sort of thing, does she? Clueless. Completely clueless."

The downstairs door slammed.

"And now we're about to be disturbed again, Pembers."

The footsteps on the stairs were light and quick. Into the room dashed a breathless Timmy Flatboot carrying a sack under one arm.

"Mrs Churchill! I found summink int'restin' under Grampa's caravan!"

Chapter 46

"SIT DOWN, BOY," said Churchill, pointing to the chair opposite her.

Timmy Flatboot removed his cap and did as she had instructed. As he dropped the sack to the floor it gave a loud clatter.

"Well done, lad," she said. "It sounds as though you've found a good few things under Grandpa Flatboot's caravan."

"Oh yeah, lots of 'em."

"Would you like a jam tart?"

"Fanks, Mrs C." He grabbed one and gobbled it down in a single mouthful.

"So what is this unusual item?"

"I'm too shy ter say it!"

"Come now, boy. There's no need for shyness."

"There might be when yer sees what it is!"

"And what is it?"

"I'll show yer."

Timmy Flatboot bent down and picked up the sack. He wrinkled his nose as he peered inside and slowly slid his hand in. He carefully withdrew his arm from the sack, pinching the mysterious item between his thumb and forefinger with an expression of great distaste.

"What is it?" asked Churchill, seeing a flash of fabric. "A silk scarf?"

"Worse 'n that."

He pulled out the rest of the fabric and deposited it on Churchill's desk.

"It's a pair o' women's…." His face flushed a deep red.

"I see what they are now," said Churchill, sharing the boy's distaste. "This pair of undergarments was hidden beneath your grandpa's caravan, you say?"

"Yeah, an' they ain't been there long. I dunno 'ow—"

"There's no need for us to speculate. Was there anything else unusual?"

"Nope."

"But you found some other items hidden under there?"

"Oh yeah, but just normal stuff."

"Why don't you empty it all out so we can take a look?"

"Alright. So we got two shotguns." He pulled them out and placed them on top of the silk undergarments. And there's a slingshot in 'ere." He grinned. "It's a good 'un; I'm gonna keep it for meself." He placed it on the desk and reached inside the bag again. "There's a saucepan, some newspapers, a wood axe, a knife, a dog collar an' two bricks."

"There was no need to bring the bricks."

"I thought you might wanna see 'em. Then there's a length o' rope, a waterin' can, a revolver and three knittin' needles. Me gramma likes knittin'."

"Interesting," said Churchill with a smile. "Timmy Flatboot, you have surpassed yourself. She reached into her handbag and pulled out her purse. "I shall give you the farthing I promised, and I think I'm going to give you another as well."

"Three farthin's in all? Fanks, Mrs C!"

"On one condition." She raised a finger. "This third farthing is to ensure that you keep quiet about this item here." She pulled out her handkerchief, wrapped it around the barrel of the revolver and picked it up. "I'm going to look after this old gun here. Everything else can go back, or you can keep or sell it. Whatever you like."

"Fanks!"

Timmy pocketed the farthings and put everything bar the revolver back inside his sack. Churchill carefully popped the revolver into her desk drawer for safekeeping, using her handkerchief to preserve any fingerprints.

"Good work, my lad." She gave him a wink. "Very good work indeed."

Once Timmy had left, Churchill used her handkerchief once again to take the revolver out of her desk drawer.

"I'm no ammunitions expert, Pembers, but I'd say this was a Webley, wouldn't you?"

Pemberley walked over to her desk to examine it. "Don't touch it, whatever you do, Pembers. It'll need to be dusted for fingerprints."

"It certainly looks like a Webley to me, Mrs Churchill. Is it the colonel's missing gun?"

"I think it must be."

"Then we must take it down to the police station!"

"We will, Pembers, we will. But let's not be in a hurry to do so. You'll recall how grumpy Inspector Mappin was about that bullet casing. I paid three farthings to retrieve this gun, and I'd like to do a little more work before we share it with anyone."

"But what if someone finds it here? They'll think we did it!"

"They won't, Pembers. I'm going to put it back in my drawer and then I'm going to lock it with this little key here. It won't be in there for long. I'd say we nearly have this case solved, wouldn't you?"

"Are you saying that the Flatboots did it?"

"It's looking that way, isn't it? Oh dear, we're rather popular today," she added, hearing the door downstairs open and shut again. "Remember that impassive and slightly bored-looking poker face I showed you when I taught you how to play bridge? Now's the time to use it."

Churchill was reading the horticultural society minutes intently when Inspector Mappin popped his head around the door.

"Good afternoon, Mrs Churchill."

"Oh hello, Inspector! How are you? I thought you'd be busy quizzing your suspect."

"We don't have one any more." He removed his hat and sat down.

"You don't?"

"No, we had to let Harding go."

"Oh, so it wasn't him after all? Well, never mind. I'm sure you'll catch the culprit before long, Inspector."

"I thought I'd see you at the allotments this morning, Mrs Churchill."

"Why's that?"

"That's where the third dreadful murder took place. Poor Mr Woolwell."

"It's awfully sad. And so tragic that no one has been able to stop this murdering maniac yet. It's quite shocking."

"Have you visited the scene yet?"

"Not yet, Inspector Mappin. My trusty assistant and I

decided to leave that up to you and your colleagues. You all know what you're doing; you don't need us getting in your way or – dare I say it – meddling."

"Hmmm." He appeared to give this some thought. "I thought you'd be taking more of an interest in the case now that there have been three murders."

"I am taking an interest, Inspector, but I didn't wish to cause any disruption or inconvenience as you once put it. After all, I might get myself swatted! Isn't that what you said?"

"I was having a rather difficult time of it that day, Mrs Churchill."

"Weren't we all?"

He nodded, got up from his seat and put his hat back on. "You don't happen to know anything that might be of use to us, do you?"

Churchill smiled. "Are you asking me for my help, Inspector?"

"No!" He cleared his throat. "No, not at all."

"You have no idea who's behind these murders, do you?"

"Do you?"

"No."

"Very well. Let's all get on with it then."

"Let's! Good day to you, Inspector Mappin."

"Poor Inspector Mappin," said Pemberley once he had left. "He has no clue about any of it. Why didn't you tell him about the revolver?"

"For reasons I've already explained, Pembers. Don't worry about him. He'll get his moment to arrest the suspect and pretend he did all the hard work. In the meantime, we need to do some more reconnaissance."

Chapter 47

"I WONDER if Kitty Flatface has made use of any hiding places around here," said Churchill as she and Pemberley stood in the yard behind the tea rooms. She peered into a bucket that contained broken crockery and pushed her hand into a few gaps in the dry-stone wall.

"I can't see many hiding places," said Pemberley. She gazed in through the window at the back of the tea rooms.

"Is that the kitchen in there, Pembers?"

"Yes, and Mrs Bramley has just spotted us. Now she's heading this way."

The door opened and the familiar small, round-faced woman in her tight apron peered out.

"Crikey! I didn't expect ter see you two round 'ere!"

"Just carrying out further investigations, Mrs Bramley," replied Churchill. "We suspect that Miss Flatboot has been up to a little more than taking money from the till."

Mrs Bramley gasped. "What d'you mean?"

"We think the colonel's involved, too."

Mrs Bramley groaned. "I don't wanna hear nuffink about it."

"We'll spare your ears then, Mrs Bramley. Are you aware of any hiding places your waitress may have used to secrete something in?"

Mrs Bramley glanced around the yard. "Nope. None what I can think of."

"How about in your kitchen? Any secret nooks and crannies in there?"

"Come an' 'ave a look if yer like."

The two ladies spent a short while in the little kitchen opening drawers and looking behind the dresser.

"Pembers, can you reach that top shelf up there?"

"I'll try," replied Pemberley, finding a stool to balance on. "There's nothing up here except for some pie dishes."

"That'd be about right," said Mrs Bramley. "I only puts me pie dishes up there. What yer lookin' for exac'ly?"

"We're not quite sure, Mrs Bramley. Just anything that looks out of place, really. Something Kitty might have placed here because she didn't wish to be caught in possession of it. Anyway, I think that's enough searching about for now." Churchill felt quite tired. "I think we need to revive ourselves with a little refreshment in your tea rooms, Mrs Bramley."

"Yer do just that, ladies. I'll bring yer some extra cakes.

"Oh, thank you."

The two ladies walked through into the tea rooms and Churchill felt rather pleased that her heart gave not even the slightest flutter when she saw Mr Harding sitting at one of the tiny tables.

"Congratulations on your release," she said politely.

"Oh, thank you, Mrs Churchill." He flashed her a wide smile. "It's been a torrid few days. It's dreadful when you're treated like a common criminal. Despicable! I have every respect for the law, but it's a sorry state of affairs when a man has to defend himself against a false charge of murder! I wouldn't wish it on my worst enemy."

"I'm sure you wouldn't, Mr Harding. Where shall we sit, Pembers? Over there in that far corner?"

"How's the kettle working out for you, Mrs Churchill?" asked Mr Harding with a grin.

"Still heating up water, Mr Harding. Let's take a seat, Pembers."

They sat beside the window and Kitty Flatboot gave them a sulky stare from the other side of the room.

"You know what, Pembers?" said Churchill. "I'm in the mood to liven things up a little. You place our order with Kitty." She got up from her chair. "I'm going to pay a quick visit to the police station."

"What do you want me to order for you?"

"Anything, and don't forget to remind Kitty about the extra cakes Mrs Bramley promised."

"What are you planning to do at the police station?"

"I'm going to invite Mappin and Doo-Lally here for afternoon tea. And I'm going to ask them to fetch the colonel while they're at it."

Chapter 48

TWENTY MINUTES later the tea rooms were quite full. Churchill had instructed Mr Harding to remain where he was, and Mrs Bramley had brought him a fresh pot of tea. Chief Inspector Llewellyn-Dalrymple had turned up with the two constables from Bulchford. Mrs Thonnings had just arrived, having somehow got wind that something was happening, and Mrs Downs and Mrs Harris had also made an appearance. Mrs Higginbath pressed her nose up against the window for a short while before stepping inside to find out what was occurring.

"Keep hold of this little key," said Churchill, giving it to Inspector Mappin who had walked with her from the police station. "I will have instructions for you shortly. And get your handcuffs ready, too."

"This is all very intriguing, Mrs Churchill," said Colonel Slingsby, lighting his pipe. "Have you got something exciting in store for us?"

"Just a little theory of mine to share, Colonel. Are you ready to write it down, Miss Pemberley?"

Her assistant nodded eagerly, knowing what to expect.

Churchill had quickly whispered her plan into Pemberley's ear before everyone had arrived.

"We should do this every week," said Mrs Bramley with a happy smile. "It's good for business, Mrs Churchill!"

"Wouldn't that be fun, Mrs Bramley? I shall get on with the matter in hand now." She cleared her throat and raised her voice. "Good afternoon, everyone. I shan't detain you for long," she began. "Thank you for coming. First of all, I would like to acknowledge the sad passing of three men in this village: Mr Williams, Mr Rumbold and Mr Woolwell. Their deaths were tragic and completely unnecessary."

"Hear, hear," said the colonel.

"Who did it?" asked Mrs Harris.

"The sorry chain of events began with the disappearance of Colonel Slingsby's revolver from his gunroom," said Churchill. "The person who took it was, in fact, the first victim, Mr Tubby Williams. But why did he take it? Well, he told Mrs Williams that he intended to do someone some mischief; that he was *going to put a stop to this once and for all*. Sadly, we'll never know exactly what he meant, as proceedings were interrupted by the vicar, who had a habit of popping round to the Williams's abode. Mr Williams took that gun up to the allotment, where it was used against him later that evening. Did he intend to harm Mr Rumbold with it? We shall never know. There had certainly been some rivalry between the two gardeners, with Mr Rumbold accusing Mr Williams of spearing his onions.

"Mr Rumbold returned home safely that evening, while Mr Williams lost his life. Any suspicions that Mr Rumbold was the murderer were quickly quelled when he was incapacitated with a frying pan and drowned in the duck pond. A shocking way to go! Mr Rumbold had been in the company of Mr Harris and Mr Downs that evening. Did these two men conspire to murder him?"

"No!" Mrs Harris shouted.

"Boooooo!" yelled Mrs Downs.

"Patience, ladies," said Churchill, raising her hand. "Mr Woolwell was the enigmatic type. So *mysterious*, you might say, that he was hiding something. *Was* he hiding something? We shall never know, because sadly his scrumpy store had been poisoned, prompting his swift demise. Three gardeners dead. But what could the motive possibly be?"

"Money," Mrs Higginbath piped up. "It's always about money."

"Ah yes, the gambling," said Churchill. "The men were all keen card players, and that's why suspicion has fallen on Mr Harding here."

"Not again!" he scorned, as all eyes in the room rested on him.

"It's no secret that he owed money to these men," continued Churchill. "In fact, Mrs Rumbold confided in me that her late husband had threatened Mr Harding to hasten the repayment of his debts. So convincing was the case against Mr Harding that he was eventually arrested."

"Why are you reminding them of this nonsense?!" he snarled.

"I'm merely providing everyone with a tidy précis, Mr Harding. Don't worry, you'll be completely forgotten about and insignificant in just a moment." She addressed the room once again. "And there was even more money!" she added. "It was hidden in marrows next to the orangery at Ashleigh Grange, and routinely used to bribe Colonel Slingsby with the aim of influencing his decisions at the vegetable shows. Vast sums also passed from the hands of the colonel to the Flatboot family."

The colonel gave a gasp and exchanged a worried glance with Kitty Flatboot. Churchill smiled to herself, confident that she had everyone on the back foot.

"So, were the murders all about money, as Mrs Higginbath suggests?" she asked. "Or was the motive something else altogether? Let's not forget that although these gardeners were friends there was intense rivalry between them. My initial introduction to the case came via an invitation from Mr Rumbold to identify the person who had been vandalising his vegetables. Perhaps the motive was merely a tit-for-tat squabble that escalated into murder?"

"Bravo! Please allow me to say a few words now, Mrs Churchill," said Chief Inspector Llewellyn-Dalrymple, rising to his feet. "Thank you for the great interest you've taken in this case. There's no doubt that ordinary people like yourself and Miss Pemberley can be of great use to the police force at times like this. You have your ear to the ground, so to speak, and that is truly magnificent to see. I think this case has shown that the policeman and the civilian can work together as one, and I must say I really am impressed with the way that works here in Compton Poppleford. Many of you will know that I'm a Dorchester man myself, and I am very keen to emulate this wonderful relationship in the big town. Who can say whether or not it will work just as well there? But we must try it. I've said it before, and I'll say it again: isn't it impressive to see what two little old ladies can do when they put their heads together?" He began to applaud his words in self-appreciation.

"Sit down, Chief Inspector!" snapped Churchill. "I haven't finished yet!"

Chief Inspector Llewellyn-Dalrymple sat back in his chair, his cheeks flushing almost as red as his moustache.

"Why's the colonel giving money to the Flatboots?" hollered Mrs Harris.

Colonel Slingsby shifted awkwardly in his chair as everyone turned to stare at him.

"Ah yes, now that's a rather delicate matter." He paused to take a puff on his pipe. "The old brother liked to sow his seed, you see."

"He was a gardener as well, was he?" asked Churchill.

"No, not at all. No, erm." The colonel scratched his nose. "It's a rather sensitive subject, you see. But the truth is, many of the Flatboots are, in fact, Slingsbys."

Gasps echoed around the room.

"Nothing to do with me!" interjected the colonel. "I was in the Punjab most of the time!" He puffed on his pipe again as he waited for the chatter in the room to die down. "The money is a sort of stipend, if you like," he continued, "to help support the illegitimate Slingsbys. Had to keep it all top secret. Sure you all understand. Young Kitty over there just happens to be my great-niece."

Everyone's heads turned from side to side as they glanced between the Colonel and the waitress, each keen to spot a family resemblance.

"Thank you, Colonel," said Churchill. "I appreciate that the information you have just shared is an enormous embarrassment to your family of landed gentry."

"I have no wish to dwell on it any further," said the colonel. "Please continue."

"I wonder, Colonel Slingsby, whether you had any idea that the revolver which has been missing from your gunroom was found beneath a caravan at Cherrybrick Farm," said Churchill.

"What?" The colonel gave a look of horror and indignation.

"What?" Inspector Mappin repeated.

"It may be another gun entirely," continued Churchill. "But I'm assuming it's the same one. There can't be many Webley revolvers lying hidden about this village."

"Where is it now?" asked the colonel.

"In the drawer of my desk for safekeeping. Inspector Mappin has the key to the drawer. You'll no doubt wish to dust it for fingerprints, Inspector."

Inspector Mappin gave an officious nod.

"But how did it get there?" asked the colonel.

"Perhaps your great-niece can tell you," said Churchill.

He glared across the room at his great-niece. "Kitty?" he barked.

"I don't know nothin' about it!" she protested.

"Do *you* know anything about it, Colonel Slingsby?" asked Inspector Mappin. "Did you plant it there?"

"Plant it? Why would I want to do that?"

"What did you remove from Mr Harding's cookshop, Colonel?" asked Churchill.

"Wh-what?" he replied, not sure who to look at during this unexpected inquisition. "Why are you firing all these questions at me all of a sudden?"

"While Mr Harding was under arrest, Miss Pemberley and I saw you remove something from his cookshop. Was it the gun?"

"The what? The gun? In the cookshop? No! Good grief, woman. No!"

"What was it, then?"

"My bag. My valise! Mr Harding had borrowed it to take some money to Mr Rumbold in. It wasn't the full amount but he'd hoped it would go some way to paying off his debts. I was simply collecting the valise because I needed it so I could give Kitty her money."

"And there was nothing in the bag when you retrieved it?"

"No, it was completely empty! A darned useful bag for carrying money, actually. That's why I went to collect it. I could hardly ask Mr Harding for it, could I? He was in the cells."

"Is the colonel the murderer, Mrs Churchill?" asked Mrs Thonnings.

"No. He almost certainly had someone do his bidding for him," said Inspector Mappin. "His great-niece, I imagine. The gun was found on her family farm, after all. *She* did it."

"I never done it!" Kitty shook her head. "No, I never! It weren't nuffink to do wiv me! I didn't even know 'em!"

"Ah, but your great-uncle did," said Inspector Mappin, "and he gave you the instruction to murder them!"

"No, it ain't true!"

"Codswallop!" spat the colonel.

"I'm afraid it is indeed codswallop, Inspector," said Churchill. "The colonel and his great-niece are entirely innocent. The person you need to place in handcuffs today is Mrs Bramley."

Chapter 49

CHURCHILL HAD PREPARED herself for the incredulous snorts and derisory comments that inevitably followed her surprising revelation.

"The little old lady who runs this place?" laughed Chief Inspector Llewellyn-Dalrymple.

"Your laughter merely confirms why you never had any hope of solving this crime, Chief Inspector," retorted Churchill.

All eyes were now on Mrs Bramley. She opened her mouth to speak, then thought better of it. Suddenly, her face turned red and she spun around to run out of the room. Mr Harding stuck his foot out and she tripped over it, falling to the floor.

"You're under arrest, Mrs Bramley!" said Inspector Mappin, knocking into tables as he charged across the room to handcuff her. Churchill allowed him a generous amount of time to enjoy his proud moment.

"What are you doing, Mappin?" asked Llewellyn-Dalrymple. "There's no evidence that this old lady has done anything wrong!"

"Mrs Churchill was right the last time she named the killer," replied the inspector, "so I thought I'd better make the arrest before Mrs Bramley got away. We can release her again if Mrs Churchill is mistaken."

"And complete all the paperwork that comes with a wrongful arrest?" scorned the chief inspector, his moustache bristling.

"They all 'ad it comin' to 'em!" snarled Mrs Bramley as she tried to shrug off Inspector Mappin, her wrists handcuffed.

Llewellyn-Dalrymple raised an eyebrow at this. "By Jove," he commented. "Perhaps Mrs Churchill really is onto something?"

"It was just a little idea I had," she replied. "Shall I explain?"

"Yes, we all want to hear it!" said the colonel.

"Well, the answer to this lies with a man I've never met and who is sadly deceased," said Churchill. "His name was Barney Bramley, and he was the dear husband of Mrs Bramley for forty years. She told me they never once exchanged a cross word."

"Fiddlesticks!" said the chief inspector.

"Only it may not be; they were certainly very devoted to one another. I haven't learned a great deal about Mr Bramley, but I do know that he loved Battenberg cake and dreamt of eating a carrot cake, which he had specifically grown carrots for. Sadly, that never happened because he never managed to grow carrots properly. He wasn't even able to grow a marrow. Despite his lack of gardening success he loved the pastime so much that he applied to join the Compton Poppleford Horticultural Society. Not just once, but... how many times was it, Colonel Slingsby?"

He gave an awkward cough before answering. "Twenty-two."

"Thank you, Colonel. That concurs with what I read in the minutes from the Compton Poppleford Horticultural Society meetings. Over a period of ten years, Mr Bramley applied to join the society twenty-two times, and each time he was refused."

"It broke 'is 'eart!" Mrs Bramley cried out. "They told 'im 'e weren't good enough! Again and again and again!"

"You see before you a woman scorned," said Churchill, pointing at Mrs Bramley. "A woman who wanted nothing more than her husband's happiness. In fact, the minutes of the meetings reveal that she tried to attend herself a number of times in order to plead her husband's case. But what happened, Colonel?"

"I'm afraid the door was closed in her face."

"That's how they treated her," said the detective sadly.

"Women aren't allowed to join the horticultural society," added the Colonel.

"How very welcoming of you," said Churchill. "Only Mrs Bramley didn't want to join herself; she was merely trying to help her husband."

"Our members must demonstrate some degree of horticultural skill," added the colonel.

"'E would of learnt it!" Mrs Bramley cried out. "They could've taught 'im!"

"However, none of this justifies the cold-blooded murder of three men, Mrs Bramley," said Churchill. "It seems that after your husband's death, you grew determined to exact your revenge on certain members of the horticultural society. You were happy to bide your time, watching and waiting for the perfect opportunity to arise.

"I think you lurked in the dark at those allotments and observed the argument between Mr Williams and Mr

Rumbold. Now I don't know where Mr Williams had placed the colonel's revolver while he was arguing with Mr Rumbold—"

"In 'is shed," replied Mrs Bramley. "I saw 'im put it in there."

"I see. And my guess is that you crept in and purloined it while the men argued?"

"It was when Rumbold was leavin'. Tubby was followin' after 'im hollerin' somethin' at 'im. That's when I got it."

"And on his return you shot him?"

Mrs Bramley gave a shrug.

Churchill gave a sad sigh. "A few nights later you must have followed the drunken Mr Rumbold, Mr Downs and Mr Harris when they left the pub, clutching your frying pan in your hands. You probably hadn't decided which of them you were aiming for; it would simply have to be the one who was left on his own. Unfortunately for Mr Rumbold, it was him. A few blows from the frying pan were probably enough to stun him, and after that you tied his arms and legs together and pushed him into the duck pond along with the aforementioned frying pan. As for the unfortunate Mr Williams, I don't know exactly when you poured fungicide into his scrumpy, but I'm certain that you carried out the act and waited for him to slowly drink himself to death.

"As for the evidence, your fingerprints are no doubt on the revolver you hid under Grandpa Flatboot's caravan, knowing that it would be discovered there before long and would naturally implicate the Flatboots. Your fingerprints are probably all over the bottles of fungicide and jars of scrumpy, too. What's more, there are two frying pans hanging on your kitchen wall, but there are three hooks. One of those hooks is empty, which suggests to me that a frying pan is missing. And you also invented a witness."

"What you talkin' about?"

"The man who claimed to have seen the murderer leaving the scene after Mr Williams's and Mr Rumbold's deaths. The one you said was normal-looking, normal height and normal weight with a square chin, spectacles and brown hair. Apparently, he was a bit of a bore, with a penchant for cricket and egg sandwiches, though he never ate the crusts. That description matches no one in this village, Mrs Bramley. And it was odd that you seemed unable to remember his name. That was because he didn't exist, wasn't it? You only told us about him to throw us off the scent."

"It ain't true!"

"What's his name, then?"

"Can't remember. Somethin' Perkins."

"Rubbish! I'll tell you something, though, Mrs Bramley."

"What?"

"I think I've solved the case of the money that went missing from your till."

"Who done it?"

"Not Miss Flatboot, if that's what you were thinking. It was him!" Churchill pointed at Mr Harding.

"Me?" He grinned, then his face grew serious again.

"Every time you visited these tea rooms, Mr Harding, you claimed that Kitty had short-changed you. You'd give her a sixpence and claim it had been a shilling, and generally confused the girl so much with all sorts of coins that each time you came out with more money than you'd gone in with."

"Jeffrey!" scolded Mrs Thonnings.

"You scoundrel," snarled the colonel.

"You stole from a widow, Mr Harding," added Churchill.

Mutters of disapproval wafted around the room.

"A *murdering* widow!" protested Mr Harding, but everyone ignored him.

"All of this makes me extremely angry," said Churchill. "Why can't people just be *nice* to each other?" She picked up her handbag. "Let's go, Miss Pemberley. Our work here is done." She walked over to the door. "Come over with the little key for my desk drawer when you're ready, Inspector Mappin."

"I will do, Mrs Churchill."

Chapter 50

"STERLING WORK, MRS CHURCHILL. STERLING WORK," said Chief Inspector Llewellyn-Dalrymple, sipping a glass of champagne.

"Does this look like your Webley, Colonel Slingsby?" asked Inspector Mappin, holding it beneath the colonel's nose in a gloved hand.

"I do believe that's the fellow," replied the colonel. "Good to have him back."

"But it's a murder weapon," protested Pemberley. "Do you really want it back?"

"Doesn't bother me," said the colonel. "Guns are designed to shoot things. Otherwise they wouldn't be doing their job, would they?"

Churchill shook her head in bemusement and drained her glass. She glanced at her watch and wondered when everyone would be kind enough to leave her office.

"It's quite astonishing really," said Chief Inspector Llewellyn-Dalrymple. "You ladies don't look capable of cracking a multiple murder case."

"So you've intimated on many occasions, Chief Inspector."

"Never fails to amaze me. You certainly gave the boys in blue a run for their money."

"Perhaps the boys in blue need to stop underestimating little old ladies."

The chief inspector gave a laugh.

"Well done, Mrs Churchill!" enthused Mrs Thonnings, perching herself on Churchill's desk. "You really are terribly clever at this sort of thing. You will let me know when you next need help with a case, won't you?"

"Next time we need help, yes. Most of the time I have all the help I need, however."

"Really?"

"Yes, in the shape of Miss Pemberley over there. I may be the large, noisy one, but she does more than her fair share of the work, and I don't want to be the one who gets all the credit."

Everyone raised their glasses to thank and congratulate Miss Pemberley. The slender secretary gave a half smile and pretended to drop a pencil on the floor so that she could hide beneath her desk.

"Why's my picture on the incident board?" asked Colonel Slingsby.

"Everyone was a suspect at one time or another."

"Suppose they had to be. Fortunately you picked a flattering photograph of me. I'm quite proud of that one, remember the day it was taken."

"So, what of the Compton Poppleford Horticultural Society now, Colonel?" asked Churchill.

"It'll be disbanded now. We're three men down and our reputation has been badly tarnished in the process. To be honest with you, I never did go in for gardening very much. The society meetings were just a way to pass the time."

"Have you ever done any gardening?"

"No, never."

"Interesting. So a keen, though slightly inept, gardener named Barney Bramley wasn't permitted to join, while you were able to become president of the society and judge of the annual show even though you'd never gardened before and had little interest in the subject."

"Yes."

"That doesn't seem very fair."

"It doesn't really, does it? I suppose it's the way the class system works in this country. Anyway, I'd better be off. Anyone want Pattison to drop them anywhere?"

The remaining guests nodded and filed out after the colonel, at which point Pemberley reappeared from beneath her desk.

"I'm exhausted, Pembers," said Churchill once they had all left. "Solving a case really takes it out of you, doesn't it?"

"Oh yes. Atkins used to reward himself by taking a nice holiday somewhere."

"Where did he usually like to go?"

"Somewhere warm. St Tropez, Biarritz. Sometimes he'd fly further afield to Marrakech or Bermuda."

"Oh, would he? Well, I should think we could manage a day trip to Weymouth tomorrow. How do you fancy that?"

"I would love that, Mrs Churchill. We could even bicycle out from there to Portland Bill."

"I'm afraid there are no bicycles allowed, Pemberley. And I have banned the contraptions from all future investigations."

"That's a shame. How about a donkey ride on the beach instead?"

"That would be lovely. I may even be able to squeeze into an old pair of jodhpurs. Shall I give them a whirl?"

"I would forget about the jodhpurs and ride side-saddle instead, Mrs Churchill."

"It all sounds perfectly delightful. Sun, sea and sand and nothing at all to do with onions, mud, allotments, more mud, revolvers, duck ponds, colonels, frying pans, cookshops, orange hair, cheap blouses and tea rooms. It's going to be a long time before I can enjoy a visit to a tea room again Pembers."

Pemberley gasped. "But tea rooms are your favourite places Mrs Churchill! How will you manage in the meantime?"

"I'll find a way Pembers. Churchy always finds a way."

The End

Thank you

~

Thank you for reading *Murder in Cold Mud*, I really hope you enjoyed it!

Would you like to know when I release new books? Here are some ways to stay updated:

- Join my mailing list and receive the short story *A Troublesome Case*: emilyorgan.com/a-troublesome-case
- Like my Facebook page: facebook.com/emilyorganwriter
- View my other books here: emilyorgan.com

And if you have a moment, I would be very grateful if you would leave a quick review of *Murder in Cold Mud* online. Honest reviews of my books help other readers discover them too!

Get a free short mystery

~

Want more of Churchill & Pemberley? Get a copy of my free short mystery *A Troublesome Case* and sit down to enjoy a thirty minute read.

Churchill and Pemberley are on the train home from a shopping trip when they're caught up with a theft from a suitcase. Inspector Mappin accuses them of stealing the valuables, but in an unusual twist of fate the elderly sleuths are forced to come to his aid!

Visit my website to claim your FREE copy:
emilyorgan.com/a-troublesome-case

Puzzle in Poppleford Wood

A Churchill & Pemberley Mystery Book 3

For twenty years the villagers of Compton Poppleford have been puzzled by the fate of Darcy Sprockett who vanished in the woods one dark and stormy night. When fresh evidence surfaces, elderly detective duo Churchill and Pemberley creak into action.

A cast of suspects emerges, but Inspector Mappin is soon barking up the wrong tree. When he refuses advice from the two old ladies, Churchill and Pemberley must use their wits and mastery of disguise to unravel the mystery of Poppleford Wood. How could the newly unveiled statue of Sir Morris Buckle-Duffington be connected? And what about local Lothario, Mr Peregrine Colthrop?

And is a new member of Churchill's Detective Agency a help or a hindrance?

The Penny Green Series

~

Also by Emily Organ. A series of mysteries set in Victorian London featuring the intrepid Fleet Street reporter, Penny Green.

Books in the Penny Green Series:
Limelight
The Rookery
The Maid's Secret
The Inventor
Curse of the Poppy
The Bermondsey Poisoner
An Unwelcome Guest
Death at the Workhouse
The Gang of St Bride's

Find out more here: emilyorgan.com